THE UNWANTEDS

Island of Shipwrecks

Also by Lisa McMann

» » « «

LISA McMANN

THE UNWANTEDS

Island of Shipwrecks

Aladdin
NEW YORK   LONDON   TORONTO   SYDNEY   NEW DELHI

ALADDIN

An imprint of Simon & Schuster Children's Publishing Division

1230 Avenue of the Americas, New York, New York 10020

This Aladdin hardcover edition February 2015

Text copyright © 2015 by Lisa McMann

Jacket illustration © 2015 by Owen Richardson

For information about special discounts for bulk purchases, please contact Simon & Schuster Special Sales at 1-866-506-1949 or business@simonandschuster.com.

The Simon & Schuster Speakers Bureau can bring authors to your live event. For more information or to book an event contact the Simon & Schuster Speakers Bureau at 1-866-248-3049 or visit our website at www.simonspeakers.com.

Book designed by Karin Paprocki

The text of this book was set in Truesdell.

Manufactured in the United States of America 1214 FFG

2 4 6 8 10 9 7 5 3 1

Library of Congress Cataloging-in-Publication Data

McMann, Lisa.

Island of shipwrecks / Lisa McMann. -- First Aladdin hardcover edition.

pages cm — (The Unwanteds ; book 5)

Summary: Alex and his friends from Artimé are stranded on a newly-discovered island, and they are not alone. While in Quill, his twin Aaron's power base grows as he joins with an unlikely ally in a risky plan to finally conquer Artimé.

ISBN 978-1-4424-9331-5 (hardcover) — ISBN 978-1-4424-9333-9 (eBook) [1. Brothers—Fiction. 2. Twins—Fiction. 3. Shipwrecks—Fiction. 4. Magic—Fiction. 5. Social problems—Fiction. 6. Fantasy.] I. Title. PZ7.M478757Isf 2015 [Fic]--dc23   2014026338

For Liliana

Contents

Prologue: Under the Sea

What did he look like?" growled the old pirate captain with hooks for hands. He slammed one of the hooks on the table in front of the slave, and it made a garish clang. "Who is responsible?"

Daxel said nothing. He couldn't speak. None of the slaves that the pirates had bought from their friend Queen Eagala could speak.

But Daxel could write, and the pirates knew it. Still, he stared at the map and the blank pieces of paper in front of him and shook his head.

The captain struck Daxel with one of his hook hands, leaving a ghastly white, jagged cut in the slave's forehead. Daxel cringed and recoiled. A second or two later, the gash turned red and blood began to drip from it, down his cheek and onto his tattered shirt.

Another pirate, who'd been standing at the glass wall staring out at the broken, now-empty aquarium, turned swiftly and picked up the map. He shook it in the slave's face and slapped it down on the table. "Where did they come from? An island? Or the outside?"

Daxel closed his eyes. He could feel his forehead pulsing, and resisted the urge to wipe away the blood—not that he could reach his face, since his wrists were chained to the arms of the chair. There was only enough slack to reach the pen and paper on the table in front of him. *The pirates can hurt me all they want*, he vowed. He would never betray his friend Copper.

Out of nowhere came a blunt slam above his ear. Daxel gripped the arms of the chair and wished for enough slack in the chains to strangle all the pirates.

He tried to block out their growly noises, and fielded blows

LISA McMANN

Island of Shipwrecks » 2

for a very long time, until he was faint with pain and loss of blood. But he wouldn't give the pirates what they wanted.

It was only when the hook-handed captain bent down near Daxel's face, close enough for the slave to smell his rancid breath and hear his wicked, whispered threat, that Daxel's orange eyes opened and pooled with fear.

The captain straightened and barked out an order: "Bring the others in here!"

Daxel's breathing grew shallow as all but the captain and one other pirate stormed out of the room. He watched them go, his hands shaking, chains rattling. Agonizing minutes passed until the pirates returned, each gripping two Warbler slaves by the arms. The pirates lined up the silent workers shoulder to shoulder in front of Daxel, and they held daggers to their hearts and cutlasses to their necks. The faces of the youngest slaves showed the most fear as they stared with pleading eyes at the man who held their fate in his hands.

Determination drained from Daxel's fighting spirit. The captain returned to his side and tapped the map and the papers in front of him. "This is your last chance to answer our questions," he said. "Or do you want us to hurt your friends?"

Some of the Warblerans stood stoically, but others couldn't mask their terror.

Daxel struggled to breathe. Sweat mingled with the blood on his forehead. *I'm so sorry*, he said in his mind, like a prayer. He was left with no choice.

The rattle of the chain when he reached for the pen was startling in the silent room. Stalling for time, even though he knew no one could or would save him and the other slaves, he studied the map. Seven small islands in a slightly inverted V-shape, and a large hunk of land to the west of them.

The captain poked his hook into the slave's back. "You have five seconds before one of them becomes food for the eels," he said. He pointed to the youngest slave, whose eyes widened in terror.

Daxel's heart pounded and his head swam. When he leaned forward, a drop of blood splattered on the table. He could hardly hear the captain's countdown for the rushing sound in his ears. There was a shuffle of feet across the room as a pirate prepared to take the first victim.

Daxel gripped the pen in his sweaty hand, touched it to the map, and slowly drew a circle around the middle island, which the strangers who rescued Copper had spoken about.

The captain spoke softly in the slave's ear. "There," he crooned. "That wasn't so hard, now was it?"

Daxel refused to react.

The captain straightened up. He strolled to the glass wall and gazed out. "Now all we need in order to let your friends go back to work is a little description of the leader responsible for *this disaster*." He pointed a hook at the empty aquarium, and his face took on a horrible, pained expression. "Years and years of searching and collecting . . . and so. Much. Money," he said, tapping the glass with each word. "All of it, gone." He shook his head. "We might not be able to afford to feed the slaves anymore. If they live, that is."

Daxel stared at the blank paper.

The captain sighed loudly. "Come on now, Daxel. Do we really have to go through the countdown again?" He moved lithely to the slave's side once more. "I'm so impatient. It's not likely I'll give you any warning this time."

The slave sucked in a breath. Sweat and blood stung his eyes. He gripped the pen and began to draw. A jawline. A swath of hair. A face.

LISA McMANN

"That's more like it," said the captain, leaning over the slave, watching intently as features began to emerge. "You have such talent," he said in mock praise.

Daxel drew and drew, knowing his life, and the lives of the slaves before him, depended on it. *Forgive me, friend.*

When he finished, he set the pen down, his gaze never straying from the drawing. Two fresh, innocent eyes bore into his soul.

The captain deftly slid the paper between his hooks and studied it. And then he began to chuckle. Softly at first, and then the chuckle rolled and crescendoed into a deep, hearty, sinister belt of laughter. He showed the drawing to his pirate companions and they began to laugh too.

When the captain could breathe, he hooked a handkerchief from his breast pocket and wiped his face with it. As he put it away, he declared, "This will most certainly be the easiest attack in our thousand-year history, comrades. For the dreaded man we seek? He's nothing but a boy!"

In Tatters

When Alex opened his eyes, he saw a blurry image of Fox standing before him on the deck of the Unwanteds' pirate ship. Kitten stood on Fox's head, mewing at the top of her voice. The sound grew distant and then faded altogether, and the young mage's lids drooped once more.

Fox stepped on Alex's thigh and licked his face, trying to get the boy's eyes to stay open. Kitten pointed over the bow with one tiny paw, still mewing.

Alex groaned. He was soaking wet and his entire body ached. His arms were tangled in rope, and he couldn't pull free.

LISA McMANN

And Fox's driftwood tongue was harsh on his skin. He lifted his head to move away from it and squinted in the sunlight. The world swam before his eyes.

"Mewmewmew!" cried the tiny porcelain kitten. Alex didn't have a clue what she was saying.

Fox began loosening the knots that held Alex to the ship's bow. He paused to translate, "Kitten is wondering if you are okay. She considers you to be one of her very, very special friends, and—"

"I'm okay," Alex interrupted. He coughed. Salt water burned his throat and nose. Fox worked at the knots with his teeth, and soon one of Alex's arms was free. Fox moved to the next, and when that one came loose, Alex plunged forward and put his hands out to catch himself.

"Thanks, Fox. You're a good, um, cat," he said, which pleased Fox immensely. Alex's arms wobbled. He pushed himself up and locked his elbows, then turned gingerly to a sitting position. He coughed again and winced. "And speaking of cats, please tell me the big one is around here somewhere."

Simber flew over from a short distance away when he heard Alex's voice. The enormous stone cheetah glanced out over the water and narrowed his eyes. "I am. But we'rrre missing someone else."

Alex struggled to his feet, alarmed. "Who's missing?"

"Octavia."

Alex's breath caught. He scanned the waves. "At least she can swim."

"Yes. But I'm not surrre wherrre we lost herrr. If it was back at the beginning . . ." Simber trailed off.

Alex wasn't at all sure how far they had traveled since their ship began the insane journey down a thunderous waterfall. When they'd reached the bottom, they'd gone screaming around a forward turn so that they were sailing upside down, and then another forward turn, climbing straight up a different waterfall, and around one final forward turn, bringing them upright again, depositing them here—wherever "here" was. It was the most frightening ride Alex had ever been on, and he wasn't sure how he'd survived it.

"Oh no," he said softly, thinking about the highly regarded octogator being battered about in the surf. Especially since she hadn't fully recovered from her ordeal with the eel in the aquarium under the volcanic pirate island. "How will we find her?" He rose on shaky legs and rubbed the rope burns on his wrists.

"Spike is out therrre calling forrr herrr. Hopefully she'll shoot up the waterrrfall like the ship did." Simber was silent as his gaze swept the surface of the water, looking for the blue whale's sparkly horn, but he didn't see it. The sea grew calm, almost glassy, and the ship inexplicably moved away from the up-waterfall from whence they'd come, into the open water.

"Ah, wait a moment," the giant stone cheetah said. His regal neck stretched upward, and his eyes narrowed. He flew higher and sampled the air with a delicate sniff. After a moment, he nodded. "Yes. Herrre comes Spike now with Octavia. She's the last one." The frown on his face softened, and he let out a sigh of relief, which almost never happened unless things had been very, very serious.

Alex, his brain still fuzzy, wondered how long he'd been unconscious, and what else he'd missed. He strained to see the two creatures, but they were too far away for his eyes to detect. Instead he looked around as the fog in his head began to clear. The ship was in tatters. Ropes and nets still held various humans, creatures, and statues who had tied themselves down to keep from flying about. And some members of their party were definitely broken. Captain Ahab's hand held on to the ship's wheel, but the rest of him was nowhere to be seen.

"Captain?" Alex called out.

"Aye," came the gargly reply from the deck behind the ship's wheel, where the captain lay in six or seven pieces. "I live. My wretched existence shall waste away another day."

"He sounds about normal," Alex muttered, and mentally checked Captain Ahab's well-being off his list of concerns. He caught Samheed's eye. "You okay?"

Samheed was easing his way to his feet nearby as Fox chomped at the ropes around his wrists. "Ugh. Major head-ache." Once freed, he staggered and grabbed the railing for support. "Where's Lani?"

Alex looked up at Simber for the answer. "And Sky?" His pulse raced when he remembered that sometime during the horrible ride he'd been holding on to her. The fear cleared his head.

"They'rrre both fine. Helping the injurrred. Everrryone is batterrred but alive thanks to Spike." The cheetah swooped down to the water to pick up Ms. Octavia from Spike's broad back.

"Mewmewmew!" cried Kitten.

Fox began to interpret, but then glanced at Simber and closed his mouth.

Alex shook his head. "I don't know how any of us lived through that, whatever it was." He stepped carefully to the railing and used it to steady himself. The water sparkled with the sun hanging low over it, making a pale yellow path in front of them. "Are you sure you're okay, Sam?"

Samheed nodded and limped over. "I think so."

"We're still heading west," Alex mused. "Unless it's morning now." He narrowed his eyes and wished for a better sense of direction. "Where are we? How do we get home? Do we have to go through that thing again to get back?"

"I doubt we'll have to go through it again," Samheed said. "I'm pretty sure that was a scroll feature. We're on the other end now." He rubbed the back of his throbbing head. His fingers came away sticky with blood. "Ick."

Kitten hopped and mewed again.

Alex ignored her, completely puzzled by Samheed's words. "What do you mean, scroll feature? Other end of what?"

Samheed wiped his fingers on his shirt. "I mean it's like the scroll feature Mr. Today turned on in Artimé whenever new Unwanteds arrived to keep them from getting lost or eaten in the jungle. I rode on it our first day, remember?"

Alex frowned. He remembered Samheed getting mad and stomping off, away from the group, but he'd never asked what had happened to him. "I didn't care much for you back then, you know."

"Likewise," Samheed said with a smirk. "I don't think I actually told you guys what happened. But it was sort of like what we just went through, only on a much smaller scale."

"You mean you scrolled on a waterfall and didn't tell any-body about it? Are you joking?"

"Not a waterfall—I wasn't on water in Artimé, I was on land. It was like . . . like I got sucked down a hill that rotated, and my feet were stuck to it, so even when I was upside down, I didn't fall anywhere." He pursed his lips. "Picture Kitten with her feet glued to the ship's wheel. If we turned it, she'd stay stuck to the wheel all the way around. It's kind of like that—I just went around, and it brought me to the other side of Artimé."

"So . . . you're saying that we went around the *world*? And now we're . . . where exactly?" Alex looked left and right at the vast, open sea.

Samheed shrugged. "My guess is that since we began scrolling when we were as far west as we could be, beyond the Island of Legends, we're now as far away from the Island of Legends as we possibly can be. We're . . . we're . . . east."

"MEW. MEW. MEW."

Everyone turned to look at Kitten, whose tiny face was furious. She pointed with her porcelain toes toward the bow of the ship.

"She says—" Fox said.

"She says," Simber interrupted, "that Ms. Morning's seek spell came frrrom the west. Arrrtimé is that way."

East of the Sun

lex cringed. The seek spell from Claire Morning—
it had come just as the ship plunged over the waterfall. He'd forgotten all about it. It could mean only
one thing: Something was wrong in Artimé.

And here they were, in a broken-down ship with a broken-
down captain somewhere far from home, in a part of the sea
they'd never traversed before. No one knew exactly how far
away they were. All they knew was that there were three
islands on this side of Quill and Artimé, just like there were
three on the other side. If these islands were spaced out
similarly to the ones on the west side of Quill, it could take

LISA McMANN

many days for the battered ship to limp home.

As Alex contemplated, Lani's head appeared in the stair-well. "Alex," she said, her face full of concern. "Glad you're finally awake. Got a big problem. There's a hole in the ship. We're taking on water fast. Sky suggested we try a glass spell to cover the hole." She paused for breath. "I think it might work, but I don't know how to cast that one."

Alex looked at Sam. "Can you do it?"

Samheed nodded. "I'll go. You figure out what to do from here."

A moment later, Carina Holiday approached. "Alex," she said urgently. Her pixie hair was wild, sticking up in all direc-tions. "Sean's not doing very well."

Alex's face lit up with concern. "Where is he?"

"Still tied to the ropes. Follow me."

Alex hurried after Carina. When they reached Sean, whose leg had been badly broken by a giant eel on the living-crab island called Karkinos, they knelt at his side. Lani's younger brother, Henry Haluki, was there already, measuring a small amount of liquid from a vial and pouring it carefully into Sean's mouth. Sean's face twisted in pain. Sweat dotted his upper lip and forehead.

"What happened?" Alex said.

"Bumpy ride," Sean said between short gasps of pain.

Carina reached for Sean's hand, and he gripped it tightly. "It's his leg, obviously," she said. "He's having almost as much pain now as when he broke it."

Alex pressed his lips together. "What do we do?" he asked Henry.

Henry held the bottle of medicine to the light, frowned, and put it into his pocket. He moved to examine the makeshift splint the Unwanteds had made for Sean's leg. "Every move this ship makes," Henry said with grave authority, "feels like a knife stabbing his leg. We have to set it again."

"No," Sean whispered. His eyelids fluttered, but the medicine was beginning to work. "Hurts . . . so much . . ." He closed his eyes.

Henry looked at Alex. "And then we have to get him home."

Alex nodded. "As soon as we can figure out how to do that, we'll be on our way."

"No," Carina said. "He needs to go right away."

Alex frowned. "Look, I know he's in pain, but there's no way to turn this ship into a speedboat. We have a leak, Captain Ahab is in pieces, and Ms. Octavia is—"

"Alex," Henry interrupted. "You don't understand. We're almost out of medicine."

Alex sat back. "What? How could that be? I thought you brought a lot."

"We had plenty for a trip to rescue Sky's mother," Henry said, sounding a little defensive. "But then we kept going, and we used two whole bottles on Lhasa before Kitten brought her back to life. And Sean's been taking it regularly for days. Even after all of that, we would have been fine, except we lost the medical bag when we went over the waterfall. So all I have left is what was in my pocket." Henry, who was quite young for having such excellent healing abilities, blinked hard, as if he were trying not to cry. "I should have hung on to the bag better."

Carina patted his shoulder. "You did just fine."

"Yes, and you saved one bottle, which Sean desperately needed," Alex reassured him. "I understand—I'm not blaming you for anything. I was just surprised." He sucked in a breath and blew it out, thinking hard about how to handle things. "How long do we have?"

"I've got a few drops left in this bottle," said Henry. "Not enough for a full dose when this wears off, but it'll help him get through the rest of today."

"Oh boy," Alex muttered. He doubted there was a way they could get home in several days, much less by nightfall.

"And we need to set his leg now, while he won't feel it as much."

Alex blew out a heavy, frustrated breath. Setting Sean's leg had been bad enough the first time. He looked around and saw a slightly bedraggled Ms. Octavia coming toward them, almost appearing to float through the air on her many tentacles. Alex waved her over.

Henry filled her in on the plan and explained how they were going to do it. Ms. Octavia wound two tentacles around Sean's leg and Alex held Sean's upper body steady. At Henry's command, Ms. Octavia pulled while Henry and Carina set the leg. Sean cried out in his sleep. Once the leg was set, Alex rushed over to help Carina replace the splint and secure it.

When Henry and Carina no longer needed him, Alex slipped away to assess their situation, beckoning Ms. Octavia to join him. "I need you to fix Captain Ahab as soon as possible," he said. "We're out of medicine. We need to get Sean home."

LISA McMANN

"Do we know where we are?" she asked. "How far is home?"

Alex shook his head. "I don't know for sure. We think we're at the easternmost end of the world. But all we know for sure is the direction that Ms. Morning's seek spell came from."

"So the seek spell doesn't require us to go back the way we came, around the world?" asked Ms. Octavia.

"Thankfully, no," Alex replied. "It must have rerouted once we made it through the waterfalls. It was gone when I woke up, but Kitten saw it before it faded away."

"Well that's good, but we're still a long way from Artimé, and the ship is barely moving. What will we do with Sean in the meantime? He'll need something for the pain."

Alex looked up at the top of the battered mast, where six squirrelicorns rested. "I was thinking maybe the squirrelicorns could . . . you know, take him. Back home."

The two looked at each other—once teacher and student, now peers solving a dilemma. After a moment Ms. Octavia shook her alligator head. "The squirrelicorns aren't like Simber—they can't fly indefinitely. We don't know what's out there or if there's any place for them to land if they need to rest."

"Oh," Alex said, his thoughts whirling. "Right. Of course you're right." He pushed back a lock of tangled hair that had fallen over his eyes and sighed, defeated. "Then I guess there's no other choice," he said, turning to gaze at Artimé's grand protector who circled the ship above. "But it worries me. I just wish it wouldn't leave us so vulnerable."

"You mean Simber?" Ms. Octavia said, her voice grave.

Losing Simber was the last thing Alex wanted to do. He had no idea what dangers awaited them. But it was the only way to save Sean. He nodded slowly, even as his gut twisted. "We'll have to make our way home without him."

Aaron Loses Someone Important

As he ran away from Artimé through the jungle, the High Priest Aaron Stowe tripped over a root and fell hard to the ground. He lay there for a minute, panting, trying to get the horrible image of Secretary being attacked by the panther out of his mind, but he couldn't.

He touched the pocket where the heart attack spell components had been. The fabric lay flat against his leg now. Had he killed Panther? He wasn't sure. All he knew was that after that attack, there was no way Secretary was still alive. And it was his fault.

It was almost like he'd murdered the woman himself.

His chest tightened. He sucked in a breath and choked on it. He tried to tell himself that she'd have died eventually anyway since he'd sent her to the Ancients Sector. But it wasn't the same—because he'd actually *seen* her die, which somehow made it more real. Besides, his plan had been to get her out of there again. To scare her into being more obedient. The plan had backfired.

"It's *her* fault," he said weakly. He pressed his elbow into the moist jungle floor and sat up. "What was she doing in Artimé, of all places? If she'd gone to the Ancients Sector right away like she was supposed to, she'd still be alive. Probably, anyway." He couldn't catch his breath, and his chest wouldn't stop hurting. He didn't know what was wrong with him. Only that he wanted Secretary back.

He got to his feet, eyes stinging, and stumbled toward the clearing where the tube was, hoping beyond hope that the rock was nowhere in sight. He had to get out of there. He had to go home.

Finally he reached the clearing and saw the little dog swinging by his teeth from tree branch to tree branch. There was no one else there. Aaron hid behind a tree and waited for the dog to move out of sight, and then he ran for the tube and stepped inside. When he turned to push the button, he caught sight of something moving toward him through the jungle. It was the panther, as alive as she'd ever been. Beside her was a large gray wolf.

The wolf's cool, blue eyes met Aaron's, and for a brief moment Aaron felt like he'd seen the creature before. But of course he hadn't. And he had no desire to see it ever again. He slammed his hand down on the button and disappeared, spending less than a second in the mansion's tube before redirecting himself to Haluki's house.

In no time at all, the high priest was making his way out of the house, up the gravel driveway toward the portcullis, and past the guards to the palace. Inside, he shoved past Liam Healy without a word, leaving the new governor speechless, and continued to his office, where all was quiet. Too quiet.

Aaron closed the door, walked to his desk, and sat down. Then he dropped his head into his hands and stayed still for a very long time, thinking about Secretary. Thinking about how he'd made yet another rash decision, and he'd messed up again.

Thinking about how there was no fixing this. Not this time. Because the woman who always fixed things for him was dead.

After a while, the pain in his chest grew so large that it began to push its way out in low groans and ugly sobs.

Aaron's only friend in the entire world was dead.

What was he going to do without her?

Meghan Gets Mad

When Gunnar Haluki returned and the confusion from the panther attack on Artimé finally began to clear, three truths emerged:

Eva Fathom was dead . . . and she appeared to have been on Artimé's side all along.

Aaron Stowe had unleashed the panther, but he'd also released the heart attack spells to stop its attack.

Meghan Ranger was one seriously ticked-off Unwanted, and she'd had about enough of Aaron Stowe.

Her component vest pockets bulging, Meghan marched past the girrinos at the gate without a word and headed into Quill, up the road toward the palace. Every step she took brought her simmering anger closer to its boiling point, and by the time she reached the palace, she was in no mood to converse with the guards who stood there. Before they could issue a challenge, she hit the men with scatterclips that sent them flying backward, pinning them to the portcullis. She finished with a silent spell and left them hanging noiselessly as she released the lock and slipped inside the grounds.

At the entrance, Meghan dog-collared each guard with clay shackles. After only a moment's hesitation to take in the unfamiliar surroundings, she straightened her vest, headed up the stairs, and began opening doors and looking inside rooms until she happened upon the right one.

Aaron emitted a small gasp when he heard the noise at the door, and Meghan thought she detected a hint of hope in his face. But it soon turned to confusion and perhaps even fear.

Meghan didn't care. Hope, confusion, fear—none of it mattered. Before he could move, Meghan flung a handful of scatterclips at him. He and his chair soared backward and stuck to the wall. His arms stuck too, spread out, leaving him helpless.

"Wha-a-a-t?" Aaron asked. He sniffed wildly and tried to wipe his eyes on his shoulder, but he couldn't quite reach.

Meghan stepped right up to him, her face pinched in disdain. "I saw what you did. What is your problem?" she said, not caring that she spoke the words loud enough to be heard outside the office. "I hope you know Eva Fathom is dead! Where did you find that horrible panther creature?"

Aaron stared. "It—it was a mistake," he said. It made him feel weak to say it, and he didn't like that feeling at all. He cleared his throat and changed his tone to something much more menacing. "I intended to kill you all," he said, lifting his chin. "And if you don't release me immediately, I will do just that."

Meghan's sneer melted in confusion as the scatterclips clattered to the floor. The sudden freedom took Aaron by surprise. He scrambled off the chair, tripped over its leg, and fell. He looked startled for a moment, then his countenance cleared, and as he got to his feet, he seemed quite pleased with himself.

"How did you do that?" Meghan demanded. She pulled more spells from her vest pockets, ready to fight.

"Yes, Aaron. How?" came a voice from the doorway. "I'm so curious."

Meghan turned to see a red-faced, eyebrowless woman stepping into the room. The girl eased back, pointing spells at Aaron and the woman, but neither seemed to take any further notice of her. The two stared at each other.

"Do what, Governor? I didn't do anything," Aaron said, his voice cool. He wiped the dust from his pants. "This Unwanted is such a failure that she can't even cast a proper spell."

Meghan's jaw dropped in indignation, but she remained silent, fascinated by Aaron's lie. She hadn't cast a bad spell, and she hadn't released it. Aaron had. Whether he knew it or not remained to be seen. But clearly the woman in the doorway had seen it, and was keen enough on magic to know something strange had just happened.

The woman walked in. "Who are you?" she asked Meghan.

"Who are *you*?" Meghan replied. She held a backward bobbly head, ready to fling it at the woman if she got any closer.

"I'm Gondoleery Rattrapp, of course. Tell me, nameless girl, did my eyes deceive me? Or did our fearless leader just release himself from a spell you cast?" The woman stepped closer to Meghan.

Meghan's eyes darted to Aaron, who gave her a small, panicked look, which confused Meghan dreadfully. What was going on here? "If you take one more step toward me," Meghan warned Gondoleery, "I'll—"

With that, Gondoleery pointed at Meghan. A tiny fireball shot from her fingertip, hitting Meghan in the shoulder and singeing her sleeve and the ends of her hair.

Without thinking, Meghan cast the bobbly head at Gondoleery and shot a highlighter spell in Aaron's eyes, blinding him. And while Gondoleery's head spun a hundred and eighty degrees, bobbling loosely, and Aaron cried out in pain and pitched into his desk, Meghan Ranger ran from the office, down the stairs, and out of the palace like her life depended on it, passing Liam Healy in the entryway. He turned and watched her go, confused. And then he sprinted up the steps to Aaron's office, finding Aaron and Gondoleery looking most peculiar.

When Gondoleery Rattrapp's head was finally on straight and she could think clearly once more, she faced Liam and

Aaron, whose sight was beginning to come back.

"Is it true what she said?" Gondoleery asked. "Eva's dead?"

"What?" cried Liam.

Aaron wasn't sure if he could speak. He was glad he could blame the highlighter spell for his moist eyes. "It's true," he said finally. "She was killed by . . ." Aaron's thoughts whirled. "By a creature in Artimé," he said carefully.

Liam's shock turned to disbelief. "Why? How could that happen? That's against everything they stand for!"

"Artimé attacked and killed the secretary to the high priest?" Gondoleery cried out, dumbfounded. "And you just stood here and let that Unwanted cast spells on *us*? What kind of pathetic ruler are you? She could have killed both of us, leaving Quill at their mercy!" Gondoleery moved her face close to Aaron's—so close he could feel draconic heat emanating from her pores. "You are a terrible leader!"

Aaron stared at her. He could smell her rank breath.

"Gondoleery," Liam said quietly. "Step back."

"Yes," Aaron said, coming to his senses, his chest heaving. "Back off immediately. Or I'll summon the guards."

Gondoleery cackled, and a bit of spittle landed on Aaron's

LISA McMANN

cheek. He narrowed his eyes and wiped it away. After a moment, she took a step back. "You're a scared little dog," she said. "You're afraid to attack Artimé, aren't you? Aha, you are!" She laughed again. "You know, if you don't take control of Quill soon, somebody else will, and happily."

The words cut Aaron hard because he knew they were true. He had failed to keep the Restorers together. He'd failed to train the jungle animals to do his bidding and the panther ended up killing the only person he actually cared about. There was only so much more he could do before somebody figured out he didn't have a clue how to run Quill . . . especially now, without Secretary by his side.

But he couldn't show any weakness—not in front of Gondoleery. Not now, when she had seen him release the spell. His magical abilities *had* to remain his secret weapon. "My dear Gondoleery," he said, his words like ice, "if you don't get out of this room immediately, I'll send you back to the Ancients Sector where you came from."

A flicker of fear crossed Gondoleery's face before her self-assured smile returned. She extended her singed fingers, examined them, and loudly cracked her knuckles, knowing she had nothing to worry about. Still, she made no reply, and after a moment, she turned and marched out of the office.

Aaron let out a breath and dropped into his chair.

Liam moved to speak but Aaron shushed him. "You too," the high priest said gruffly. "Out."

"But . . . about Eva—what happened?"

"I said get out!"

Liam hesitated, fists balled in frustration and grief, and then turned on his heel and left.

Once Aaron was alone, the realization was almost too much for him to take. Gondoleery was so right it hurt—Aaron *was* a terrible leader of Quill. He didn't know what he was doing. He made hasty decisions that had awful, senseless outcomes. He started things that had potential, but he continually failed to follow through. And now, the worst thing of all had happened. Gondoleery had figured out his secret—he was a complete and utter failure.

And he was scared to death.

A Painful Truth

On board the ship, Octavia quickly weaved a large square hammock out of rope while Alex talked over the plan with Simber. When the hammock was finished, Alex and Octavia spread it out on the deck, and then they and Carina lifted Sean and gently lowered him onto it. Simber glided above the deck and let his legs hang down low so Alex and Carina could attach the four corners of the hammock to them. They tested the rope to make sure it was secure, and then tied a few more ropes to one side of the hammock, tossed them up and over Simber's back, and attached them to the other side to be completely certain Sean

LISA McMANN

would be safe and secure. Hanging in the hammock would give Sean a fairly smooth ride, or at least that's what everyone hoped.

Carina grabbed a bag of necessities and climbed on the cheetah's back. She would accompany them.

"Come back as soon as you can," Alex said to Simber. He tried not to sound anxious. "We'll be fine out here, I'm sure. I hope you can find us."

The stone cheetah growled in response. Alex knew Simber didn't want to leave, but he had no choice. Slowly the statue ascended with his strange-looking cargo. Carina tapped her fist to her chest and gave a solemn wave, and soon she, Simber, and Sean were on their way home.

Home. It seemed like forever since they'd been in Artimé. Alex stood at the bow and watched the three grow small against the blue canvas of the sky, and tried not to think about all the things that could go wrong without Simber there to save them.

"Alex!" Lani called from the stairs, breaking his reverie. Her hair was disheveled and her clothes dripping wet. She followed Alex's gaze and saw the dot in the sky. "Ah, they're off, then," she said softly. "Poor Sean."

"You heard?"

"Yes," she said. "The ship feels so naked without Simber overhead. Makes me nervous."

Alex nodded. "I'm nervous too." They watched the dot disappear, and when Alex was sure there was nothing more to see, he sighed and looked at Lani, dripping next to him.

"Oh," he said. "Sorry—I was lost there for a minute. How's the leak? What can I help with?"

Lani touched his arm. "Nothing. Just coming up to give you an update. The hole is patched for now, at least. We're bailing out the rest of the water."

Alex shoved his worries about Simber aside for the moment. He had more pressing matters right below his feet. "Do you need help?"

"No, it's crowded enough down there. Thanks, though."

"Sure," he said. "Octavia is looking for the rest of the captain's body parts so she can put him back together, and Florence is repairing broken railings, equipment, and sails. We should be on our way soon."

"We'll have to take it slow. We don't want the waves to break open our patch job."

"I know." Alex looked at her. "Is Sky . . . ?"

Lani offered a sympathetic smile. "She's fine. Working hard. We all are."

"Of course I know that."

Lani cringed. "We're all *fine*, I mean. Just bruises and scrapes."

"Oh. Yes, Simber told me. I'm glad."

Lani held Alex's gaze for a moment. "Just give her some space," she said quietly. "She says you two weren't meant to be. She's given up on you. But I don't know." She looked over her shoulder down the stairwell. "I've got to go. There's a lot of water. I'm working on creating a larger sponge spell to try and soak it up that way, but I don't have the right components here on the ship." She turned and headed down the steps. "Maybe a bigger bucket spell . . . nah. Too heavy. Come on, Haluki," she chided. "Think it through." Her mumblings grew too soft to hear.

Alex watched her go and almost went after her to see the damage, but decided to heed her advice. Her blunt words hurt—Sky had told Lani that she'd given up on him? It made him feel terrible. After a moment Alex began to pick up broken

LISA McMANN

chunks of the railing and other items strewn about the battered ship, flinging them a bit harder than he intended into a pile on the deck near Florence.

But why wouldn't she give up on him? He deserved it. Things had been tense with Sky before their harrowing journey around the world, and it was his fault. Completely. He knew that. He'd realized that he liked her so much that he couldn't seem to do his job properly. Whenever she was around, he got distracted. He'd made a lot of mistakes, like when he almost killed Spike before she had a chance to really live. And when he'd been too careless to find out if Florence could swim, which had caused intense worry for days when Florence was captured by the giant eel. These were big mistakes. Life or death mistakes. The kind he couldn't afford to make again, not under any circumstances. All of which had led to awkward tension and a vast failure on his part to communicate the problem to Sky.

If only he could explain it to her. But according to Lani, he didn't have to now. Sky had given up on him.

He stared long and hard at the pile of rubbish on the deck, hardly remembering that he'd built it. Of course she'd given up on him. She wasn't the kind of person to wait around for someone to be done acting out all of his foolishness. If Alex couldn't tell Sky the truth, at least she could be free to find whatever it was she wanted from life, whether alone or with someone else. And as long as threats to his people existed, Alex would have to keep away from romantic relationships.

It was for the best. Alex had a million other things to do, and there was no way he could keep making such enormous mistakes with all of the Artiméans' well-being at stake under his leadership.

Even so, his heart twisted and pain shot through him in a most deep and intense way, more painful than any injury he'd ever sustained, because it came from inside. And while the pain surprised him, it brought with it an even more shocking revelation. For the truth was that in the time since the girl on a raft had washed up on shore, Alex Stowe, Unwanted, head mage and restorer of Artimé, in the midst of turmoil from all sides, had slowly—and quite tragically—fallen in love.

And, unlike Sky, he was having quite a lot of trouble falling out of it.

The Pieces Begin to Come Together

A few days later in Artimé, Meghan sat on the lawn with Ms. Morning, Mr. Appleblossom, and Gunnar Haluki. They had much to discuss.

"Is it too soon to be concerned about Alex and the ship?" Ms. Morning asked. "Shall I send another seek spell?"

"It might be just a little premature," replied Mr. Appleblossom in his traditional rhyming iambic pentameter speech. "And we don't want to worry them, do we? I'll visit *poste d'observateur* to check if there is any ship out there to see."

Meghan flashed Ms. Morning a curious glance.

Ms. Morning smiled and explained, "Ever since he climbed up Florence to the top of the gray shack, he can't get enough climbing, so he's been visiting the mansion rooftop daily to watch for Alex. He calls it his observer position."

Mr. Appleblossom cleared his throat and looked pointedly at Ms. Morning.

"*Poste d'observateur,*" Ms. Morning said carefully, trying not to mangle the strange words. "He thinks it's some other language."

Mr. Appleblossom beamed.

"What, from another island you mean?" asked Gunnar.

"Another island or another world, it is unknown; the truth remains unfurled." He pointed to the book on the table next to him, which he'd gotten from the vessel that crashed into the sea near Artimé some weeks before.

"Anyway," Meghan prompted, "Mr. Appleblossom is right. I think if we send another seek spell it'll make us seem like we're in scads of trouble when all we really want is to let Carina know about her mother's death." She paused. "Which is kind of a big deal too, of course. But we've only used that spell in times of danger, so I bet they'll be imagining the worst. We

LISA McMANN

don't want them to botch up the mission on account of them rushing to get back here."

"All right, we'll wait," said Ms. Morning. "Now, what is this I hear about you going into Quill? Did you see your parents?"

Meghan scowled in the direction of the girrinos, who apparently couldn't keep a secret. "Not exactly," she said. She knew Ms. Morning would be mad if she found out what had happened at the palace with Aaron and Gondoleery Rattrapp. It had been reckless of Meghan to go there alone, and she could have gotten killed. "I just, um, went for a walk like my brother often does. When he's here, that is. Obviously."

Ms. Morning, seemingly distracted, accepted the explanation. She looked at Gunnar. "I'm still not sure what to think about Eva Fathom. Do you believe what she said? That she was on our side?"

"I do," Gunnar said. "Marcus told me about the plan he had with Eva to fake his death and take control of Aaron. It all backfired when Marcus and you took the tube to my house in Quill and Aaron was there. That unfortunate turn of events was out of Eva's control."

"But all that time she *knew* you and I were being held captive! She knew and she didn't do anything about it!"

Haluki smiled grimly. "She let me know you were there. I don't know if I would have survived without that information."

Claire Morning looked at her hands. "But why wouldn't she rescue us?"

"I don't know for sure," Haluki said, "but I believe she was doing the best she could under the shocking circumstances. She couldn't help us, not with the others there. Not without risking everything."

He scratched his chin thoughtfully and went on. "She had to prove her loyalty to Aaron so he would tell her things. She'd been the one keeping us informed since she went back to work as Secretary. Matilda can only hear so much from the closet where Aaron stashed her, and then only what happens in the office. Eva was our second set of ears. She stopped Aaron from doing a number of very stupid things. I just wish . . ." He trailed off, thinking of the old woman. "I will miss her. She was a good woman, and we need to let Carina know that. I'm sure it broke Eva's heart to keep the truth from her daughter. But she did it for the sake of Artimé."

LISA McMANN

Ms. Morning frowned. "How did she keep us informed? She hadn't been on the premises for months until she came rushing in here the other day."

Meghan listened, holding her breath. She didn't know any of this, and she felt very important to be a trusted part of this conversation.

Gunnar glanced sidelong at Meghan. His look told her this was a secret she should keep. "Eva had a confidant. Someone she met with regularly to exchange information. I am quite sure that person will vouch for her."

Ms. Morning sat up, indignant. "Why doesn't he or she come forward, then?"

"Because he's on the ship," Gunnar said in a low voice.

"You mean Alex?" Ms. Morning asked.

"It must be," said Meghan.

Gunnar Haluki looked down.

Mr. Appleblossom, silent all this time, brows knit together in concentration, soon leaned in confidently and looked at Meghan. "The confidant would not the head mage be—for who else but Sean Ranger? It is he."

LISA McMANN

Meghan gasped. She looked at Ms. Morning, whose lips parted in wonder. They both turned to Haluki.

"Is it?" demanded Ms. Morning.

"My brother?" asked Meghan.

Haluki's silence gave no answer. But Meghan thought his eyes said yes.

"Well what about Liam Healy, then?" Ms. Morning asked after a while. "Eva mentioned him. That he was on our side. I hardly believed it, but now . . . I'm not sure what to think."

"Liam's loyalty is something I know nothing about," Haluki said gruffly. He hesitated, looking carefully at Ms. Morning. "I only know how poorly he treated you."

Ms. Morning looked at the grass. "Don't worry," she said bitterly. "I haven't forgotten that."

Meghan, sensing tension, looked anywhere but at Haluki and Ms. Morning. As Meghan craned her neck, pretending to admire the budding trees near the shore, she spotted something in the sky.

"Look." She squinted, then got up and ran toward the beach, while Mr. Appleblossom headed for the corner of the

LISA McMANN

mansion and climbed sprightly up the side of it to his observation tower on the roof.

The spot grew bigger. "What in the world?" Meghan whispered.

"Hurrry!" came the familiar roar from the dot in the sky. "Prrreparrre forrr incoming wounded!"

Island Number Five

The ship drifted slowly to the west with the current while the people on board grew restless and tired of fixing things. It had been days since they'd raced over the waterfall. Water continued to seep in through the edges of the patched hole in the ship, and sometimes the pressure of the waves knocked the glass out completely, causing a blast of seawater to fill the bowels of the vessel at an alarming rate. Samheed and Alex had cast more glass spells than they could count, and everyone else was getting sick of bailing around the clock. Sleep came in snatches, and on the minds of everyone was Simber's glaring absence.

LISA McMANN

One of Captain Ahab's ears was still missing and probably lost forever, and his head rattled a bit, but there was nothing Ms. Octavia could do to stop it short of taking his entire head off, and she didn't want to risk doing that at sea when they needed him at the wheel. Half-deaf, the captain spoke even louder than usual, and his nonsensical outbursts put everyone on edge.

Spike surfaced now and then, staying near the ship in case she was needed, and always eager to learn more about the ways of the sea by watching and listening.

Florence was unusually quiet and lost in thought as she repaired things on the top deck, no doubt revisiting in her mind the island of Karkinos and its inhabitants, most specifically the bronze giant Talon, whom she'd grown very fond of. She thought often about the dying crab and racked her brain to think of something the people of Artimé could do to help. But so far, she hadn't come up with anything.

Energy was down all around. Not unlike Karkinos, the ship had pretty much turned into a floating island with no other land in sight.

In the quietness of the late afternoon, Lani took a worn map from her pocket. It was the one she'd been studying through-out the journey to Pirate Island and the Island of Legends. She'd been convinced the map held a secret to what lay beyond the string of seven islands, for on the map, to the west of a staggered row of seven dots, was a drawing of a much larger piece of land. That land was what she'd hoped to find on their journey beyond the westernmost island, Karkinos.

Now she studied it one last time and shook her head. There was no larger land to the west. The world was only seven islands, and the map was probably just something some writer imagined in her world of make-believe stories. Lani's theory had been wrong, and Samheed had been right. Oh, how she hated to admit it! But with her chin held high, and making sure Samheed was watching, Lani took a fire-breathing origami dragon from her component vest pocket, commanded it to light, and used it to set the corner of the map on fire, intending to let the ashes whirl around and fly off to meet the sea.

But Samheed didn't gloat—he sprang into action. He grabbed the map, threw it to the deck, and stomped the fire out. Then he picked it up and handed it back to Lani, smooth-ing the blackened corner and seeing that the map was still

LISA McMANN

fully intact. "You should keep this," he said. "It might not be what you thought, but it could still be important." He put his hands on Lani's shoulders and pulled her close. They stayed together, talking quietly for a very long time.

Alex noticed them and paused to watch their intimate conversation from his spot at the stern, where he continued to retreat to despite the fact that Simber was no longer hovering above. Feeling lost and alone, he sighed softly and turned to stare out over the sea.

Sky also noticed the couple and looked away. After an awkward moment standing near the stairwell, pointedly not looking at Alex, she descended to check on her mother, Copper, whom they'd rescued from the pirate island. Soon after, Crow and Henry, who had been watching and snickering at Sam and Lani from behind a crate, lost interest in the mushiness and snuck belowdecks too.

As darkness crept over the ship, the exhausted sailors, creatures, and even the young whale failed to detect in the distance what Simber no doubt would have noticed, had he been there. It was the easternmost island.

And it was not a nice one.

Aaron Grows Desperate

A aron lifted his head from his desk. His hair was disheveled and his jawline wore an uneven layer of fuzz. Shadows hung below his bloodshot eyes. The desk was strewn with recent sketches—this time of Quillitary vehicles and soldiers. "There's no other way," he muttered, stabbing the drawings with his pencil. "I need their help. And there's no more time to waste."

Gondoleery had said out loud what Aaron had refused to admit to himself all this time—that he was going to lose everything. His power, the palace . . . probably even his life if he didn't do something drastic. And fast.

LISA McMANN

In retrospect, this was probably something Aaron should have done from the time he'd been kicked out of university, but back then there was no way it would have worked—after all, the Quillitary soldiers had been the ones who removed him. But now? Maybe. There was a chance.

All Aaron knew was that if his new plan didn't work, he might as well throw himself into the Great Lake of Boiling Oil, because he'd be more unwanted than the Unwanteds themselves.

He'd already sent Liam and Gondoleery out on the streets of Quill to spread the word about the new threat from Artimé, having them preach far and wide that one of the magical land's creatures had killed his beloved Secretary. And he'd pushed aside the twinge of guilt that went along with the little white lie. Technically the panther *was* a creature of Artimé if Mr. Today had created it. And it lived in the jungle, which was a part of Artimé. So it seemed a fair assessment. He just conveniently left out the part where *he* had been the one to unleash the wild beast.

His mouth went dry as he remembered the horrible scene that had kept him up every night since it happened. He couldn't understand why he kept thinking about it. For much of his life he'd been able to push thoughts aside, because the laws of

Quill required it. Sure, he'd had dreams about his brother now and then even though it wasn't allowed. He'd felt *something* when Justine had died, even though he wasn't supposed to. But Secretary . . . something about her death tore apart his insides in a way that was foreign and extremely frightening.

He stood abruptly and began ripping his drawings into tiny shreds and throwing them into the trash bin. "No!" he shouted. But even he wasn't sure why.

"Secretary! I require a meeting with the Quillitary—" He stopped short and set his jaw. The old habit of calling for her seemed impossible to break. He had no one now.

There was a noise in the hallway, and soon Liam appeared at the door. "Can I help you, sir? I mean, I heard you calling. I'm happy to, um . . . assist. . . ."

Aaron looked at Liam. "Yes," he said. "Yes, indeed. Get me a driver. I need to visit the Quillitary." He paused. As Liam turned to go, Aaron added, "Come with me." It was a demand, not a plea.

"Certainly," Liam said. "I'll fetch a driver now."

Ten minutes later the man who had driven Eva Fathom to her meeting with death was driving Liam and Aaron to the

LISA McMANN

place where all the weapons in Quill were kept, as well as all the people who knew how to use them.

Liam focused on his hands, folded in his lap. His eyes were bloodshot from mourning Eva Fathom's death in private. But now he knew he had to step up and do what she'd prepared him to do.

"May I suggest, High Priest," Liam said tentatively, looking up, "that we stop at the Favored Farm on our way? A basket of nuts and produce might be a welcome gift to the Quillitary general."

Aaron scowled. He thought about it for a while as the vehicle puttered along. It sounded like something Secretary would have suggested, and she was usually right with such things. "Fine," he said.

Liam leaned forward to tell the driver, who maneuvered the vehicle to the side of the road and made the stop.

"I'll take care of collecting the goods," Liam said.

Aaron remained in the car, staring sullenly out the window at the wall that surrounded Quill while Liam fetched an enormous burlap bag full of nuts, fruits, and vegetables. When the driver got out of the vehicle to help Liam load the produce into the back of the old jalopy, Liam palmed him some oranges.

The driver glanced at the backseat to make sure Aaron wasn't looking, then slipped the oranges inside a hidden compartment in the trunk. "Th-thank you," he said in a voice so soft Liam could scarcely hear him. "I'm sorry about Secretary. When I saw what happened, I had to go. I had to—for my—"

Liam held a hand out. "I know," he said, his voice quiet too. "She wouldn't have wanted you to get into trouble." He glanced at the car. "We need to go." The two exchanged a look of trust and returned to the vehicle.

"Let's get on with it, then," Aaron said. He was cross and a little bit anxious to get the Quillitary visit over with. And he was disgusted by having to ask the Quillitary for help after the way they'd rejected and ridiculed him and kicked him out of university. As they proceeded, he continued to stare moodily out the window at the dingy wall that encircled them, wondering what was going on beyond it, but glad he didn't have to face that fear.

As they neared the Quillitary, Aaron's thoughts moved toward wondering whom exactly he'd have to grovel *to*. Who was in charge now? He hadn't visited the Quillitary since before he and Justine had discovered Artimé. After the battle,

LISA McMANN

the Quillitary had been very angry with Aaron for messing everything up, and they'd blamed him for Justine's death—it was no wonder that Aaron wanted nothing to do with them. Aaron hadn't paid any attention to them ever since.

But now that a meeting was imminent, Aaron realized he had absolutely no idea what had been going on behind the closed doors of the Quillitary since Quill's defeat. It struck him finally how odd it was that he, the high priest of Quill, wasn't exactly sure who was leading the Quillitary or what they'd been doing in the yard all this time. All he knew was that General Blair, notorious for tossing the dead body of his own son Will into Artimé, had been killed—Aaron had read it on the death post in the burial grounds more than a year before. *Perhaps*, thought Aaron, *the new general will be easier to deal with*.

With that in mind, it was all the more surprising when Aaron and Liam got out of the jalopy, opened the Quillitary gate, and entered the yard for the first time in a very long time. For not only was everything quite different from what Aaron remembered the last time he was here, but striding toward him at an alarming pace was the very last person Aaron had ever expected to see.

The Return of the General

Aaron and Liam stepped back in shock.

"General Blair," Aaron said under his breath, trying to keep his composure as much as one could expect to when a huge angry man you thought was dead came barreling toward you. Was it a ghost?

"Who invited you?" boomed the towering general. He wore a threadbare Quillitary jacket that strained at the shoulder seams, and his shirt placket was open to mid-chest. As he drew close, Aaron gaped at the jagged red scar that swept from his ear to the hollow of his throat. One end of it looked swollen and angry.

LISA McMANN

"We came of our own accord," Aaron said, trying not to look at the hideous scar. Was that pus oozing from the swollen end? Aaron's stomach churned. He focused on the general's sun-chapped face. The man had distinct wrinkles now, and his hair was decidedly gray in the parts that framed his face. "And you'll address me as High Priest," Aaron added. His voice wavered but his confidence returned. "I thought you were dead."

"Apparently I didn't stay that way for long," the general growled. "What do you want? Excuse me . . . I meant, what do you want, *High Priest?*" he asked, a sneer in his voice.

Liam's eyes widened but he remained scared speechless.

Aaron lifted his chin. "Keep working on that," he said lightly. He picked up the large sack of produce and nuts from the Favored Farm.

"Why, I'll . . ." General Blair's threat died in his scarred throat.

"I've brought you a gift." Aaron opened the sack and showed General Blair.

The general remained skeptical. "In exchange for what?"

"Nothing at all," Aaron said.

Liam found his voice once more. "It's just a gift," he added. "Nothing, um—"

"Who are you?" interrupted the general.

"Liam Healy, sir. Governor, that is. I mean *I'm* a governor. Not you." Liam cringed and was silent.

General Blair looked him over. "Ah, yes. I heard about you."

"Oh?" Liam asked weakly. "From whom?"

The general didn't answer.

Aaron let his gaze wander past the hulking man to the stations of workers who had begun clanking metal together once more or working on broken-down Quillitary vehicles. "You've changed things," he said. "How are the vehicles running?"

"Poorly," General Blair said, his voice retaining its sharp edge despite him taking the sack from Aaron.

Aaron stepped forward and then turned. "Do you mind if I have a look?"

The general glared. "Fine," he said through gritted teeth.

"You see," Aaron continued, acting as if conversation had suddenly become his strong suit, "I know a little bit about these things." He walked over to a soldier working on a vehicle and looked under the hood. "You need something more slick to make this work properly. Rain water just won't do. You may remember that I once suggested using the Great Lake of Boiling Oil—"

"Yes, and how did that turn out?" boomed the general. It was clear he didn't like Aaron nosing around his soldiers, undermining him.

"Not well at all," Aaron said. He saw his opening, took a breath, and lied his face off. "I'm sorry about that, and about . . . Justine. I am. Truly. I never expected my plan to impersonate my Unwanted brother would result in Justine's death. I was foolish." He didn't think he could say anything more without gagging, so he closed his mouth and left it at that, hoping it would be enough to win the man over.

General Blair frowned. "Yes, you were very foolish. Too foolish to have in my Quillitary, which was why—from my deathbed—I ordered you removed from the university."

Aaron nodded. It was as he'd thought. "But I did have some good ideas back then." He pointed to the sack of goods from the Favored Farm.

The general harrumphed.

LISA McMANN

"And I have some today." Aaron inspected the vehicle more closely, and then slowly walked around to the other side and leaned over the engine, saying nothing more.

Liam followed the high priest's lead, having no idea what he was looking at but pretending to be quite absorbed in what he saw.

"Hmm," Aaron said eventually. He straightened and looked around. At one end of the yard was a house, where General Blair most likely had taken up residence in order to remain hidden from the rest of Quill.

Aaron turned suddenly. "Why hasn't it been announced that you are alive? Your name is on the death board."

"I know." The man frowned again. "Artimé believed me to be dead from that Unwanted boy's attack. And I was close, but I'm too stubborn to die."

Aaron nodded and remained silent, hoping the man would go on.

He did. "When I recovered," the general said, "I decided it was better for everyone to believe I'd been killed. And because of it, no one has expected the Quillitary to be doing anything at all without me. It's kept visitors away. Until now," he said

LISA McMANN

wryly, softening a little. "I wish it to remain a secret, because when my Quillitary has fixed our vehicles and become well-equipped enough to battle Artimé once more, I'd very much like to see the look of shock on Samheed Burkesh's face when he sees me . . . right before I kill him."

A Potential
Alliance

Aaron's and Liam's eyes widened at the general's statement—Aaron's in delight, Liam's in fear. But Liam remained quiet, focusing intently on the rusty, dust-covered engine before him.

Aaron, containing the thrill of excitement that threatened to leap out of his throat, merely nodded. "So you're out for revenge on Samheed. Well, he certainly has it coming."

"Yes," the general replied, drawing a finger across the wide scar on his neck, "he certainly does."

"You know, General Blair," Aaron said, "you and I have

very similar goals. If we worked together, don't you think the battle day would come a lot sooner?"

The Quillitary soldier paused in his work and squinted up at the general, then hurriedly resumed working.

General Blair narrowed his eyes at Aaron. "Follow me," he said abruptly. "Please, High Priest," he added diplomatically.

Aaron, smiling inwardly, nodded to Liam to pick up the bag of goods, and together the two followed the general into his house. It looked very much like Haluki's house, not nearly as sparse as the Necessary housing.

"Sit."

Liam held out a chair for Aaron, then set the bag on the table. Aaron urged him with a nod to empty the bag, so Liam began setting the fruit, vegetables, and nuts in a makeshift display that would, with any luck, keep General Blair on speaking terms.

"You don't have any Quillitary soldiers in here protecting you?" Aaron asked, surprised.

"They saw who you were when you arrived. Sorry to say no one's afraid of you." He laughed.

Aaron frowned and sat up straighter. He opened his mouth

to explain just why they all *should* be afraid of him, then hesitated.

Liam, whose senses had finally returned to him, stepped in. He waved his hand over the goods. "Twenty pieces of fruit, a cornucopia of vegetables, and enough nuts to last you many weeks," he said.

The general picked up a handful of nuts. He broke one open with a small hammer, picked the meat from it, and tasted it. "Not bad," he admitted. He ate another. And another.

Aaron forgot about being offended and stared at the almonds, lost in thought.

"So, High Priest," the general continued while chewing and swallowing, "you said you know something about engines. I rather doubt it, but perhaps you'll surprise me." The general popped the rest of the handful of nuts into his mouth and then grabbed an orange and peeled it. "Never seen so much food in one place before," he muttered. "Sure beats having to send someone out to the Favored Farm every day for four measly items. Waste of time."

Liam looked sidelong at Aaron, who was clearly concentrating deeply on the pile of nuts on the table. "It surely does,"

Liam said. "High Priest Aaron, do you have anything to say about engines?"

Aaron startled. "What?" He looked at Liam.

"The general asked you what you know about engines."

"Oh. I, uh . . ." Aaron trailed off, still deep in thought. And then he looked straight at General Blair. "General, I think I can fix the oil issue. It'll help you get the fleet of broken-down vehicles back in service again so you can be prepared to fight Artimé once more." He leaned in. "If I do that for you, will you work with me on a plan of attack?"

The general looked even more skeptical than before.

Before General Blair could say no, Aaron hastened to tell the general about his plan to enclose all of Artimé into Quill once he'd taken over the magical land, and he promised the general a section of the mansion, should they succeed.

At those words, Liam's lips parted a little in surprise, since by offering a portion of the mansion to the general, Aaron ensured the governors a smaller stake in the place. But he said nothing.

When Aaron had finished, he sat back. "What do you think? Can we work together?"

The general scratched his chin and glared. "I'm still not convinced working with you would do me any good. You'll probably mess everything up. But more importantly, how do I know you aren't a coward? Will you have the courage to do what needs to be done in order to succeed? Your track record is pretty bad."

"I managed to become high priest," Aaron said. "That doesn't seem very bad to me." Still, a wave of fear washed through him. He couldn't screw this up—it was his last option. "Look, General Blair. It's true I've made mistakes; I've already admitted that. But I've learned from them. You can trust me. I'll—I'll—I'll do whatever you say," he said recklessly.

"Oh, will you now?" For the first time, General Blair smiled, showing his sharp, yellowed teeth. "Prove it."

"I will," Aaron said. "What do you want me to do?"

The general put his elbows on the table and leaned forward, staring hard at Aaron, his hideous scar pulsing to the beat of Aaron's own heart. "Son, do you know the reason why we lost the battle last time?"

Aaron tried not to flinch, but the scar was getting closer and closer to Aaron's face. "Because Justine was killed—"

LISA McMANN

"No!" General Blair shouted, slamming his hand down on the table.

Aaron and Liam jumped.

"No," the man said again, pointing at Aaron's face. "Not because Justine was murdered." He stood abruptly and lurched forward, his hands on the center of the table and his face inches from Aaron's. "We lost because we couldn't sneak up on Artimé. We walked right through the gate, our vehicles going single file into their battlefield, and we couldn't get back out again. We lost," he seethed, "because the High Priest Justine wouldn't let me do what I needed to do to succeed."

Aaron gulped. The general's breath was hot on his face. Shaking, Aaron pushed his chair back and rose slowly to his feet. It took him several seconds before he trusted himself to speak. "General Blair, what is it *exactly* that you're asking me to do?"

The general straightened up, his face blotched red and purple. When he spoke, his voice was one of quiet anger. "I think you understand quite well what I am asking you, *High Priest.* I want you to take down that blasted wall."

LISA McMANN

Shipwrecked

Spike Furious, the whale that Alex created in the Museum of Large, was an intuitive creature, so she was the first to sense danger. "Where is the Alex?" she asked from alongside the ship in the darkness.

Alex's eyes flew open. "I'm here. At the back of the ship." He scrambled to his feet and peered over the side, but he couldn't see her. He couldn't see much of anything. A troubled wind stopped and started. The stars were hidden, and only a hint of moon lit their way tonight.

"Something bad is coming," Spike said. "It is not a waterfall." She spoke simply and without fear, for she was a very new

LISA McMANN

creature who was still learning the ways of the sea. Each experience the Artiméans went through gave Spike the information on which to build her predictions.

"How do you know it's bad?" asked Alex. His eyes grazed the sky, where a faint glow from the moon revealed a thick layer of clouds. Clouds were a rare sight for the people of Artimé, and immediately Alex wondered if they had something to do with Spike's premonition.

"I can feel the badness tugging at me. It's like the waterfall, but different."

The sky lit up with a flash, followed by a low rumbling. Alex thought he saw a mass of land in the distance. He trained his eyes on the spot and waited for lightning to come again. "It's just a storm, Spike. You're safe under water. I hope it doesn't get too rough though, or we're going to be in trouble."

"It's tugging at me."

Alex frowned, not sure what the whale meant. Maybe there was an undertow churning below the surface. He glanced at Florence, who was watching him with concern as she listened to the conversation.

Lightning flashed again, and this time Alex clearly saw the

outline of an island, closer than he ever expected. "Captain!" he shouted, waking up several others in the process.

Captain Ahab, whose rattling head was still missing an ear, hadn't been the same since before the waterfall. He couldn't hear well, his balance was off, and rumor aboard the ship was that his head must have hit the deck pretty hard . . . about a hundred times. He also dozed off occasionally, which actually gave the rest of them some peace and quiet.

Now, though, he jumped to attention. "Is she there? Do you see her?"

"Captain," said Alex, "it's land. We've reached the eastern-most island. See?" Lightning lit up the sky again, and a light spattering of rain began to fall. The wind picked up. "Can you guide us there? A storm is coming."

"What? What? Aye, how treacherous be the night storm," muttered the captain, looking all around. "Rocks! Rocks! Every-where! May as well toll the bell and surrender to death himself!"

The rain fell harder.

"Well, can you steer clear of the storm without picking up speed? I don't want the glass patch to break again, so we've got to keep it slow."

LISA McMANN

Florence, who had been aligning her gaze with the looming land whenever lighting lit the sky, spoke up. "Guide us in over there, Ahab. To the north side, see? When we get close enough for me to touch the sea floor, I'll step out and try to guide the ship around the rocks from below."

The captain mumbled something unintelligible as thunder exploded and the crew came to life, tying down their personal goods. The sea grew rough. Rain pelted down at a furious pace. The wind whipped about, and lightning played out more and more frequently.

At the next earsplitting crash of thunder, the Artiméans needed no instructions—they sprang into action. Samheed, Lani, and Octavia headed belowdecks to keep an eye on the leak. Sky, Copper, Crow, and the others secured the ship. Henry came up the stairs to the main deck to see if Alex needed him. The storm grew, and the wind began to sing around Alex's ears.

"Stand by, will you?" Alex shouted to Henry, grateful for the extra set of eyes. "Look at the land when it's lit up—we're moving awfully fast. We're heading straight toward it!"

Henry squinted and shielded his eyes from the rain. "The

storm is centered right on top of the island; did you notice that?"

"Yeah," Alex said, "and it isn't moving. But we definitely are—right toward the rocks." He looked at Florence as the rain poured down, sounding like a thousand drumbeats on the deck. She leaned over the side, making the boat shift with her weight and almost throwing Alex off balance.

"Florence!" he called. In a flash of lightning, Alex could tell the warrior was talking with Spike. He motioned to Henry to follow him, and the two maneuvered their way on the tilting vessel over to Florence. Waves roiling in all directions, seemingly undecided on their path, slapped at the ship, splashed up, and soaked them.

"We're being pulled toward the island!" Florence shouted when the boys drew near. "Spike is having trouble hanging on to us!"

"I *thought* we were moving way too fast," Alex muttered. "Why isn't Captain Ahab doing anything?"

"I don't think he realizes it. He's not well, Alex." She gave him a serious look. "I think you need to take over the ship's wheel."

LISA McMANN

Alex looked at Florence in alarm. "Me? I don't know how to steer this thing!"

Florence pointed at the island in the flickering light. "We're turning, see? Watch the island. We're moving in a circle around it, picking up speed." She looked at Alex. "Take over. I'll coach you. I'd do it myself if I could reach the wheel, but I need to get centered on the deck for everyone's safety, especially now that the waves are swelling." She shifted carefully back to center, trying to counterbalance her weight against the rocking ship.

Alex nodded—there was no one else who could take Ahab's place, so it was up to him. *If only Simber were here!* he thought. *Simber would have seen this coming before it was too late.* "Henry," he said abruptly, turning to the boy, "I need you to distract Captain Ahab and coax him away from the wheel. I don't know how happy he'll be to leave his post right now."

"I can do it," Henry said.

They braced themselves against the wind, and as the ship rocked, they lurched along with it until they reached the captain. Henry distracted the statue, suggesting to him that the whale he sought might be on the other side of the ship.

When they'd moved away, Alex grabbed hold of the wheel and peered into the storm. Florence called out instructions and Alex did his best to follow them and try to turn the ship away from the island, but at every lightning flash he saw they were growing closer and closer. Soon their wide circling of the island became a tighter spiraling motion around it, as if they were caught in the water of a draining bathtub. "No! Stop!" he shouted. Then, "Hang on!" His words were all but snatched up by the wind.

Alex tugged and pulled at the wheel, fighting the impossible current and wind, until his whole body ached. His muscles began shaking, and he knew he couldn't get the ship to turn away. "It's no use!" he shouted. "We're caught in this storm and it's not letting go!"

The ship rocked and the sea churned. Even in the confusion, Alex heard the glass-patched hole explode. The shouts of Samheed, Lani, and Ms. Octavia assured him they were still alive, but they would have trouble aiming a new glass spell accurately with all the rocking.

Spike jumped nearby, trying to fight the current by traveling through air rather than water.

"Spike!" Alex called, struck by an idea. "Can you use part of your body to plug the hole in the ship?"

"I will try, the Alex." Immediately the whale dove down and disappeared. Alex listened, and soon he heard faint cheers from below. Spike had saved them once more. Alex just hoped he wasn't putting the whale's life in danger by trapping her in a runaway vessel. He focused on the island, looming very close now. Alex could see the rocky coast, and he didn't know what to do.

"We're going to crash!" he shouted. "If we don't slow down, we'll have to abandon ship!"

Word spread quickly from statue to creature to human, and before Alex knew it, Sky had arrived at his side, soaking-wet hair stuck to her face and shoulders. She was furious. "My mother can't swim!" she shouted. "She can't abandon ship— what are you thinking? We have to do something else!"

Alex gave her a frantic look. He whipped his head around, looking for any possible solution to this latest problem, and his eyes landed on Florence, who was a rock in stressful times. "Get your mother," Alex said to Sky in a voice more assured and calm than he felt. "Bring her up here."

She hesitated, skeptical.

"I mean it. We don't have much time."

Sky turned and made her way below.

"Florence?" Alex called.

"Yes, Alex," she replied, not taking her eyes off the looming rocks.

"I need the squirrelicorns to deliver Copper safely to the island. They can take up to two others who want to go by air—Ahab, probably, and someone else. Can you prep them? Sky's coming up with her mother now."

"Of course," Florence said. "I think Lani or Samheed should go too, or someone with magical ability, in case there are unfriendly islanders to greet us."

"Yikes. I didn't even think of that."

"That's why you have me," she replied with an uneasy grin. Florence called the six squirrelicorns to attention and gave them their instructions. Within moments they were carrying Copper, Lani, and Captain Ahab—despite his protests—through the storm and out of sight in the dark torrent. With the hole plugged by Spike, the rest of the Artiméans trickled upstairs, some carrying supplies, prepared to jump.

The wind and current forced the swirling ship uncomfortably close to a bevy of rocks near the island's shore. Alex, grasping the railing for balance, pointed a blinding highlighter toward land, but it was useless—the rain was too heavy in his eyes, and he couldn't see much beyond the rocks. He looked at Florence and she nodded. It was time.

"Everybody, listen up!" he shouted. All of the Artiméans gathered together on the top deck, hanging on to the nets and railings as rain and wind stung their skin. "We can't wait for the squirrelicorns to come back—we're going to wreck. We've tried to control the ship but we can't. Without Simber here, there's nothing more we can do. So I'm ordering you to jump now, and swim for the rocks. Okay? Don't try to make it all the way to shore. The squirrelicorns will come out for you. Pair up and keep track of each other!"

The ship lurched and Alex lost his balance. He caught himself as lightning lit up the rocky scene, just yards away. "Go now!" he cried. "We're going to hit! Watch out for the rocks!"

Without a moment's hesitation, Ms. Octavia wrapped her tentacles around Henry's and Crow's wrists. The three climbed to the top of the railing, and at the octogator's signal, jumped into the water. Samheed grabbed Kitten and shoved her into his pocket. He helped Fox to the ledge, then held his hand out to Sky. She glanced at Alex. Samheed did too.

"You okay?" Samheed asked.

Alex nodded. "Go. Hurry!"

Sky pressed her lips together. She took Samheed's hand, and they jumped.

"Now you, Florence."

Florence gathered as many supplies as she could hold. "Climb on my back," she said.

"I'm fine. I'll jump after you."

"Simber will break me in two if I don't take you. You know that. Besides, if I step over the side, you'll go flying when I let go of the ship."

Alex hesitated. He couldn't see how close they were to the danger, and there was no time to argue. "We don't know how deep it is here, and you sink like a rock. I'm better off swimming on my own."

"Alex." Florence would have none of it. "Grab on. If it's not deep, I'll get us both on land faster. And if it is deep and we keep sinking, let go of me."

LISA McMANN

Alex frowned and lurched toward the statue. "All right, fine. Let's go." He took one last look at the pirate-ship deck, thinking about all the conversations he'd had here, and wondering how in the world they were going to get home if this ship was destroyed or lost at sea. But he couldn't tackle that problem right now. He let out a defeated breath, and as Florence bent down, he moved to grab on to her neck.

Alex's hands barely skimmed the warrior's broad shoulders before his world turned upside down. With a deafening crash the ship struck the rocks, and with a thousand *cracks* it split asunder. Mage, statue, and hole-plugging whale went flying headlong through the stormy sky and dropped into the sea.

Home Again

After flying nonstop for days with Carina on his back and Sean in the makeshift hammock below, Simber glided over the lagoon and the jungle trees toward Artimé's welcoming lawn. It was a sight for sore eyes indeed.

The cheetah was relieved to see that his presence and strange cargo were recognized by Artiméans on the lawn, who had gathered, pointing, and now began to prepare a space for Simber to land. Simber lowered the hammock to the ground and then touched down over and around it, careful not to step on any part of Sean. He folded his wings for the first time in

LISA McMANN

many days. Carina slid off. She stumbled and fell on the grass, her stiff muscles unable to support her properly at first.

Mr. Appleblossom, Ms. Morning, and Gunnar Haluki came running to greet them.

"Simber, what happened?" cried Claire, helping Carina to her feet. "Where is everyone else? Is Sean okay?"

"Could you be verrry kind and untie the rrropes frrrom my legs?"

"Of course!" Claire said. She and Mr. Appleblossom began working the knots to release Simber from the hammock ropes so that he could step aside and make room for Sean to be assessed. Others crowded around to help Carina and hear the news. Someone ran off to get Meghan.

"Sean's leg is brrroken and he's in trrremendous pain. He needs medicine quickly. Carrrina is okay, I think, but she's prrrobably exhausted frrrom rrriding on my back forrr a few days. Everrryone else on the ship is fine, but we had some trrrouble and the ship can't move fast."

Once Simber was freed, he stepped aside to reveal Sean, his face ghastly gray and twisted in pain. "Hurrry! Take him inside," Simber said, a bit louder than he'd intended. It had been a frustrating trip, longer than he'd hoped, and Sean had cried out many times.

Meghan came running over as several Artiméans lifted Sean and carried him into the mansion.

"What happened?" she exclaimed. She followed closely behind. Carina, who now stood on shaky legs, gave Simber a silent hug and a kiss on the neck, and slowly walked to the mansion as well.

"Did you find Sky's mother?" Ms. Morning asked Simber. "Tell us everything!"

"Yes. We've got herrr." The cat shook his head slightly, dazed. "A lot happened."

"I noticed you came home from the wrong way," Mr. Appleblossom said, pointing to the east. "The opposite direc- tion, if you will. I wonder what adventures you'll reveal when we have time to listen to your tale." Mr. Appleblossom winced a little at the imperfect rhyme, but left it hanging there all the same, as the moment was urgent.

"Yes," Simber said. He arched his back and took a few steps gingerly, testing the ground. "It's quite a storrry." Simber looked up, as if suddenly remembering something. "But firrrst, is

LISA McMANN

everrrything herrre all rrright? We got yourrr seek spell, Clairrre."

"Oh," Claire said, her voice troubled. She glanced toward the mansion, but Carina had disappeared inside. "I—well, I'm glad to know you got the seek spell. It's—everything is fine. I mean, it's not fine, but we're not in danger."

Simber regarded her. "I'm sorrry it took so long forrr me to come," he said quietly.

"Don't worry, Sim," Ms. Morning said, resting a hand on the cheetah's neck. "I would have sent more spells if it was really urgent. I just thought if you were nearby, well . . ." She tilted her head toward the mansion. "We need to talk to Carina. Right away."

Simber looked at Mr. Appleblossom and Gunnar Haluki. All wore solemn expressions. "Verrry well. Therrre's not much she can do forrr Sean rrright now. Shall we find herrr?"

Claire nodded swiftly, and the small group went into the mansion. In the hospital ward they found Meghan and Carina sitting next to Sean's bed. Sean's eyes were closed. He seemed to be resting comfortably now.

"How is he?" asked Simber.

"Handling the pain again, it seems," Carina said, not looking up. "Thankfully. But he hasn't woken up yet. He was lucky to have such a smooth ride thanks to you, Simber." When Simber remained silent, she turned her gaze toward the group. Seeing their serious faces, she asked, "Is something wrong?"

Ms. Morning pulled a chair next to Carina and sat in it.

"What is it?" Carina asked, fear creeping into her face. "Is it little Seth? Is he all right? What's going on?" She gripped Ms. Morning's hand. "You have to tell me at once!"

"Your son is fine," Ms. Morning assured her. "He's down for his nap now. He missed you, of course, but he is doing wonderfully well. He's taken quite a liking to Siggy."

Mr. Appleblossom blushed. "The lad likes costume closet frippery," he said. "He plays 'ship,' like Mum—quite the skipper, he."

Ms. Morning grinned. "Yes, Siggy built a replica of the pirate ship for Seth to sail in, and one of the boys made him a costume so he'd look like Captain Ahab. Such a special one, your Seth. He'd be considered quite the Unwanted in Quill."

Carina held a hand to her chest. "Oh, that's wonderful. Yes, he's showing great signs of creativity already." She sighed in relief. "So what's wrong, then?"

LISA McMANN

Ms. Morning offered a grim smile. "I'm afraid it's your mother, Carina."

Simber's eyes narrowed.

Carina's did too. "What of her?" she asked, her voice turning cold.

"I'm afraid she's . . . gone."

"Gone?"

"Dead."

Silence hung over the room. Sean stirred in his sleep.

"Dead?" Carina asked finally.

Ms. Morning nodded. "It happened here, you see. . . ." She struggled to find the right words.

"*What* happened? What was she doing here?" Carina sat stiffly in her chair, her face wiped of emotion.

"She came here to tell you—to deliver a message to you, that is, that she loves you. Apparently Aaron got tired of her and sent her to the Ancients Sector. She stopped here on her way, and . . ."

Carina stared blankly. "Did you tell her I don't care? Did you tell her I don't need love from traitors, nor do I accept it?"

Meghan interrupted. "She didn't actually end up going to the Ancients Sector, though. That's not how she died." She put her hand on Carina's shoulder. "She died saving the Warbler children."

"*What?*" Carina shook her head, trying to understand.

"She came here to say good-bye, Carina," Meghan said, "and to tell you she loves you and little Seth, and then practically out of nowhere, from the direction of the jungle, came a horrible creature. A panther. One of the jungle creatures that Mr. Today warned us about when we first came to Artimé. The evil thing came bounding toward the lawn and all the children, and then . . ." She stopped.

"And then," Haluki continued, "your mother saw the panther coming and she threw herself in front of it to stop it. She didn't hesitate. She sacrificed her life for Artimé's new children. She saved them."

Carina sat numb, unable to comprehend the words.

Simber's brow furrowed, but he remained silent for the moment.

"I'm sorry," Meghan said softly.

Carina looked up. "What?"

"I'm sorry. I mean, I wouldn't know how it feels, but I'm guessing it must be hard to hear this." Meghan pressed her lips together.

LISA McMANN

Carina's eyes flashed. Her head began to shake ever so slightly, and her breath escaped her nostrils in tiny bursts. "Well, I'm not sorry," she said, perhaps louder than she intended. "I'm not sorry at all. She deserved to die after what she did." Her face crumpled. "She's a traitor!"

She swallowed hard, shrugged Meghan's hand roughly off her shoulder, and stood up, her chair making a painfully loud scrape on the floor as she shoved it back. Then she turned away from the others. Her hands trembled on the bedside railing.

Haluki took a step toward her. "That's just it, Carina. We're no longer sure that she *was* a traitor, despite all the evidence."

Carina didn't react.

Ms. Morning and Haluki exchanged glances, while Simber looked on, skeptical.

"She said she knew we wouldn't believe her," Ms. Morning continued, and her own voice cooled substantially now, for she was even more skeptical than Simber, "but said she was working for Artimé all along, even when she appeared most loyal to Aaron after Artimé disappeared. She said she had proof—that someone in Artimé could vouch for her—but she wouldn't reveal the individual's name."

Simber spoke for the first time. "You sound as if you don't believe herrr, Clairrre."

Ms. Morning raised her chin. "I admit I find it hard to believe after what she allowed to happen to me, locked in Gunnar's pantry all that time. She was well aware of my presence, and of Gunnar's in the closet, and she did nothing to help us. But I'm trying to keep an open mind in hopes that her so-called confidant comes forward."

She looked around at the small group and went on. "I can only assume that person is on the ship with Alex—or perhaps it is Alex—for no one so far has come to vouch for her honor in the days since the attack." Her eyes landed on Sean, but she didn't offer him up despite Mr. Appleblossom's previous suspicions.

Carina's knuckles turned white as she gripped the railing harder. "Because there isn't anyone! I don't believe her. She was lying. She must have been. I bet she lied about having to go to the Ancients Sector, too. She was Aaron's little slave—he would never get rid of her." She shook her head. "How could a woman—a mother—do such horrid things, and lie so complexly, so frequently, that she'd lose her own child's devotion . . . ?" She trailed off and clutched at her heart now, as if it were being torn out. "For what purpose? Wasn't giving me up at the Purge enough? Did she have to come back into my life, only to betray me *a second time*? What absolute heartlessness, which is just so typical of someone loyal to Quill! Is there any purpose great enough to cause someone to turn her back on her family for the sake of it?"

She turned and looked at the others, her eyes rimmed red. "Well?" she demanded. "Is there?"

Simber, Ms. Morning, Mr. Appleblossom, and Meghan had no answers. They could only reply to Carina's tormented gaze with sympathetic eyes.

"I didn't think so," Carina muttered. "Her whole life was dedicated to hurting as many people as possible." She looked up at the ceiling to contain her tears and sighed bitterly. "Excuse me. I need to get out of here. I need to see my son—someone I would *never* betray."

Simber moved aside to clear a path for her escape. As she reached the door, a hoarse voice called out after her.

It was Sean.

"Carina," he said, his breath labored. "Wait."

Sean Shares a Secret

At the sound of Sean's voice, Carina paused in the doorway to the hospital ward. She turned and looked at his bed, and saw that his eyes were open. "You're awake," she breathed, and rushed past Ms. Morning, Meghan, Simber, and Mr. Appleblossom to Sean's side. "Are you feeling any better?"

The others crowded around to see him, conscious for the first time since well before arriving in Artimé.

Meghan reached out and ruffled her brother's hair. "He's looking a little better, at least."

LISA McMANN

"Yes, he is," Carina said. "Sean, I'm so glad to see you awake. I was awfully worried. . . ."

He lifted a weak hand and Carina grasped it. They stared into each other's eyes.

"Excuse me for a moment, *Artimons*," Mr. Appleblossom said gently. "Carina, I shall go and find your son."

"Oh, thank you, dear Mr. Appleblossom," she said, offering him a half smile in spite of the tears that were still wet on her face. "Bring him here to me right away, will you? I miss him so."

He nodded and slipped away without another word.

Carina turned back to Sean. "You're feeling better, then?" she prompted.

"Yes, a bit better," Sean said. His eyes remained half-closed and his speech was slower than usual, but the color was back in his face, and the near-constant grimace he'd worn since the ride around the world was gone.

"You should rest. Can you sleep? Were we talking too loudly? I'm sorry."

He shook his head and gripped her hand tighter. "No, it's okay. I have to tell you something," he said. "I heard you all talking . . . about Eva." His chin quivered. "I'm so sorry."

"It doesn't matter," Carina said. "We can talk about it another time, when you're well. I'm—I'm fine. Really. She means nothing to me." She set her jaw. "She was an enemy of Artimé."

Meghan watched her brother's face carefully, and wondered. Had Mr. Appleblossom guessed right the day of the attack? Was Sean the one working with Eva? "I think he really just needs to say something," Meghan said carefully. "Don't you, Sean?"

Sean turned his head. His eyes connected with his sister's, and she nodded encouragingly. He frowned, puzzled that she seemed to know something, but too tired to contemplate it. "Yes," he said. He turned back to Carina. "Please. Let me explain."

Carina glanced from Sean to Meghan, and back to Sean again. "All right, if you're sure you're feeling okay."

He nodded. "Now that Eva's gone, I-I feel like it's my duty to defend her."

Carina turned sharply back to Meghan. "Do you know what he's talking about? Is he delirious?"

Meghan shrugged.

LISA McMANN

"Carina," Haluki said in his fatherly voice, "let him speak."

"Please," Sean said. "I am—I was—your mother's confidant."

Carina's lips parted in shock.

"It's true," Sean said. He struggled a little, and Meghan quickly slipped an extra pillow under his head and shoulders to prop him up. "Thanks," he murmured. "I'd been meeting in secret with Eva since the rise of the Restorers, back when you were high priest, Gunnar." He paused, breathing hard from the effort, and continued.

"Eva was a spy. She told me everything Aaron was doing. She's the reason Aaron held off from fighting us all this time. The reason," he said, taking several breaths, "we are not under attack right now."

This was news to everyone. They all listened intently, waiting for more.

When Sean was able, he continued. "She knew Alex and the rest of us were going to be gone, but Aaron didn't. And we didn't want him to find out. He's planning to fight. She convinced him to wait to attack us. I spoke to her the night before we set out, and she promised to do everything she could to keep Artimé safe for as long as possible."

Simber and Claire Morning exchanged glances. Carina stared, unbelieving.

Sean took a sip of water and continued. "She felt her days were numbered, so she took a chance on saving Liam Healy, knowing how remorseful he was about the part he played. Eva had secretly kept him alive in the Ancients Sector, waiting for a chance to get him out of there. And it finally came. She convinced Aaron that he was loyal, and talked him into taking Liam on as a governor."

Claire Morning stood abruptly and began to pace, visibly angry but keeping her thoughts to herself.

Sean struggled to lift himself on one elbow, and Meghan hurried to help him. "Claire," he said. His face cracked as he watched her begin to cry. "Claire, please listen."

Ms. Morning blew her nose in a tissue and nodded.

"Eva Fathom was our friend. And Mr. Today knew it."

"Don't," Ms. Morning said.

"She and Mr. Today had a plan."

"It's her fault he's dead!"

"No. No. I know it looks that way, but it wasn't her fault."

Ms. Morning paced a bit more, then stopped at the end of

LISA McMANN

Sean's bed and folded her arms. "All right. Tell me, then."

Sean closed his eyes momentarily to collect his thoughts, and then opened them and spoke. "Aaron had been plotting to kill Mr. Today for a long time. When it all came down to the final planning stages, he didn't dare. So he told Eva to do it to prove that she was truly on his side, because he didn't trust her." He leaned forward and winced. "And we needed him to trust her."

"*We?*" Carina said sarcastically. "You mean *you.*"

Sean winced. "I'm sorry, Carina."

She held up a hand to stop the apology. "Just . . . just go on."

Sean nodded and turned back to Claire. "Like I said, we needed Aaron to trust Eva. So she and Mr. Today concocted a plan: They would go on holiday together. Eva stole heart attack spells from Carina to show Aaron she had the means to kill Mr. Today. He took some from her, so she lied and told him that one heart attack spell was deadly, in case he ever decided to use it. Then she told Aaron she'd kill Mr. Today on their holiday, and when she returned to Artimé, she'd tell everyone he'd died on the journey."

Simber frowned but said nothing.

Sean went on. "But really, Eva and Mr. Today planned to fake his death. They were going to send Mr. Today to another island for a time, where he knew and trusted the inhabitants. He'd bide some time there until word got back to Artimé and Quill that he was dead, which would give Aaron a false sense of security, and perhaps he'd delay an attack, thinking he had more time to build up support."

Sean looked around the room at the faces. "I promise every word of this is true."

"Why wouldn't my father tell me about this plan?" Claire asked, eyes blazing. "Or Simber, for that matter?"

Simber lowered his head. "If only I had known . . . ," he said, but didn't finish.

"He was going to tell you and Gunnar at your meeting at the palace that night," Sean said to Claire. "And I'm sure he planned to tell you, Simber. I'm sure of it. And maybe even Alex, too."

"So Alex doesn't know any of this?" asked Claire.

Sean shook his head. "If he does, he never said anything to me about it."

LISA McMANN

"Not about your secret cavorting with the enemy either?" Carina asked sharply.

"He knew I was up to something from the time Artimé disappeared, but I begged him not to ask me about it, and he trusted me. Besides, he had a lot of other stuff to handle back then."

Claire frowned. She looked at Gunnar, who was listening intently, reserving judgment for the full story.

After a moment, Claire nodded. "All right. Go on, please, if you're feeling up to it."

Sean nodded and took another drink of water. He sank back in his pillows and closed his eyes. After a moment of rest, he continued, his voice softer now, and pained. "No one but you and Haluki and Mr. Today knew about the tube in Haluki's office, Claire."

Meghan's eyes darted from one face to another, then back to her brother's.

"No one expected you and Mr. Today to magically appear smack-dab in the enemy's headquarters. Mr. Today had always walked into Quill when he met with Haluki. *Always.* Why would anyone expect there to be a different route?"

Claire's face was ashen. "Did you know Aaron was working from Gunnar's house?"

Sean shook his head. "Only a few of the Restorers knew. Eva didn't—not until after. When Mr. Today walked out of that closet, he couldn't possibly have been more surprised in his life to see the house lit up and Aaron standing ten feet away. And Aaron, even in a state of panic, actually managed to do it. To . . . to kill him." He opened his eyes and stared at the ceiling. A tear dripped from the corner of his eye, and he didn't wipe it away. "If Aaron had only used one heart attack spell, Mr. Today might still be alive . . . but he didn't. He lunged for the pile and threw a handful of them. He used a lethal dose without even knowing it."

The room was silent. Claire's lips twitched, and tears streamed down her face.

After a while, Haluki looked up. "He used two more heart attack spells the other day," he said, "to subdue the panther."

The others turned toward him.

Meghan nodded, thinking back to her secret visit to the palace. "Yes, I'm pretty sure it was him."

"I'm almost positive of it," Haluki said. "I saw him later in the jungle by the tube."

"There's a *tube* in the *jungle*?" Meghan asked, incredulous.

"There are tubes in several places," Haluki said. "I'm sure I don't know all of them. But there's definitely one in the jungle. I've used it myself."

"Whoa," Sean said. "I didn't know either."

"Almost nobody did," Haluki said. "Marcus had many secrets. I imagine there are hundreds of things we'll never know. Unless he wrote things down, his secrets went to the grave with him. Perhaps we'll stumble across some now and then."

Carina, who had been silent and brooding during this last bit, stood up, her face a mask. She looked at Sean. "Well," she said, her words cold and sharp, "this has been a very informative session." She struggled to control her anger. "I'm just *so glad* to know you were such *great* friends with my lying mother. Nice of you to tell me—it's not like you and I had anything else to talk about during the entire time I *took care of you*." She clenched her jaw. "And to think I could have had the chance to . . . to understand all of this and maybe speak to her before . . ."

She shook her head and pointed a shaking finger at Sean. "You are quite possibly the worst person anyone has ever

LISA McMANN

known. You're a worse human than . . . than Queen Eagala. You're a . . . you're a world-class jerk, Sean. An absolutely hideous man, inside and out. And I never want to look at your ridiculous lying face again."

She looked like she wanted to say more, but instead she turned and walked swiftly toward the hospital wing doorway, where Mr. Appleblossom stood with Seth, listening to the conversation from afar.

"Mama!" cried the toddler.

"Thank you, sir," Carina said to Mr. Appleblossom as Seth reached out to her in glee. She took him and held him tightly, then retreated into the mansion's entryway, ran up the stairs to the family wing, and disappeared.

Sean, weak and exhausted, could only watch her go, and when she was out of sight, he put his hand over his eyes and groaned. "Crud," he muttered.

Aaron Strikes a Deal

Y ou want me to do what?" Aaron asked the general, trying not to sound incredulous. But what General Blair was asking was something Aaron, even on his most adventurous days, had never seriously considered. Tear down the wall? Completely? That went against everything Justine had taught him—everything Justine believed in. The wall was their infallible protector. Their safety. Their *hope*, for Quill's sake. Sure, he'd taken down a tiny portion in the past. But even opening that window in the wall near the palace had made Aaron so uncomfortable he'd filled it again. It was dangerous! Clearly the general had lost his mind. Maybe the gunk oozing from his wound was his brain leaking out.

That forty-foot-tall wall that encircled Quill had taken months, maybe even years to construct. It had kept them safe from enemies for Justine's entire reign. And clearly there were enemies out there. Aaron knew well enough that Artimé was fighting them. Did Aaron really want to go that route, when that route looked like the most wrong of all possible wrong ways to go?

"Take down the wall," General Blair repeated. There was menace to his voice. A dare. Almost as if he expected Aaron to say no.

And why wouldn't he? It was a ridiculous request.

Yet the general had a point. The bottleneck issues of the original battle had been Quill's downfall—that was easy to see when the general pointed it out. Once vehicles had been rendered useless inside the gate, there was no way to get the working ones out past the ones that had broken down. And each platoon that entered was small compared to the Artiméan groups that awaited them. No wonder they'd lost that battle. They couldn't descend on the enemy in any sort of successful way.

What Aaron had to decide now was whether it was worth it to take down the wall and risk being attacked from other islands in order to defeat the one true enemy, Artimé.

Liam fidgeted next to Aaron. Aaron averted his eyes. He had to concentrate. He had to think this through. What was more important? Protecting Quill from some unknown enemy who might not ever attack—and had no reason to attack Quill, because they hadn't done anything? Or giving Quill the opportunity to control the entire island, including the magical world . . . and the beautiful mansion?

And even more important—if Aaron said no to General Blair, would that alienate their relationship forever? General Blair was Aaron's last possible ally. The Quillitary was his only remaining option for ultimate success.

Aaron frowned and pinched the bridge of his nose as a headache began to pound. Was this his moment to make a bold move? Was this his moment to shine? Was this the moment he would look back on one day and say, "That's when I *really* took over. That exact moment, when I decided to tear down the wall."

Even though it was basically the only option he had left,

he could still say no and hope for something better to present itself. But he didn't expect there would be anything. He'd exhausted his other resources—the Restorers, the jungle creatures—and now the Quillitary could be his with a single nod of his head. The question was, did he dare?

Did he?

Aaron looked up at the general. "All right," he said, his words like ice.

Liam sat up straight. "But, High Priest—" he began.

Aaron held up a hand to the governor, shushing him. "Please," he said with disdain.

Liam was silent.

"I'll order it done," Aaron said. "First thing in the morning, the stretch of wall nearest Artimé will come down."

"That's not good enough," General Blair said. "We need the entire wall removed. All of it."

Aaron scowled. "Why the entire wall, if the problem was in the area around Artimé?"

"Because," General Blair explained with an air of annoy-ance, "think about it. If the wall stays up around part of Quill, the Artiméans can fan out around the perimeter of the island, behind it. They can use the wall as a bunker. They'd be able to hide behind the two ends of the wall and set up sneak attacks. And with their quick method of warfare, they'll take us down every time. Our Quillitary fights better in the open. So it's all or nothing, High Priest." He leaned toward Aaron. "And if it's nothing, then you may leave now, and good luck making it to adulthood."

Aaron studied the general's stony face. His lungs felt like they were squeezing all of the air out of him, and his heartbeat pounded in his eardrums. *The entire wall?* Under the table, Aaron gripped his kneecaps until his fingers were numb. "What about outside enemies?" The words came out almost in a whisper.

The general laughed. "Do you really think we have any? We haven't been attacked in over fifty years. Anyone that Justine was guarding against fifty years ago is dead or extremely old by now. Whether the wall is partially standing or completely removed, enemies would get to us eventually anyway." He coughed and cleared his throat. "But in the end, I'm simply not concerned about it. We have only one enemy, and it's encroaching on our island already. Stop looking beyond it for more when the most offensive one is practically upon us! Let's do the job and take them out. This is really simple, High Priest." He rolled his eyes.

Something about what the general said made Aaron feel even more unsure. But he was stuck. He needed the Quillitary. "Fine," he said with a small squeak in his voice. "We'll take down the entire wall."

General Blair didn't give Aaron the satisfaction of witnessing his surprise—he hadn't been expecting Aaron to go along with him. Instead he nodded stiffly. "Very well. I'll send my troops to assist your Necessaries in tearing it down. We'll make quick work of it."

"We'd better," Aaron said in a voice as calm as he could command. But his heart filled with more fear than he had ever known.

Island of
Shipwrecks

O f the three, Alex flew the farthest. Experience had taught him to suck in a deep breath before he hit the water. Florence and Spike narrowly avoided crashing into one another, and all fortunately managed to miss the jutting rocks.

The water was cold and rough. Alex struggled against the weight of it, pushing toward the surface as soon as his downward momentum slowed. His thighs and lungs burned as he fought against the current, and then moved with it. Eventually, because of the darkness, and because he was unsure if he was swimming toward the surface or away from it, he stopped struggling to see if he would naturally right himself.

It wasn't long before he felt a nudge, and soon Spike was solidly below Alex, pushing him upward. Alex grabbed on to the whale's spike and hung on for the ride. They burst through the waves with a small jump, Alex hanging on tightly.

"Hello, the Alex. I am sorry about the jumping," the whale managed to say before they were plunging back underwater. Alex accidentally inhaled water and choked. A moment later the whale took another jump and said, "This jumping is the only way for me to get to the island because of the current."

Spike waited for Alex to cough the water out of his lungs. As soon as Alex could manage to eke out "Okay, go," Spike obliged, and down they went again. Alex learned quickly to grab a breath of air the next time they surfaced, and as he figured out the whale's pattern, he actually thought he might enjoy the ride if he weren't so worried about the rest of his crew.

As they traveled through the water, more Artiméans found themselves sliding onto the whale's back, for every time Spike saw someone struggling in the current, she swam under them and vaulted them to safety. By the time they reached shallow water, the whale had collected Fox, Sky, and Samheed

LISA McMANN

in addition to Alex. As soon as they neared land, the load of passengers jumped off Spike's back and staggered through the roiling water, and Spike went out again to rescue anyone else she could find.

The group waded to shore, guided by near-constant lightning. Alex could see the outlines of several shipwrecks on the rocks. And no wonder, the way the storm seemed to stay centered over this island. But right now Alex wasn't looking for shipwrecks, he was looking for people, creatures, and statues. And he was hoping that daylight would come soon, and the storm would end.

"Lani!" he called, and Samheed chimed in.

"Over here!" she said. "There's an overhang."

Alex and the others headed toward Lani's voice, and soon they saw her cast a highlighter spell, keeping its light low so as not to blind anyone. With her under a small, stone overhang they found Captain Ahab and Copper, delivered safely by the squirrelicorns, who had now gone out once more to search for others.

Soon Ms. Octavia and the squirrelicorns made it to shore, followed by Henry and Crow, and then out of the water rose Florence, unscathed.

Alex craned his neck and squinted to scan the water. "Have you seen Spike?" Alex called out to her. "Is she okay?"

"She's great. And having more fun than anyone else under the circumstances." Florence's wry smile was evident in a burst of lightning. "Apparently she found a lagoon on the leeward side of the island where the water's not as rough," Florence said. "She'll be fine there. I told her to hole up for the duration and we'd find her when we need her."

"Good." Alex sighed in relief and batted at a sodden lock of hair that kept dripping into his eye. He looked around in the dim light from the highlighter. "We're all here, then, right? Where's Kitten?"

"I've got her," Samheed said. Kitten emerged from his pocket and ran down his leg and over to Fox to perch on his head.

"I feel bloated," Fox said to no one in particular.

"Okay, good," Alex said, ignoring Fox for the moment. "Squirrelicorns?"

"Over here in the corner," piped one of them. "Six in num-ber, sir!"

"Great. Everyone's accounted for."

"Except the ship," Florence said. "And it's too dark to see if any of it survived."

That took the mood down considerably. For several minutes the cave buzzed with questions, mainly, "How are we going to get out of here?"

Finally, Alex quieted the group. He didn't have an answer, but he knew things weren't completely dire. "Look, everyone," he said. "I know this feels bleak, and we're all cold and wet, but we're safe, and we have to stay positive," he said. "We're smart. We'll figure this out. Once the storm is over we can see what the ship looks like. And at the very least, we'll have Simber back here soon to rescue us. I'm sure he'll find us. It's hard to miss Florence when you have eyes as sharp as his." He sounded more sure of himself than he felt.

"Alex is right," Ms. Octavia said. "Simber will be back to save us. All is not lost." She looked at Florence, then tapped a tentacle to her lips as her face clouded. "Well, except for you," she said.

"We can't leave Florence here!" Lani said.

"Don't worry about me," Florence said. "But did you notice all the shipwrecks? I'm feeling a bit of an itch to explore and maybe see if we can build something that will take us home." She grinned. "We don't need Simber to save us. We're perfectly capable of rescuing ourselves. Right, Alex?"

Alex laughed uneasily. "Right, of course!" His gaze automatically went to the sky, as if looking for the flying cat would bring him soaring in. But there was nothing to see but driving rain and lightning. "Of course," he said again with less enthusiasm this time, but trying his best to stay heartened. "We managed to bring back Artimé without him, didn't we?" he asked, glancing at Sky.

She smiled. "We did."

"Well then," Alex said, "I figure we can get out of here no problem, ship or no ship!" But his insides felt extremely uneasy.

The words seemed to reassure everyone, and eventually they settled under the overhang, spreading their wet outer layers of clothing over rocks to try to dry them—though the hope for that was minimal as the air around them seemed almost as wet as the rain itself.

The mood changed once more as the group fell silent, each member lost in his own individual fears.

"We may as well try to sleep," Alex said presently. "And hope the weather clears up by morning."

There was nothing to eat and only rain to drink, and no dry wood for a fire. So the Artiméans huddled together, trying to get comfortable under the shallow overhang in the storm, occasionally struck by slaps of wind and rain so strong they stung. Florence, who couldn't fit under the overhang, sat outside trying to block the flying debris from the others. The rain didn't really bother her. She kept watch so those who needed sleep could get it, just like she would do back home.

It was at times like these that Florence's thoughts often turned to Talon. But tonight, her mind was on Simber. After a few hours of silence, Florence overheard a whisper from the back of the cave. It sounded like Lani.

"What are we going to do if Simber doesn't come back, Al? We don't have any food or fresh water. . . ."

There was a long silence, and for a moment, Florence thought the storm had drowned out Alex's response. But then she heard it.

"We'll do the only thing we can do," he said, his voice tired and defeated. "Try not to die."

Copper Steps Up

A dreary morning dawned. The wind died down and the thunder and lightning quieted, but a steady drizzle remained. Florence reached under the overhang and nudged Alex awake.

He groaned and rolled over, finding Crow's feet in his face. His eyes shot open. He sat up and looked around, and then seeing Florence beckoning to him, he crawled out from under the overhang and got to his feet. She stood as well, and Alex followed her around their shelter so they could talk without waking the others.

The island was simply rocky and barren. There were no

LISA McMANN

trees anywhere, only large slabs of moss-covered rock peppering the landscape, with an occasional scrubby bush growing sideways because of the wind. Near the water were pods of wet sand, and the sea churned dark gray all around—no gently lapping waves on the beach here, like in Artimé. It was the ugliest place Alex had ever seen. Even Quill couldn't compete with this.

"Wow," he said, taking it in. "It's bleak. Any inhabitants?"

"None that I can see," Florence replied. She pointed and said, "It's a pretty small island. When I stand up I can see between rock formations to the water on the other side. I think I saw Spike's spike flashing a minute ago in the water over there."

"Oh, good," Alex said. "Do you see any animals? Food or water? Anything?" His stomach growled loudly, and his tongue felt thick with thirst.

Florence shook her head. "Not even a bird. There's not much plant life on the island either, as far as I can tell, but I haven't explored everything yet, and obviously I don't have Simber's infallible sense of smell to detect things. The shipwrecks all seem old, weathered, and abandoned—I can't imagine anyone surviving a violent wreck like the one we

LISA McMANN

had, without also having the swimming capabilities of our Artiméans." She looked at Alex. "Other than the wrecks, there's nothing much here but these giant rock formations with moss and lichen growing on everything. It must rain a lot here."

"I wondered last night if the storm is permanently stationed above the island," Alex said, looking up at the circle of dark clouds above their heads that didn't seem to be moving any-where. The thought didn't seem as weird now that the weather had remained so consistently stormy throughout the night. He looked beyond the shoreline and could see far enough to discern sunshine on the water in the distance. He ventured farther into the drizzle. "All those shipwrecks," he said.

"Yes," Florence said. "I counted at least ten. Ours is over there."

"You found it?" Alex asked, looking up at her. "It didn't sink?"

"It's lodged on the rocks, split in two. Or maybe it's in more pieces than that, but there are two large ones for sure."

Alex and Florence walked to the island's edge and stared at the wreck.

LISA McMANN

"Oh dear," Alex muttered.

"You said it," Florence said.

Alex absently raked his fingers through his damp, tangled hair, setting it on end, not unlike Mr. Today used to do. He took in the scene. The ship sat half underwater, split from port to starboard. Its gaping maw made a V, like a giant window allowing them to view the water on the other side of it.

"Do you, um," Alex began, and tilted his head as he studied the ship. "Do you think it's something we can . . . repair?"

"Not out there."

"Right, right. No, of course not. We'd all get swept away." He squinted. "Well then what?"

"I don't know."

"I can try to put it on land, you know."

Florence tapped her lips with her finger. "So you can. I'd forgotten about the transport spell."

Alex sized up the land nearest the water, trying to figure out if there was a flat enough spot on the shore for the ship, and then he looked back at the wreck. "I don't know if it'll all come in one piece, though, if it's a complete split."

"I fear it is, or it's close, anyway—look at the angle. It can't

LISA McMANN

be held together by much, if anything. We'll have to try it and hope for the best."

"Yeah, that spell is a little finicky," Alex said, remembering how hard it had been to find Spike when he'd transported her to the water. "I'll do what I can to land it in a good place. I just hope . . ." He trailed off, wondering what sort of mess it would be if he had to transport it in pieces, and whether they'd end up anywhere near each other. He decided to put that out of his mind. "You know," he said, "if we can find a rope, I bet we can attach one half to the other with it. That way it'll technically be one piece."

"Good thinking, kid," Florence said. "You're smarter than you look." She grinned. "We may as well try now while no one's wandering about to get crushed to death."

Alex laughed. He was really starting to enjoy Florence's sense of humor, and he liked it when she teased him. It made them feel like friends. "You should take cover then too—or better yet, will you carry me out there so I don't have to get wet again now that it seems to have stopped raining for the moment? My skin is shriveling up."

"Oh, sure," she said drily. "*Now* you let me carry you, when

LISA McMANN

there isn't any danger. Stubborn mages. You're all alike."

"Sorry," Alex said sheepishly.

"Shall I clear an area on the beach so you can aim for it?"

"That would be excellent."

While Alex ran back to the shelter to tell everyone to stay there for a while, Florence quickly uprooted a few scraggly bushes and tossed several large boulders out of the way near the flat, open area of the beach. She approached the remains of an old fishing boat that had somehow made it through the maze of jutting rocks and all the way to the mainland before wrecking. After peering inside it, she carefully picked it up and moved it to another area, leaving behind a small army of crabs scuttling across the wet sand. When she was finished, she met up with Alex again, hoisted him up to her shoulders, and set off through the rough water to their ship.

"You know, we used to climb on you when you were frozen," Alex confided. "You happened to be standing in a very convenient spot when the magic disappeared."

"Is that so?" Florence said. She narrowed her eyes. "Who is we?"

"Oh, me and Sean and Carina and Sky and Mr. Appleblossom—"

"What? Siggy, too? I-I'm actually somewhat embarrassed by this information."

"It wasn't for fun, believe me. It was to get to the roof of the gray shack so we could escape from the masses of people and try to figure out how to fix things. I never thought I'd tell you—we were so scared you'd come back alive while we were climbing on you. We didn't know what you'd do to us."

Florence chuckled. "Well in that case, I'm glad I could be of some use."

By the time they reached the rocks where the pirate ship rested, Alex had scrambled to the top of Florence's head to stay dry. She grabbed on to a boulder, found a foothold, and pulled herself up out of the water, finding a place to perch on the rocks that had split the pirate ship.

Alex stood on Florence's shoulders, reached for the ship, and peered over the railing. There wasn't much left inside, but he spied a few ropes floating there, attached to the ship at one end. He reached out for one, grabbed it, and climbed deftly along the inside of the ship to a spot where Florence could take it. He handed off the rope to her. She quickly wound it around the mast on the other half of the ship and tied it tightly. They did the same on the other side.

"There," Florence said. "Now the two pieces are connected."

Alex scrambled back out of the ship to climb on Florence's shoulders again. Once settled, he leaned out and touched the side of the ship. "I can see some of our water containers tied up," Alex said, relieved. "Let's get this ship on shore."

"Sounds good."

"Are you ready?" he asked. He took a deep breath.

"Whenever you are, but take your time. There's no need to rush. Focus on that open spot on the beach."

"I know." He realized all too well that if the ship didn't transport properly, they could end up with nothing but an unfixable mess. After a moment of panic at the gravity of the situation, he shoved the fear aside and removed all other thoughts from his mind. He focused intently on the open space on land. He made sure he had his hand firmly placed on the ship's side, and then, in an intense whisper, he said, "Transport."

Both halves of the ship vanished.

Florence and Alex whipped their heads around to scan the

shore. An instant later the battered vessel appeared almost exactly where Alex had intended it to land. Upright, and nearly perfectly placed. Seawater gushed out of it onto the sand.

"Yes!" Alex shouted, pumping his fist in the air.

Florence held a hand up in triumph. "You did it! All in one piece—just barely, thanks to the rope idea. Nice work." She climbed down the rock into the sea with Alex crouched on her head to stay dry, and began the walk back to shore. When they reached land, Alex gave a shout. The others came running to see the ship and assess the damage. Alex slid off of Florence's shoulders and landed with a thud on the ground.

"Oh my," Copper said, peering at it. Her voice was still a bit raspy from the thorn necklace she'd worn up until her recent rescue. "I wonder if it's something we can fix."

She came up to the broken edge of the ship and took an expert look all around inside. She'd worked on plenty of Queen Eagala's ships on Warbler.

Florence joined her. "I think so," she said. She reached inside the ship and began loosening the knots that held the containers of freshwater, then brought the containers out and placed them in front of the thirsty humans.

LISA McMANN

As they drank in careful, measured sips, Florence glanced at the variety of shipwrecks poking up out of the water nearby or crashed onto the rocks. "We'll need a little help. We don't have any tools. We're also missing some really important items, like the sails, rigging, ship's wheel, a rudder . . . and plenty of material to patch this thing. We're going to need to scavenge some of these shipwrecks to find what we need."

Sky flashed her mother an adventurous smile. She and Crow knew quite a bit about shipbuilding too.

At the word "scavenging," Samheed and Lani looked at each other and grinned.

Henry and Crow both stopped in their tracks and looked at Florence, eyes wide. "What did you say?" Crow asked. "We get to explore the wrecks?" He could hardly contain his excitement.

"You swimmers can scavenge," Copper said. "I'll stay on shore and help Florence. I'm glad to finally be able to do something to help after all you have done for me."

"I'll be glad to have your help," Florence said.

Ms. Octavia seated Captain Ahab nearby to rest and watch, and then joined the humans to figure out their work plan.

But soon a peal of thunder rattled the sky and rain pelted the ground, leaving tiny, perfect divots in the pods of drying sand. The wind shifted and began to swirl around them. The short reprieve from the storm was apparently over.

Sky ignored the storm. She scurried toward a wreck a little ways offshore to explore. But just as she ran through the wind and rain, something caught her eye near the center of the barren island. She stopped short and looked more carefully. It was a small person, raggedly clothed, standing still and watching them.

Sky gasped. The figure disappeared behind a rock.

She turned back to the ship. "Alex? Florence?" she called out softly. "We're definitely not alone on the this island."

LISA McMANN

Aaron Tries to Rile Up the Crowd

Aaron realized the best way to show General Blair that he was serious was to start tearing the wall down immediately—but that wasn't necessarily the best way to go about it from the perspective of the high priest of Quill. So the morning after his meeting with the general, Aaron called the people of Quill together so he could tell them what to believe.

"People of Quill," Aaron said in the monotone manner of Justine, "some of you already know that my faithful secretary was attacked and killed by a creature of Artimé." He paused and allowed the small murmur of the crowd to grow and fade,

LISA McMANN

for some of them with fuzzy minds had forgotten the news already.

"It's an unfortunate situation," Aaron continued, "and one that we must swiftly address. Artimé is dangerous. And we must no longer tolerate their infiltration and attacks on our good people. Comrades, have you any rage inside you?"

The people of Quill looked up at Aaron.

Aaron frowned. "You may respond. Do you have any rage inside you?"

The Quillens looked at one another, unsure of what the right answer was. It seemed like a trick question. Were they supposed to have rage inside them, or was that against the law? They couldn't remember. Mr. and Mrs. Stowe exchanged a worried glance, and then both immediately looked down at their daughters in their arms, as if they didn't want Aaron to read their thoughts.

Gondoleery, standing nearby with Liam, leaned over to Aaron and hissed, "You have to tell them what to say, idiot."

Aaron blinked, pretending not to hear. His cheeks burned. "My dear people," he said, trying again. "As you know, the High Priest Justine taught us to bank our rage, saving it up for a time when we would need to fight against our enemies. Remember?" He frowned. "I am telling you today that our enemies in Artimé must be extinguished for what they have done. We will be attacking Artimé soon. It is now time for you to get angry. Do you understand?"

A few people in the audience murmured. Others looked around fearfully. They liked this high priest . . . didn't they? He was the one who gave them extra food. But it was hard to remember. . . .

"Very good," Aaron said. His eyes darted anxiously around the lethargic crowd. "We can use that kind of energy, and perhaps even a little more than that would be quite helpful. Okay." He ran his fingernail nervously along a sliver of warped wood on the podium and winced as it broke off and stuck fast under his nail. He stepped back and clasped his hands in front of him, his finger throbbing.

"Now," he said, growing increasingly short-tempered, "in order to fight against Artimé, we must do one thing that may come as a surprise to you. We must tear down the wall that surrounds us."

This brought a slightly more lively response, but Aaron

held his hands up for silence. "I know what you're thinking," Aaron said, though it seemed more likely that only a few of them were actually thinking anything. "But the only way to attack properly is to have full access to Artimé. The wall was a hindrance in the past and it will be the cause of our failure in the future. We must take it down. Don't argue," he said, though none of them were. "You need to understand that the risk of an enemy from far away is not nearly as great as the risk from the enemy in Artimé, where, as you may recall, they are now sending beasts to kill us! We must hurry to tear down the wall and move toward an organized attack before they have time to prepare a defense against us. Once we have defeated them, we will finally be at peace."

He looked around the bland faces of the people of Quill, and for a moment, Aaron felt disgusted by them all—every last one of them had no opinion, no goals, no fire inside them. Not like he did. His fire to take over the island was stronger than ever. Why couldn't he get them to call up their anger, like he had done within himself? He felt like giving them all slivers in their fingers to see if that would garner a response.

"Look alive!" he pleaded, and the people of Quill started,

afraid. "Allow your rage to build so we can let it loose against the enemy!"

A few more weak responses came from the audience, but it was disorganized at best, and soon everyone was quiet again.

Aaron sighed, exasperated. This wasn't going at all the way he'd planned. Maybe the Quillens had used up all fifty years' worth of their rage in the last battle.

"Just . . . okay, we'll work on the rage part. But now, you will please help me take the wall down," he said, beginning to feel very impatient. "Necessaries, you will join the Quillitary efforts, beginning in the area next to the gates of Artimé and moving out in both directions, all the way around the island. It will be dangerous, but you'll see it will be worth it in the end. When I'm finished here, please make your way to the Quillitary officers and await your instructions."

Mrs. Stowe gave her husband a searching glance, then silently reached for the twin he was holding. He put the girl into Mrs. Stowe's arms alongside the other, and before he let go, he gripped his wife's hand and squeezed. Mrs. Stowe looked up into his face. She squeezed back.

Aaron, feeling more and more like he was losing the attention of his entire audience, wrapped up his speech. "And everyone—get ready to fight."

This time he didn't wait for any lackluster reaction. Instead he marched out of the amphitheater to the road and climbed into the car that waited for him. He put his arm out the window and waved Liam over to join him, leaving Gondoleery behind to go in the next car.

"Take us to the Quillitary," Aaron barked to the driver.

The ride was silent but for the chug and squeal of the jalopy. Aaron stared stone-faced out the window, and Liam looked at his hands, clasped in his lap.

Soon they arrived at the Quillitary grounds. Aaron and Liam went inside and made their way to the little house where General Blair lived. The door stood ajar. Aaron pushed it and found the general alone.

The man looked up from the table where he was eating a lunch of Favored food. "Well?" he asked, his voice dripping with sarcasm. "What kind of response did you get? Lots of cheers?"

Aaron's face burned. "My people are exactly as responsive as we trained them to be," he said. "What more would you expect? A shout? A rousing song? None of that's allowed, so of course their silent stares indicate all are properly ready to proceed with this plan."

"Fair enough." The general finished chewing and wiped his mouth with his sleeve. "When the wall is down, and when you have solved my oil problem, we'll talk about this plan of attack."

"Good," Aaron said, but he'd forgotten about the oil problem. He looked down his nose and said with a hint of disdain, "I've prepared the Necessaries to start the work on the wall. Your Quillitary is instructing them now, so I'm assuming you have an excellent idea of how to carry out the task after so many years of wanting the wall down." He shoved his hands in his pockets. "I'll get to work on the oil problem and will return with a solution after your work on the wall is done."

The general, his eyes narrowed and the wound throbbing at his neck, nodded. "I'll be waiting."

Aaron glared back at him. "Not for long, I assure you," he said. "So be ready."

The general laughed. "I give the orders, *High Priest*."

Aaron scowled. He turned, Liam followed, and they walked out of the house and across the Quillitary grounds, back to the road. They climbed into the vehicle and chugged back up the dusty road to the palace.

As the barbed-wire ceiling's shadows rolled across Aaron's cheek, his mind whirled with the overwhelming promises he'd made. Not only did he promise to tear down the wall, but now he had to fix the oil problem—a problem that had existed since Quill began over fifty years ago. What had he gotten himself into? His breath came out in short bursts as he tried to control the panic that welled up inside him. He was so tired of this feeling. Would it ever end?

Liam looked at Aaron curiously but said nothing.

When the vehicle came to a rest in front of the palace door, Aaron and Liam climbed out. Aaron paused in the driveway as the vehicle pulled away, and looked at the forty-foot wall. His moving gaze stopped when he reached the filled-in spot, where he'd once opened a window to the sea. How strange it would be to see the water again. Despite the heat, Aaron shivered.

Liam paused at the door and stood uncertainly, waiting for him.

"Send someone out to collect all the cashew fruit and other nuts growing in the Favored Farm," Aaron said brusquely.

LISA McMANN

"Every last one. And deliver them to my office. Oh, and tell the Farm guards to plant more immediately. We'll need a constant supply."

Liam knit his brows. "Yes, sir."

"And then make sure the Necessaries understand their instructions from the Quillitary so they can get moving on the teardown."

"Yes, sir," Liam said again. He hesitated, and added, "Are you sure about this? The wall coming down, I mean?"

Aaron looked sharply at Liam. "What do you think? Of course I'm not sure! This plan could ruin me. And it could ruin you, too. So if you do not wish to participate, you may gladly take yourself back to the Ancients Sector once and for all, and you'll be dead by morning."

Liam stood, mouth agape. He couldn't stand Aaron's arrogance and considered walking away. But then he closed his mouth. If he left, there would be no hope for Artimé. For the sake of Eva and for the hope of Claire's forgiveness, he uttered the words as Eva had taught him. "You have my utmost loyalty."

"I should hope so," Aaron snarled.

LISA McMANN

As Liam turned to go, Aaron grabbed his arm. "Wait. I'm not finished," he said, his voice strained.

"I'm sorry. What can I do for you?" Liam could see the fear in Aaron's eyes. It was there all the time now. For a moment, he almost felt sorry for the high priest.

"I want you to steal as many magical components from Artimé as you can get your hands on, and bring them to me. I need to know how they work, and the words you have to say with them, so you'll have to find somebody over there who you can torture for secrets. I don't care what you do or how you get them—just get it done."

Leaving Liam speechless as he had done so often lately, Aaron fled into the palace, wondering if he was making an extremely dangerous mistake, and hoping with everything he had in him that his reign—and his life—was not about to end.

Underwater Exploration

When the figure disappeared behind the rock, Sky ran back toward Alex. "What do we do? Go after him?"

"It depends," Alex said, thinking frantically. What would Simber do? Alex hated not having him around to consult with. The wind gusted, spraying them all with rain and salt water from the sea. "If this place is like Warbler, there could be thousands of them."

Florence interrupted. "There aren't thousands. This island isn't big enough to hide them all, and it's solid rock—there's no going underground here. I can see over

LISA McMANN

many of the boulders, and I don't see anyone else."

"That doesn't mean they aren't there," Samheed said, his voice anxious. He gripped Lani's hand. "We should get out of here now." Samheed and Lani were rightfully afraid after having spent a month captured underground on Warbler.

"Why did Sean have to break his stupid leg?" Lani muttered. "We need Simber."

"Simber couldn't transport all of us anyway," Alex pointed out weakly.

"The safest way out is by fixing the ship," Florence said. "We don't know how far we are from home. And nobody said this person—or these people—are going to harm us. They could be friendly, like on Karkinos."

"Friendly people don't hide," Sky muttered. She looked at Alex. "Mean people and scared people hide."

Alex shifted uncomfortably. He wasn't sure if her statement was aimed at him, but he'd learned to assume most cryptic comments were. And it was true—Alex had a tendency to hide when he was scared to confront a problem, especially when it involved a girl. That's how he ended up in this current predicament with Sky. They talked at, about, and around each other

LISA McMANN

rather than directly with each other. He knew it wasn't right, but he didn't know how else to function. He had to focus on leading his people out of this mess. There simply wasn't time for difficult relationships. But he missed her.

"Sky's right, of course," Alex said carefully, eyeing her to see her response.

She smirked and looked at the ground, then stole a glance his way. But then she recovered her serious approach to the issue at hand. "I don't think there's enough food on this rocky island to sustain very many people. We need to get to work on this ship and have people keep watch. See if he or anyone else approaches us. Don't forget how scary Florence is when you haven't seen anything like her before."

Florence popped her biceps. "Right. Don't ever forget."

Alex nodded. "It's probably just someone in the same predicament we're in. A lucky victim of one of these shipwrecks. Or maybe not so lucky, depending on how you look at it." He looked around to assess his team. "Whatever the case, we're stuck here, so I imagine we'll run into him again. So is everybody in agreement? Shall we get to work?"

"We should at least have a lookout," Lani said, wringing

out her hair, which was soaked with rain by now. "I'll do it. I'd feel a lot better about this that way."

"Great," Alex said. "We can take turns." He looked up at the sky. It was growing darker. The clouds weaved restlessly together.

Lani ran a few yards away, climbed up a tall rock formation and perched on top of it. The steady rain beat down on her. She held her knees and mopped her eyes with her sleeve.

"Florence," Alex said, "what are we looking for?"

"Whatever we can find to patch this ship together. Planks, sheets of metal. Waterproof stuff. Cloth for sails, ropes, tools— you name it. If it looks useful, bring it to me and Copper. And let's make it beautiful and creative, Unwanteds! That's our specialty, after all." She stood up, a giant against the small barren island. "If things are too big for you to carry, you know how to find me."

"Can we go, please?" Crow asked. He and Henry jiggled impatiently, excited to explore the shipwrecks that littered the area.

"All right, go," Alex said with a grin as they bounded away. "Stay together and be careful! There could be sea critters about." He thought briefly about the eel they'd fought on Karkinos and wondered if it had any friends out this way, lurking and waiting for a meal, and his smile faded. "Be careful!" he shouted again.

LISA McMANN

Everyone scattered, some staying on land to explore the smashed fishing boats and wreckage, and others heading out toward the rocks in the water to see what lay below the surface.

Alex watched as Sky followed her brother into the water. He wished he could follow her. He longed to talk with her the way they had before things got complicated. Was she really over him, like Lani had said? It seemed that way. He sighed and joined Ms. Octavia. They swam carefully amidst the rocks and headed toward the weathered stern of a sunken ship that just barely stuck up above the water.

They couldn't see much through the murk until they got close. Once they reached it, they dove down and followed the line of the ship's side, Octavia going first. The ship rested at a forty-five-degree angle, its snout planted firmly in a bed of rocks and mud. It was hard to see much of anything, but Octavia lit several highlighter components to guide them.

Alex followed close behind Ms. Octavia, marveling at the beautiful sides of the near-perfect ship. He wondered how it came to be here. He'd never seen anything like it in the waters or on any of the other islands they'd visited.

Nestled in the rocky sea bottom nearby was an enormous

technical instrument that had apparently dislodged when the boat sank. Alex knew he'd have to check that out later. It looked fascinating, and he couldn't imagine what it was used for. It probably wouldn't be of any use to the shipbuilders, but maybe he could convince Florence to try to bring it on shore sometime.

Ms. Octavia reached the sea floor, swam across the bow and up the other side. Alex went after her, peering through the water and peeking into the ship's many orifices. Schools of fish flashed and disappeared in and out of the openings. Alex wondered how they all knew just when to turn. It was like they were dancing, moving to some music only they could hear.

Clumps of sharp barnacles gripped the ship and the rocks nearby. As Ms. Octavia swam upward, Alex knew he'd have to surface soon—even all of Ms. Octavia's training had not enabled him to hold his breath forever.

As they neared the surface, Ms. Octavia stopped and peered at the side of the ship. She looked at Alex and motioned him to come closer. When he did, she drew her tentacle across the ship's side, underlining the faded letters she found there.

Ka o aru o. 5.

Scavengers

I t seemed like a strange name for a ship, but when Alex really thought about it, he admitted he wasn't an expert on ship names. After all, he'd only known one vessel with a name, and that was Mr. Today's boat, named after his daughter, Claire. And there were a lot of spaces in the name, which made Alex wonder if some of the letters had been washed away. They would probably never know the answer.

He and Ms. Octavia broke the surface, giving Alex a chance to catch his breath and check the weather before taking a closer look inside the vessel. On shore, Henry and Crow carried a long red plank between them, heading toward Florence. The rain and wind continued on all around the island, and clouds were thick above them, but the sun was still visible beyond the strange storm's perimeter. Looking out to sea, Alex could tell where the rain field ended, about half a mile offshore, and it seemed to be consistent all the way around—at least from what Alex could see. When he was ready, Alex and Ms. Octavia headed underwater once more.

This time they swept across the deck, both holding highlighters, looking for anything useful. Alex spotted a fine-looking rope, perfectly coiled around a stairway railing. And the sides of the ship were in good shape. Not wooden like the pirate ship, but made of some hard material. If only they could cut a portion out of each side and attach it to the pirate ship like a bandage over the split . . . but there was no way to cut through material like this.

Alex followed Ms. Octavia, swimming down the stairwell to see what was belowdecks. Moving cautiously, they swam back and forth, taking in everything. Tools, equipment, rigging, giant trunks that were padlocked and bolted to the floor. Alex wondered if they'd be able to pry them open, and if so, what they'd find inside. There were doors with the windows broken out and vast rooms filled with strange machinery.

They went down another level to find even more strange equipment: Telescopes and giant instrument panels, all sitting politely in place, as if the ship weren't resting at a forty-five-degree angle under water.

When Alex began to run out of air, he motioned to Ms. Octavia, and the two weaved back through the ship. Along the way, Alex unwound the coil of rope and pulled it with him through the water, and Ms. Octavia enfolded several arms around a large wooden box of tools and carried it upward, showing her tremendous strength.

They rose to the surface with their goods and struggled through the water to drag them along to shore. The water was much rougher near the surface, making the journey tougher than Alex expected. By the time he reached the shore, he was spent. He heaved the coil of rope onto the land next to a small pile of other useful items that had been retrieved from other wreckage. He went back to get the waterlogged toolbox from Ms. Octavia, helped her drag it ashore, and dropped it to the ground with a thud. Water trickled out of it through cracks in its sides.

Fox and Kitten, who weren't able to collect much, instead hopped around the recovered items, observing and commenting on them. Every now and then a gust of wind bowled Fox over and sent him across the rocks like a misplaced tumbleweed. The storm was getting worse.

Alex, still breathing hard, approached Florence and Copper. "There's a ton of stuff on the ship Ms. Octavia and I found. Machinery and strange-looking equipment—I don't know what any of it is, but it might be worth you taking a look. Almost everything is too heavy for us to carry. The ship is in really great shape—except for the rip in the side that caused it to sink."

"That's very encouraging," Florence said. She stood near the split in the pirate ship's side, and Alex could tell she had managed to align one half to the other, which must have taken every bit of strength she had. "We're going to need a lot of help putting this thing back together. This will be an interesting patch job, and it won't be easy to ensure it'll be waterproof." She shifted her bow and looked down at Alex. "Do you have any magical components left or did we lose them all in the wreck?"

LISA McMANN

"I have what's on me," Alex said, patting his pockets.

"Do you have any preserve spell components?"

"A couple. I'll ask around. Do you think that would help?"

"Marcus used that spell on Simber. So my thought is that if it keeps the water from seeping into the cat, it'll keep the sea from seeping into our ship. So yes, I think it would help tremendously once we've got this thing put back together."

Copper approached. She could no longer squeeze inside the ship through the split now that Florence had pushed it closed and propped up the bow and stern with rocks to hold the ship in place. "Can you let me in?" she asked. "I want to check the stability of the structure to make sure it's not compromised. No use fixing a ship that'll split apart on a rough sea with all aboard. We'll need to be certain we shore up the beams properly."

"We'd be in deep trouble without you, Copper," Florence said. She hoisted Copper into one half of the pirate ship so she could assess the condition from belowdecks, where Florence couldn't go.

Alex nodded. "We can try to make some new preserve components too. And we could sure use a saw or something that would cut metal things," he said, shoving the toolbox with his foot, "like this padlock."

Florence turned her attention to Alex and the box. She leaned down, grasped the padlock, and squeezed. The lock snapped and dropped to the sand.

"Okay," Alex said with a grin. "Well, knowing you can do that is slightly frightening."

Florence smiled and turned back to analyzing the ship's needs while Alex opened the toolbox and began to pull things out. The wind grabbed hold of the lid and slammed it open wide. Thunder pounded overhead. The rain grew more insistent. Alex squinted at the sky and shook his head. They'd just begun working and now the weather threatened to shut down their efforts. "How are we supposed to get anything done?" he muttered.

A moment later, a shout rose from the shore. "Guys, come and look!" called Henry. "Down here—you won't believe it!"

Alex and Florence looked at each other and headed over to where Henry and Crow stood on the shore. Copper climbed up to the top deck and watched from there. Lani hopped off her post and, after a quick surveillance, ran toward the boys. Fox,

Kitten, Ms. Octavia, Samheed, and Sky came running as well.

"What is it?" Alex asked.

Henry and Crow, streaming with water, grinned from ear to ear. Their eyes shone.

Sky laughed at her brother's mischievous face. "Come on, what is it?"

Henry looked at Crow. "I think they're going to have to see it to believe it."

Crow nodded.

The two boys ran back into the water and struck out toward a wreck that looked like an enormous barge. The rest of the Artiméans went after them.

When Alex dove into the water and swam down, following the boys, he nearly sucked in a noseful of seawater.

Littered across the sea floor, as if in a giant traffic jam, were no fewer than twenty military vehicles . . . exactly like the ones the Quillitary used.

The Strange Figure

S ome of the vehicles were lodged up to the tops of their wheels in mud. Others were on their sides or upside down. It was a crazy sight to see—all of those vehicles, covered in rust and slime, green tufts of seaweed growing on the seats and doors. The seat covers rotten. Giant bites ripped out of the cushions. Lani tugged at Alex's shirt and beckoned him to follow, casting a highlighter spell as she swam. They went closer to see inside one of the vehicles and scared a school of fish.

They explored the fleet of vehicles, finding few useful items among them, but marveling at the strangeness of so many

LISA McMANN

vehicles all submerged and useless. Alex couldn't stop wondering about them. How long had they been here? It had to be many years. And where did they come from—Quill? It seemed impossible that any of the islands Alex had visited in the chain had enough material and machinery to manufacture these complex vehicles. Were the vehicles created by magic somehow? But if Mr. Today had created them magically, why did they work so poorly in Quill? And why didn't Artimé have any?

Puzzled and tired, Alex swam to the surface, only to find the skies growing black and the sky sparking with lightning. As Alex swam toward the shore, thunder rumbled and the wind whistled around his head. "Florence," he called, "tell everyone to come on shore and find shelter. It's too dangerous."

Florence summoned the Artiméans and everyone began swimming back to land. As Alex neared the shore, he saw Copper waving and jumping from the top deck of their ship. He could barely make out her raspy shouts, but he could tell she was alarmed. He ran deftly across the rocky shore toward her. Sky wasn't far behind.

Copper began using hand motions to communicate with Sky.

Sky caught up with Alex and translated as they ran. "She says the man I saw earlier is stealing something."

"We don't have much to steal," Alex muttered. They rounded the curve of the ship and stopped short when they saw a short, thin man tugging fruitlessly on the toolbox. The man looked very old, his olive skin set with deep wrinkles, but he didn't seem terribly fragile for his age. He wore black-rimmed cat-eye glasses and a floppy sun hat on his head, despite the weather. There was no way he could carry the heavy box of tools, yet he kept trying to drag it. He was going nowhere.

Alex looked at Sky and raised an eyebrow.

She flashed a crooked half smile, and the two communicated without words, like they'd done many times in the past. The man was harmless, and they both understood it. Sky touched Alex's arm. "Shall I talk to him?"

Alex nodded. He felt the familiar flutter in his stomach at Sky's touch, and it made him miss their friendship even more. He *had* to get things back to the way they were when they spent so much time on the roof of the gray shack. He would give anything to have that again. Why did they have to complicate things by kissing? Though he admitted he liked that part too.

Sky approached the man, who hadn't noticed them yet. She cleared her throat to announce her presence, and he still didn't notice her—either that or he was ignoring her.

"Excuse me," Sky said. "Sir, what are you doing?"

The man looked up. He didn't seem afraid. He tilted his head and said something neither Alex nor Sky could understand.

"I'm sorry," Sky said, speaking more slowly. "What did you say?" She wrapped her arms around herself to stay warm as the wind and rain beat down on them.

The man narrowed his eyes at Sky. He didn't seem to notice the storm. He spoke rapidly, but neither of the Artiméans could understand a word.

Sky glanced at Alex, who shrugged. She turned back to the man and tried signing to him.

He regarded her curiously, then shook his head. He tried speaking again, slower this time. "*Kore wa watashi no monodesu.*"

"I'm afraid I don't know what you are saying," Sky said in a gentle voice. "Do you understand me at all?"

The man held up a finger and closed his eyes, a pained expression on his face, as if he were trying to recall something.

When he opened his eyes, he tapped the box and said very slowly, "This . . . mine. Understand?"

This time Sky nodded, and she spoke slowly too. "This is your toolbox?"

The man smiled, revealing a mouth void of teeth. "Mine." He pointed to the stern of the ship that Alex and Ms. Octavia had explored. "My ship."

"Ah," Alex said. "So you are stranded here?"

"*Hai.* Stranded." He leaned in and, hesitating now and then, said, "I speak your language. Long time ago. I am old . . . must think for the words." He tapped the side of his head. "But it comes back. You'll see."

Alex nodded. "I can understand you very well, sir. Thank you."

By this time, the rest of the Artiméans had gathered, with Florence hanging back, keeping an eye on the island but also realizing that her looming presence might be a little intimidating. Still the man noticed her—she was impossible to miss. He pointed excitedly at her, looking at Sky, and asked, "Robot?"

Sky stared. "Um . . . what?"

"That is a robot?" the man asked, trying very carefully to sound out his words.

LISA McMANN

Sky shook her head and looked around. She didn't know the word.

Lani pushed forward. "Wait. Did you say 'robot'?"

When the man nodded, Lani covered her mouth and tried not to laugh. "No. Not a robot. Statue."

Alex and Sky exchanged puzzled glances.

The man frowned. "Statue is alive." He peered more closely at Lani, then looked at the ship. He pointed at it. "You are pirates?" He seemed extremely puzzled.

"No," Lani said. "Not pirates. We just use the ship. Florence is a living statue. It's . . . it's magic, you see. . . ." Lani trailed off. Magic was hard to explain, and she didn't know if the man understood.

The man's face perked up. "Oh, magic!" He nodded. "Magic. So. This is why ship . . . arrives . . . on the land, like this. It is for you to fix." He pointed to the pirate ship, clearly happy to finally make sense of how the damaged ship managed to be sitting entirely on land.

"Yes," Lani said, tickled. "How do you know about magic? Can you do magic?"

"Me magic?" the ancient little man said, pointing to his

wrinkled old chest. A gust of wind took his hat high into the air, and he laughed, unbothered by it. "No. I know magic from another visitor. Visitor I do not see in a long time. He comes through the magic tube. You know him? His name is Marcus Today."

Another Tube

Wh-what?" Alex sputtered. "You knew Mr. Today? There's a tube here?" Could this be their way home?

The little man held up his hand as the storm grew worse and a gust of wind sent Fox rolling across the ground. "Come quick," the man said to them all. "I will show you."

Alex exchanged looks with Florence and his friends, and they all nodded. The man seemed harmless and trustworthy.

The man trekked to a cluster of rocks not far inland, and held his hand out, presenting it. "Magic tube," he said proudly.

Alex and Samheed ran to look inside the rock formation.

L I S A M c M A N N

There, indeed, were the remains of a tube, tilting slightly as if years of wind had begun to push it over. Its glass was opaque with salty grime from the sea. Moss grew on the floor of it, and a puddle of water collected in the lowest area. The panel was cracked and there were several holes in it where the directional buttons should be.

Alex's heart sank. It was completely useless. "Very nice," he said to the man. "Thank you for showing us." He looked back at the others and gave a quick shake of the head. "Sorry, everybody. Not functional," he said. "I wouldn't have the first clue about how to fix it." He squinted at it. "I'll certainly give it a try, though."

A blast of lightning split the sky and a howling wind sent Fox tumbling several yards. Henry ran to pick him up, and Kitten too, though being so small and low to the ground had kept her from sailing anywhere thus far.

The man beckoned the Artiméans to follow him. "Hour of calm is over," he said, and his words were starting to come out more smoothly the more he spoke. "We must shelter from the hurricane." With that he shielded his eyes and squinted toward the shore, looking longingly at the toolbox, and shook his head. "My box," he muttered. He turned and moved quickly toward the center of the island, where the largest rock formations stood. The Artiméans exchanged glances once more. Faced with a choice between the worsening storm and the unknown, they chose the unknown and went after him.

When they reached the tallest rocks, everyone but Florence followed the man through a small, sheltered doorway into a large open room.

"I'll stay out here," Florence called out.

Alex came running back to the doorway, realizing Florence was too big to fit through it. He looked at her, concerned. "Are you sure?"

"The weather doesn't bother me. If anything strange happens, yell, and I'll rip these rocks out of my way so fast and be at your side in no time. But there's no use destroying the poor man's place unless it's necessary." She gave Alex a reassuring smile. "Besides, I can see and hear what's going on inside that main room from here."

Alex frowned. "Okay, if you say so," he said.

"I do."

Alex slowly turned and went back inside.

LISA McMANN

Off the main room were smaller, semi-closed nooks. The nooks were modest in size, but plentiful, which made the shelter feel quite spacious, yet cozy. There was easily enough room for thirty or forty people, Alex guessed. He looked around and automatically reached for a spell component in case they were being set up for an ambush. But the little man just stood and waited patiently, a wide grin on his face, as he watched the Artiméans look around. No one else appeared.

The entry room where they stood was by far the largest space they could see, and though there was no physical door that could be closed to shut out the storm, the wind and rain coming inside was vastly minimized by intricately positioned rock slabs outside.

While the others wandered through the shelter, Alex stood by the door and looked out, seeing the pattern of rocks that protected him from the elements. It was so cleverly designed that he quite wished he'd thought of it, and for a moment he longed to be back in Artimé, working on art for a change. He needed something creative to do. The voyage had gotten long and arduous, and now that they had rescued Copper, he just wanted to go home and draw things.

He could see Florence just outside the door, sitting against the rocks, wiping down her bow and arrows with a bit of moss she'd pulled up.

Sensing Alex hanging back, Florence spoke up. "I may try to work on the ship if the storm lets up a little. For now, though, I can barely hang on to this arrow even though I'm partially sheltered in this corner. The wind wants to take everything. So I imagine out on the open shore it'll be nearly impossible to do anything in these conditions." She looked at Alex. "I mean it, Alex. Get out of the rain. I'll be fine here."

Alex, finally convinced, nodded and went inside to find the others settling in nicely. The little man scurried over and gave him a towel and some dry, ragged clothes to change into, then disappeared into one of the nooks. Alex could tell the clothes had once been adorned with a colorful pattern that had now faded almost completely away. Alex changed quickly and hung his clothes to dry by the others, then wandered about through the open space, visiting the different nooks where his friends had settled. He checked on Captain Ahab, making sure the statue was comfortable. He spied Sky with Lani and Samheed, all talking animatedly in one nook, Samheed acting something out to the others' enjoyment. Alex looked away. He'd join them later. Maybe.

On one side of the shelter was a nook that led to a large enclosed area with a door. Alex peered inside the doorway. To his surprise, he found it was a greenhouse, brightly lit. The little man was inside with his back to Alex, working intently on something.

Alex looked up, wondering where the light was coming from. Instead of a rock slab ceiling, there was glass to let in whatever natural light there happened to be, and strange glowing orbs hung above a healthy assortment of vegetation.

The man noticed Alex and pointed to the glass overhead. Loud sheets of rain swept over it. "You see this?" the little man asked. "Marcus Today makes magic glass for us."

The words sank in and Alex's eyes clouded with emotion. He was surprised by how much this information affected him. Mr. Today had been here, in this place. He had been kind to this man. Yet he'd never spoken about it. And there was a tube here! If there was a tube in this desolate place, how many other tubes could there be? And all of those Quillitary vehicles buried at sea . . .

LISA McMANN

He looked at the man and then suddenly frowned, replaying his words in his head. "Wait a minute. Did you say 'us'?"

The man nodded. He pointed to an area of the shelter that had been thus far unexplored, and he held up two bony fingers. He went to the opening and called out in the strange language. After a long moment, two equally ancient men appeared from deep inside the shelter. They nodded politely at Alex, who smiled and gave an awkward wave.

The three island inhabitants had a conversation, and then the first man invited Alex to follow him. "If everyone is ready, may I speak, please?"

"Of course," Alex said. He went back to the main room and called the Artiméans to gather. The man asked everyone to sit down on the floor around a blackened area. He disappeared, returning a moment later with dry firewood, and began to work two pieces of wood together with a bit of dried moss. Samheed offered up a damp origami dragon, which was able to spit a few sparks to help the process along.

When the fire was going strong, and the smoke was funneling itself neatly out a nearly invisible vent hole near the ceiling, the man sat back on his haunches.

Alex and the two men joined him by the fire. Florence leaned in and poked her head through the doorway to listen.

"This is home of many and few," the man said to the tune of the wind and thunder. "We did not build it. The ones who came before us did not build it. We are all visitors here, like you."

Sky smiled and caught Alex's eye. The both swiftly looked away.

"These are my friends. They only speak our native language," the man said. "We are . . . scientists." His hesitations and stutters lessened the more he spoke, as if the Artiméans' language was swiftly coming back to him.

"I am youngest," he said with his gummy grin. "My name is Ishibashi Junpei. You may call me Ishibashi-san." He nodded at Samheed, who sat closest, prompting him to repeat it.

"Ishibashi-san," Samheed repeated.

"Good." Ishibashi drew some symbols on the dirt floor with his finger. "I am ninety-six years old. My friends are ninety-eight and one hundred and ten," he said, pointing to them. "Ito and Sato. They are *very* old." Ishibashi cackled. The other two islanders smiled politely, not understanding. They were mostly toothless as well.

"We are pleased to meet you and grateful for the shelter, Ishibashi-san," Alex said. "My name is Alex." He introduced the others. Fox, who was embarrassed at being pointed out, and Kitten, who decided to be embarrassed too, scampered around the shelter, to the delight of the islanders.

"Are you the only people on the island?" Alex asked.

"*Hai*, that is correct. There were more, but dead now. Some lived here with us for a time. I am sure more in the future will smash upon our rocks during the hurricane. But now, we are only three."

Lani edged closer, her eyes ablaze with the fire's reflection. "How long have you been here? Are all three of you scientists? Don't you want to escape? What is a hurricane?"

Ishibashi's laughter rang out and echoed in the stone chamber. "Slower please; I am very old."

Lani repeated her questions.

The old man nodded after each one and began to answer slowly. "Our ship carried a great number of scientists and crewmembers. It was lost here many, many years ago."

He paused, a faraway look in his eye, and continued. "At that time, there were ten or twelve others from shipwrecks living here. They were old. Most died soon after we came. Also there are outcasts."

"Outcasts?" Sky asked.

The man nodded. "There is an island of pirates—you know of it?"

The Artiméans all nodded.

"When the pirates capture intruders or enemies, they hurt them, drag them near our island. Set them adrift in little fishing boats. They have done this for hundreds of years—or so the legend goes. The little boats get caught in the hurricane and crash on rocks. Only a few outcasts lived and made it to shore."

"Where is everybody now?"

"Gone." Ishibashi looked at the floor. "Most cannot withstand the constant storm. They go crazy. Then they try to escape. The current and the wind always drive them back against the rocks, to their deaths. Only one time someone escaped—just last year."

Crow and Henry exchanged horrified looks. Copper leaned over and whispered something to them, but they didn't look relieved. Alex's stomach knotted.

LISA McMANN

Ishibashi went on. "Some from our ship died that way—trying to get off the island. The rest died from accidents or old age."

"That's horrible." Alex shifted uncomfortably as fearful, questioning eyes turned his way. There was so much pressure being the head mage! How were they going to get out of here? He was pretty sure he could transport the ship to calmer waters, but that presented a new set of problems, like how would they get to it without Simber? Living things didn't transport, so they couldn't board the ship before moving it. And poor Spike had had a hard enough time getting them safely to the island, and that was swimming *with* the current. She couldn't possibly carry them that great distance fighting the current the whole way. And of course there was Florence, too heavy for everyone present to lift for long. It had taken Simber and Spike combined to bring her up from the pirates' aquarium, and that was in calm water. There was simply no way to get off this island without Simber—they'd have to wait . . . and hope he'd find them.

But what if he didn't?

Outside the wind howled and thunder crashed. Ishibashi

looked out the stone doorway at Florence, who remained unaffected by the horrible weather. "Are you okay, robot?"

Florence, disturbed by the hopelessness of escape, murmured, "Yes, I'm fine. Thank you."

Ishibashi turned back to the other Artiméans. "You know by now a hurricane is a terrible storm. Every day the hurricane comes. It howls all afternoon and through the night. In the morning the storm rests, only to return a short time later, more fierce than the day before."

"Every single day?" Sky asked. She couldn't imagine it. She had seen very little rain in her life, and she didn't like it. Automatically her hand went to her throat, which had once worn the thorns that had silenced her voice. She wasn't sure which was worse—that, or living in a hurricane like this every day of your life. She found herself longing for Artimé. And she wasn't the only one.

Ishibashi's face wore the effects of many years of sorrow and hurricanes. "Every single day," he said softly.

Trying Not to Panic

After the gathering, Ishibashi and the other two scientists left the Artiméans to get settled. Once alone, fear and worry spread through the group. How were they going to get out of here? When would they have time to fix the boat with the hurricane pounding them every day and blowing away all their supplies? And once Simber returned, how was Alex going to transport the ship far enough outside of the treacherous hurricane zone to keep it from crashing on the rocks again?

Henry was the one to say it out loud. "If Simber had been

LISA McMANN

with us, he would have seen this coming and steered us away. We wouldn't be stuck here."

Crow couldn't hide his fear. "I don't like this place. Are we stuck here forever?"

"We have to get out of here," Samheed muttered. "We have to." He clenched his fists and began to pace the floor.

"Everybody, please stay calm," Alex said, not feeling calm in the slightest. "We will get out of here."

Samheed stopped in front of Alex, his face intense. "How?"

Alex flinched. "We'll fix the ship and wait for Simber."

"Fixing the ship will take forever!"

"We'll get it done, Samheed," Alex said through clenched teeth.

"Yeah, well what if Simber doesn't come? We're stuck here!"

"Sam," Lani said. "Take it easy. We'll figure it out."

"Of course we will," Ms. Octavia said. "We always do."

But her words didn't sound as sure as everyone wanted.

Copper spoke up. "In fixing the ship, we just have to be efficient with timing. We can do the salvaging and repair work during the morning reprieve from the storm," she said. "And

LISA McMANN

any leftover material we have each day, why, we'll drag it into the shelter so it doesn't blow away, and work on it in here. That way the next day we'll have material to build with as soon as we can head outside safely."

She paused, and then leaned forward, putting a gentle hand on Samheed's shoulder. "You don't know me very well. And maybe I seem weak because I was a captured slave to the pirates. But I promise you that I know what I'm doing. I know how to fix ships, and so do Sky and Crow." She looked at her children, and they nodded solemnly. "You have to trust us and Florence. Together we can get this done."

"And what about the rest of the time?" Samheed prompted. "Sit in this cave? Endlessly? I'll go crazy. I'm already going crazy just thinking about it."

"The rest of the day we'll do what we do best," Alex said. "We'll make spell components. I don't know about you guys, but I'm almost out of them, and we lost a whole crate full of them when we wrecked."

The others checked their supplies and reported minimal components remaining. "What are we going to use to make them?" Lani mused. She peered out the door as the rain pounded the rocky ground like a million footsteps. "All there is here is rocks and moss."

Alex's face was troubled. "Then we use rocks and moss," he said weakly. "I can think of five new spells to create without even trying."

Samheed smirked, clearly calming down a bit. "Oh yeah? What are they, Stowe?"

Alex could feel his ears growing hot. Of course Samheed was going to call Alex out. That's what Samheed did. And that's why Alex liked him so much, even if Sam was a little intense. He scrambled to think of something to say as a retort. "If I told you, you might steal my awesome ideas," Alex said.

Samheed laughed. "Nice try. Come on. What are they? You don't even have one, do you."

Lani hid a grin. The two had been sparring since they were boys in Quill, and clearly it wasn't about to change now.

With all eyes on him, Alex knew he had to say something or risk looking stupid. Even if he couldn't make the magic work, he had to save face and show his leadership right now.

He coughed to stall for time, shuffled his feet, and finally blurted out the first thing that came to him. "A flying carpet. That's one idea."

Samheed blinked. "A flying rock carpet? Ha! Yeah, that'll work."

Alex shook his head as the idea took form in his mind. "No, you dolt," he said, and stood up a little straighter. "A flying *moss* carpet." And then, as it dawned on him, he added triumphantly, "And that, my friend, is what will help us get off this island."

Liam Does the Dirty Work

After Aaron gave him the impossible task of stealing components from Artimé, Liam Healy retreated to his room at the top of the stairs, in the palace tower. It was a room chosen for him by Eva Fathom, who had become his dear friend in the short time they'd spent together. She'd given him this room because it was the highest point in all of Quill, and anyone who spent day after day awaiting death in the Ancients Sector before finally being rescued deserved to have a high point in life.

Above him, the point of the tower held up the barbed-wire sky that covered all of Quill. If he stood by one window, he could see nearly all of Quill spread out before him. And if he stood on his tiptoes by the other window, such that his hair brushed the sloping ceiling, and pressed his face against the top pane of glass just so, he could barely see over the wall to the sea.

He didn't bother to look at it now, though, for he was quite perturbed about the task at hand. Instead he arranged his chair by the window, just outside the realm of the sunlight that streamed in, sat down, and thought about how he could possibly convince anyone in Artimé—through brutality or otherwise—to give him multiple magical spell components and tell him how they worked.

Brutality was clearly out of the question. It was only something Aaron had suggested, and something Liam would have done without much thought in the past. But Liam was done with that life. And once his eyes had been opened, he realized he hadn't really liked hurting people in the first place. In fact, he now looked back in horror at the attacks he'd made on Artimé when he was a Restorer, and at doing one of the most horrendous things a human could possibly do—hold another human hostage and treat her, well, treat her terribly. He had pushed aside their former friendship, and worse, intentionally ignored the fact that she was a human with feelings and goals and . . . and a life. An actual, good, helpful life to live. A life completely unlike his own had been.

He didn't even know that man now. The old Liam was obedient to Quill's high priest. He didn't dream. He didn't express emotion. He followed the law and never had an original thought. From the time he was thirteen, when his friend Claire was sent to her death, until he and the other Restorers attacked Artimé and he'd seen her there, *alive* after all these years, Liam had given his entire self over to the power of Justine—the power she had to take away a best friend without anyone objecting. The power to make a person give up everything and obey, because obeying was easy, and standing against her seemed impossible.

And even when he saw Claire, and knew she was alive, he still did those horrible things to her because the high priest had more control over him than his own conscience. What a weakling.

It's too late to change, he'd told himself back then. *It's the only way to get by.* And then later, *Aaron forced me to do it.* That's the

LISA McMANN

weak excuse he offered himself whenever the guilt pushed its way to the surface of his bland, recycled thoughts.

How he wished he could take it all back. How he regretted the man he had become. How he longed to go back in time and live his life the right way, even if it meant he'd be put to death for it. Anything would be better than living with this torment.

But he had done all of those things, and he had made those mistakes. There was no one else to blame for his own bad decisions. He knew that now. Boy, did he know it.

And if it truly was too late for forgiveness from Claire and from Haluki and from all of Artimé, too, well, then Liam would get what he deserved. But he wasn't going to stop trying to fix things. Eva Fathom had given him another chance. Another life. A new life.

He was going to live this one right, even if it killed him. But he had to go about it the right way if he was going to make a difference, make things better. He had to pretend for a while. He couldn't lose Aaron's trust—Eva was counting on him. All of Artimé was counting on him, though they didn't know it yet. He couldn't mess this up.

Ugh. Poor, stupid Aaron. Making all the same mistakes

Liam did, and more, for the sake of an errant goal.

Liam leaned forward and cupped his face with his hands.

After a while he rose up out of his chair and walked down the winding, uneven tower staircase, down the hall past Aaron's closed office door, and down the main staircase to the door. He left the palace and continued down the driveway. His steps were firm and his jaw was set, and the guards opened the portcullis without question for the governor. They trusted him, though they shouldn't.

He walked toward Artimé in the shadow of the wall, which would soon be coming down. When he drew near to the most desolate part of Quill, he could hear the distant sound of workers assembling, preparing to begin deconstruction. And when he reached the gates of Artimé, he weaved through the crowd of Necessaries and Quillitary and stepped inside the magical world. He presented himself to the girrinos, and behind them, hundreds of Artiméans had gathered on the lawn when they noticed the commotion in Quill.

An authoritative-looking young woman with reddish hair and freckles came forward at the sight of him.

LISA McMANN

"Greetings," Liam said. Hadn't she been the one who rushed past him in the palace a few days ago? He wasn't sure.

She folded her arms across her chest and glared. "What do you want?"

"I would like to request a meeting with Ms. Claire Morning."

The first hammer slammed against the wall behind Liam. He ducked, glanced over his shoulder, and took a few tiny steps toward the girl, which he immediately regretted, as she did not move along with him.

"My name is Liam Healy," he said as another hammer hit. Bits of rubble pattered on his back, and he lifted his shoulders to keep stones from slipping down his shirt collar. "And I am not with them."

Ms. Morning Stands Her Ground

O h, I know who you are, *Governor Healy*," said Meghan, "and if I remember correctly, the last time you came here, my friend Samheed warned you never to come back or he'd kill you. Do you remember that?"

"I-I-I—ah, yes," said Liam, beginning to stutter and sweat profusely, both of which he did frequently when nervous. "Actually, I do recall that. Is he," he said, his eyes darting all around the crowd, "ah, is he here?"

Meghan glared. "Maybe he is and maybe he isn't. I guess you'll find out eventually."

LISA McMANN

Liam swallowed hard. This wasn't going at all how he'd planned it. "I s-s-suppose I shall. And—and what about Claire? Ms. Morning?"

"Do you really think she'd want to see you? Really?" Meghan asked. "You are quite an idiot, aren't you?"

"I—yes. Yes, I am." More rubble, including a large hunk of rock, showered onto Liam. He stood there, completely miserable, but not ready to give up.

Meghan laughed. "Well, at least you admit it. That's certainly something." She looked around him to the Quillitary. "What in the world are they doing?"

"Oh!" said Liam, glad for the change of subject. "Aaron has—that is, the High Priest Aaron—has ordered the entire wall to come down."

Meghan stared. "You're joking."

"No, no, he's done it. We Quillens don't joke, you may recall. And it's, ah, as you can see, coming down. Quite explosively, I might add." He looked down at his feet. The rubble was beginning to gather around his shoes. "If I stand here long enough," he said brightly, "your friend Samheed might not have to go through the effort of killing me. Or, ah, burying me, either."

Meghan's face twisted with delight and puzzlement at the man before her. But she quickly remembered what he had done to Ms. Morning, and her expression soured. "I'll see if Ms. Morning wants to see you." She turned to the girrinos. "Don't let him move a single step."

"Oh, we won't," sang the three ladies. They lumbered over and made a triangular cage around him with their bodies.

Meghan darted through the crowd and disappeared.

A moment later Simber appeared from the mansion and walked regally toward Liam. The governor hadn't expected to find the creature here today. Eva had told him the cheetah had accompanied Alex on his journey, but perhaps she'd been mistaken. Or perhaps they'd returned home. He began to perspire even more heavily now, but the enormous creature sat down a good bit away. Liam wiped his brow and hoped he didn't faint here in his girrino prison. That would look very bad. The Quillitary would no doubt report that to Aaron.

More rubble.

Soon Meghan returned, and the girrinos moved away to offer them privacy to speak. Liam lifted his chin and searched the young woman's face.

"Will she see me?" he asked, his head swimming.

Meghan looked at him. He was pitiful, really. The back of him was covered from head to toe in gray dust and pebbles, and his shirt was soaked through with sweat. "Sorry," she said, and as she said it, she actually did feel a little bit sorry for the man. "She told me to tell you to go away and never come back."

Liam's face fell, and his heart sank. He closed his eyes, letting the sweat drip in and sting them, and he wavered a moment on his feet. He should have expected this, he knew.

"Oh," he said. He opened his eyes and found the girl looking curiously at him. "Did she . . . did she say anything else?"

"Actually, yes, but I chose to edit out some of the unsavory words." Meghan offered a cool smile.

"I see." Liam stood there another minute, lost in his thoughts, and then he turned to go. "All right," he said, pausing and looking back at Meghan. "I do understand. Thank you, and I'm sorry for the intrusion."

A spray of rubble peppered his front side and he put his arm up to shield his face. He took a step toward Quill.

"She also said she knows you were friends with Eva,"

Meghan called after him. "But you should still go away. So if that's what you came for, she already knows."

Liam stopped in his tracks. He turned slowly, oblivious to the pelting rocks now. He returned to Meghan, slipping a little over the gravel, and whispered harshly under the pounding noise, "Please don't shout that information, miss, I beg you. But tell me, how in Quill could she possibly know that?"

Meghan shrugged and lowered her voice. "Sean told us."

"Sean—Sean's . . . *here*? Has the ship returned?"

"No, just him and Carina. He broke his leg, so Simber brought him back."

Liam glanced at the cheetah, who was coming closer now. He turned back to Meghan. "*Sean's* here," he said, thinking very hard. "Sean's *here*."

"I think the rocks may be affecting you."

Liam didn't hear her. "That's it," he said under his breath. "Sean's here."

"Yes," Meghan said, rolling her eyes. "I know."

"May I . . . may I speak to *him*, perhaps?"

LISA McMANN

Meghan frowned. She looked at Simber, who shrugged. It was her call.

She sighed loudly. "I'll go ask." She ran back to the mansion, leaving Liam once more to think through his assignment. Maybe, just maybe, there was a way to do this. And if he succeeded, and saved Artimé . . . perhaps Claire would speak to him again.

A few minutes later Meghan returned, slightly out of breath.

"He says sure, come on in."

Liam blinked.

Meghan turned to lead the way. Liam stared for a moment, then he shook the rubble out of his shoes and followed.

Liam Finally Finds a Friend

S ean was alone in the hospital ward when Meghan led Liam into the mansion, trailing pebbles behind him as he walked. A young Unwanted descending the stairs frowned at the mess, pulled a tiny broom component from her vest, threw it, and muttered, "Sweep." Immediately the pebbles bounded to one spot on the floor. The component grew to a dustpan, scooped the pebbles up, and closed inward upon itself several times until it disappeared.

Liam watched over his shoulder, eyes wide. Everything he saw here was so incredible and foreign, and so colorful. He didn't know how to handle it. But he knew he had to stay focused.

Meghan pulled two chairs to Sean's bedside.

Sean, who was propped up on his pillows, reached out a hand. "Pleased to meet you, Liam," he said, but his voice held a hint of reserve. He only had Eva's word on Liam's character, and the man very likely could have been conning the old woman—though he didn't think so. Eva was one of the smartest people he'd ever known, and he was still in shock over the news of her tragic death.

Liam quickly wiped his grimy hands on his pants, sending a fresh shower of pebbles to the floor, and reached out to shake Sean's hand. "I'm pleased as well," he said, though the phrase was foreign to him—people didn't talk like that in Quill. "And, ah, I'm glad you were willing to see me. Eva spoke so highly of you."

Sean gave a grim smile. "That's actually nice to hear after the day I've had."

Liam nodded, and though he had no idea what Sean was referring to, he didn't feel right about asking.

There was a moment of awkward silence as Liam looked at Meghan. She narrowed her eyes, and then her face cleared. "Oh, I'm Meghan. Sean's sister. You don't mind if I sit in on your little chat, do you?"

Liam shot Sean a fearful glance. He was already taking such a risk, and the young woman didn't seem to understand the enormity of situation he was in, nor the secrecy of it.

"She's smarter than both of us, Liam," Sean said. "She's staying."

Liam let out a small, shuddering breath, and nodded. "All right, then." He bit his bottom lip, searching for words, and then he said, "Aaron has ordered me to bring him as many spell components as possible, along with the . . . the, ah, incantations that go with them."

Sean chuckled. "Has he, now? How interesting. And what does he expect to do with these items?"

Liam looked puzzled. "Use them, sir. Against Artimé. I believe so, anyway."

Sean and Meghan exchanged near-identical frowns. They were silent for a moment, considering the information.

"But—" Sean said, and stopped.

"Do you think—?" Meghan said, and she stopped too. They looked at each other again, and then Meghan turned to Liam. "Do you think he can *actually* do magic? I mean . . . he got lucky a few times. . . ." She trailed off, remembering.

LISA McMANN

"A few very important times. And if so, can anyone else in Quill? Do magic, I mean?" She knew of at least one other, that was certain. She touched her shoulder, where the burn from Gondoleery's fireball still smarted.

Sean shook his head. "I don't think so. When Quill attacked us the day Aaron killed Mr. Today, some of them cast spell components at us and they didn't work. They just bounced off us."

"But did *your* spells work?" asked Meghan, who hadn't been present during that attack. "Or did you all start fighting after Artimé disappeared?"

Sean closed his eyes, remembering the horrible day. "Oh, you're right. It was after. Our spells didn't work, either." He shook his head. "Sorry. My mind is a bit fuzzy from the medicine."

Liam waited politely until he was sure the siblings' conversation was done. "I do think Aaron can do magic, and not just by accident," he ventured. "For he's obviously done it more than once. And as for anyone else, well . . ." His face clouded as he remembered the time he and Eva had stopped by Gondoleery's house and were greeted by a wave of heat. "Yes. I think there are others."

Meghan wondered if Liam knew about Gondoleery too. But she hadn't told anyone of her visit to the palace, or what had taken place there—it hadn't been smart to go there alone, and she knew Ms. Morning would be furious to know she'd taken such a risk. She didn't know if she could trust Liam enough to say what she'd seen, so she continued to keep quiet about it. "Liam's right about that," she said simply. "There are others to be wary of in Quill." She looked at Liam. "So why are you here? Did you think we would just give you a bunch of spell components or something?" She laughed.

Liam's face paled. He cleared his throat and sat up straighter in his chair. "I'm here to see if you would consider a-a plan. Of mine, that is."

Sean's eyes narrowed. "What kind of plan?"

Liam swallowed hard. "Ah, well, I was thinking maybe you could give me . . . some spell components . . ."

Meghan's lips parted.

Sean raised an eyebrow.

"And . . . ," Liam continued quickly. "And, ah, I would show them to Aaron, so he would see I did my job, and he'd trust me more, and then I could return them to you. And I'd

189 « Island of Shipwrecks

LISA McMANN

just . . . I'd tell him that I was keeping them safe, you see. For when he needed them." He dropped his eyes and mumbled, "But obviously I wouldn't be, because you'd have them back."

Sean and Meghan stared.

"It's kind of a trick," he added. The idea didn't sound nearly as good out loud as it had seemed in Liam's head earlier. In fact, he was embarrassed by it, sitting here with two very intelligent people. *How did they get to be Unwanted if they were so smart?* he wondered.

And then it dawned on him. One more crack in Quill's philosophy. Eva could do magic. She was creative and intelligent. Sean and Meghan were too. And Claire, of course . . . Justine's words haunted him. "The strong, intelligent Wanteds go to university. The creative Unwanteds are sent to their deaths." Not even Justine herself had said that the creative children were unintelligent. It was just something the Wanteds assumed. Now, thinking about it, it didn't seem very intelligent of the Wanteds to assume such a thing as that. What a land of fools.

Liam sighed weakly and slumped in his chair. "I realize now how this sounds. I'm not, ah, not very *practiced* when it comes to ideas. Not yet, anyway. I'm sorry for wasting your time.

Forgive me." He pushed back his chair and stood up, unable to look either Sean or Meghan in the eye, and hurried out of the hospital ward to the sound of their incredulous silence.

Now what was he going to do? He thought about the options as he left the mansion and strode, head down, across the lawn and through the ever-widening opening into Quill. He'd have to admit to Aaron sooner or later that he wasn't able to complete the task. Maybe he could drag it out for a few days before Aaron sent him back to the Ancients Sector.

As he slipped over the shifting gravel below his feet and ducked to avoid the largest chunks of the wall that sailed through the air, he realized what a total failure he was. How ridiculous of him to think Claire would ever consider being his friend again. It was impossible. Especially once she got wind of his visit and his stupid request. "Oh, Liam," he chided as he walked the dusty road of Quill back toward the palace, leaving the noise behind, "Liam, you are a fool."

"Liam!" came a voice behind him.

He stopped.

"Liam!" the voice called again.

He turned. It was Meghan, running toward him.

"Wait," she called, slightly out of breath.

"Yes?" Liam asked. "Have I forgotten something? My hat, perhaps?" His hand went to his head and he absently brushed pebbles from his hair. He hadn't been wearing a hat, but in his embarrassment he could think of nothing else to say.

"You are a strange man," Meghan declared. "Very strange. But I wanted to thank you for telling us what Aaron was planning. That's helpful."

Liam looked up. "You're welcome. I'm on your side. I want you to know that. Just as Eva was. I don't know if you believe me, but there it is. I'm also very sorry—so incredibly sorry, for what I did to Claire, and if you could pass that information along, I would appreciate it very much."

Meghan regarded him for a long moment. "I will," she said.

"Thank you." He turned to go once more.

"Just a moment," Meghan said. "I wasn't finished."

"My vast apologies, Meghan." He waited.

"You see," she went on thoughtfully, "I think I have an idea to help you with your little problem. And I must say, it's a very good one—the idea, I mean. I think you'll like it." With that, she grinned impishly and started back toward Artimé.

LISA McMANN

"Come on, then!" she called out over her shoulder.

Liam watched her for a moment, a puzzled look on his face, and shuffled after her.

An hour or so later, Liam Healy, Governor to the High Priest Aaron of Quill, walked out of Artimé with his shoulders set, his head held high, and a large sack under one arm. He very nearly started to whistle as he walked, but then he remembered—just in time—where he was.

LISA McMANN

Aaron Builds a Machine

When Liam returned to the palace with the sack of spell components under his arm, the door to Aaron's office was open. He peeked in.

Taking up nearly all the space on Aaron's desk was a sparse contraption made up of rusty metal pieces. Gears were strewn all about along with other pieces of metal of every size and shape. Leaning over the contraption was Aaron. His priestly robe lay on the floor in a heap and the sleeves of his shirt were pushed up. There was a streak of dirt near his jaw. Surrounding the desk were several large burlap sacks overflowing with various nuts from the Favored Farm.

Aaron didn't notice Liam, for he was incredibly intent on the task before him. He muttered to himself now and then. Things like "If this goes here, then I need . . . ah yes" and "Where in Quill did I put my wrench?"

"It's in your back pocket, sir," Liam offered.

Aaron looked up, startled. "Oh, it's you, is it?"

"Yes."

Aaron reached for the wrench and almost grinned before he stopped himself. He was having more fun than he'd had in a very long time, but no one needed to know that.

Liam took a step inside the room. "What are you making, if I may ask?"

"None of your business," Aaron snapped out, without thinking. It was second nature to him to respond like that, even when he didn't mean to or need to. He didn't even realize he said it, and continued, "It's an oil press."

"Very nice," Liam said. He was intrigued by Aaron's ability to think of such a thing. "You seem to be very good at putting it together." He came closer and spoke in a low voice, as if he

LISA McMANN

were doing something wrong by asking, "Tell me—how did you come to, ah, to create such a thing? How did you know what to do with all the metal pieces and such?" He realized he didn't know the names of any of the instruments or parts that Aaron was working with. Most people in Quill didn't have access to such things.

Aaron frowned and didn't answer. He turned his attention to Liam, looking him over. "Where have you been? What's that in your hair?"

"Oh!" Liam said, rubbing his free hand through his hair and dusting off his shoulders. "While I was out getting the spell components, I spent a bit of time, ah, overseeing the wall destruction. It's coming along quite well."

Aaron set the wrench down on the table. "Really? That's good . . . I suppose. I mean, yes, that's very good." His eyes landed on the sack under Liam's arm. "And what's that?"

"The spell components you requested, High Priest," Liam said. He nodded politely.

Aaron gave him a skeptical look. "You got the spell components already? And you know how to use them?"

"Oh, yes. I knew you wanted them right away, so I took care of it immediately. Only had to torture two Artiméans to get what I needed," he said.

Aaron's eyes widened. "Well," he said, trying not to sound impressed, "I admit I didn't think you had it in you. Torture, you say? That's . . . that's a job well done."

"Thank you, High Priest." He began opening the bag. "Do you want to see?"

Aaron was curious, indeed, but the contraption was calling him. "I'm focused on this task at the moment, since we won't have General Blair's help until I figure this out. Save the spells for later when I can concentrate, will you?"

Liam obliged, securing the sack once more. "I'll keep these safe until you're ready."

"It may be a few weeks, unfortunately. This is slow going." Aaron turned back to his oil press, picked up the wrench, and started tinkering. Liam watched curiously for a moment, and then regarded the high priest thoughtfully before turning on his heel and heading out of Aaron's office.

"Liam," Aaron called as the governor disappeared.

LISA McMANN

He poked his head back into the office. "Yes, High Priest?"

"Be sure Gondoleery doesn't hear about those spell components, all right?"

Liam nodded. "Of course." He paused. "Where has she been, by the way?"

Aaron sighed and turned back to his machine. "If we only knew," he muttered.

The Wall Comes Down

Simber paced the lawn in front of the workers as the wall crumbled, making a huge mess along the entire border between Quill and Artimé. The work continued around the clock, with two teams going in opposite directions around the island. By the next morning, the area where the gate had been was free of all Quillens, and the people of Artimé had an expanded view of the ugly land of Quill.

Meghan and Carina met Simber and Ms. Morning on the lawn to figure out what to do about it all.

"What do you think about this, Simber?" Meghan asked.

Simber had been contemplating the action since the demolition began. "I think tearrring the wall down is an excellent idea," he said. "Which is why it's so puzzling to me that they'rrre doing it. I can't think of anotherrr time when I've agrrreed with something Quill does."

They watched as a large section at the top of the wall came down with a tremendous thud, shaking the land, and barely missing a handful of workers who scurried away just in time.

"Not only is it dangerous," Carina said, "but it seems very suspicious to me, and I can think of only one reason why they're doing it."

"Me too," Meghan said.

"Me thrrree," added Simber. "Aarrron is clearrrly plotting anotherrr attack against us."

The two young women nodded, and Meghan shared what Liam had told her about Aaron's plan to take over Artimé.

Ms. Morning frowned at the mention of his name, but she seemed grateful for the information.

"I wonder if they finally figured out how terrible their original attack plan was," mused Carina. "But if they're trying to

LISA McMANN

widen the access to make us more vulnerable, they're going to have to remove or smooth out all of this rubble to get their pathetic vehicles through."

"It'll definitely take a while," Meghan said. She glanced out to sea, wondering if she'd find Alex and the ship magically appearing in the distance. But they weren't there. "Are you and Carina going back to the ship, Sim?"

The stone cheetah growled his indecision. He felt uneasy about being away from Alex. "I don't know," he said. "Not rrright now, anyway. I'm quite concerrrned about all of this." He waved a paw at the workers.

"Carina should definitely stay here," Ms. Morning said. "We need her as a fighter in case something happens."

"I think that's a wise decision," Carina said. "And, Simber, why don't we see how things progress? There's not much you can do for the ship anyway. They just have to take it slow."

Simber nodded. "Yes, that's what I've been thinking. And I rrreally need to be prrresent herrre for the moment. I make the Quillitarrry uncomforrrtable. If they see me leave, they might considerrr Arrrtimé vulnerrrable. We mustn't let on that not

LISA McMANN

all of ourrr best fighterrrs arrre herrre at the moment."

"Or Alex, for that matter," Meghan said. "He's been away from home too long. It doesn't feel safe, you know? What if something happens? I hope they get back soon." She wanted the safety of Alex's presence, sure, but she missed him and her other friends terribly.

"So it's settled, then," Carina said. "Simber and I will remain in Artimé for now."

"I think that's the best plan," Meghan said.

"I agrrree," Simber said. "And I know the ship will be back soon. It has to be." He looked out over the sea, more worried than he was willing to say.

The Tube

S aying he could create a flying carpet component was easier than actually doing it. Alex knew it would take an incredible amount of construction, turning little bits of moss into a component sturdy enough to hold a person and fly them around. It would be very time consuming, and he didn't actually know if it would work. Secretly Alex wasn't too worried though. He wouldn't need to tackle the task at all if his own personal flying carpet, Simber, returned soon. Besides, there were a number of other things that were more important at the moment. And there was still one possible solution that would get most of them home in an instant, if only Alex could fix the tube.

LISA McMANN

Confident that Copper and Florence could direct the others in scavenging and fixing the ship, Alex's first order of business was to revisit that option. At dawn, before the precious hour of calm arrived, he sought out the island's gracious host, finding him in the greenhouse.

"Good morning, Ishibashi-san," Alex said. "I'd like to try to fix the magic tube. Do you have any tools I could use?"

"I do." Ishibashi led Alex to a small room that was filled with a hodgepodge of supplies. It appeared the scientists had done a fair amount of scavenging over the years. "You may use anything in here," Ishibashi said. He left Alex to explore on his own, but returned a moment later with an overflowing handful of broken knobs and springs, cracked buttons, and a few unidentifiable bits of metal.

Alex raised an eyebrow. "What's this?"

"Sato found these years ago after a violent wreck that sent debris crashing into Marcus Today's tube. Some pieces he found inside the tube, some wedged between rocks nearby. He collected them and saved them for Mr. Marcus Today, but our friend does not return."

Alex cringed. "I'm sorry, Ishibashi-san. I meant to tell you when you first mentioned him, but we were distracted by the storm. Mr. Today . . . he died. He was killed by my brother. . . ." He sighed and briefly closed his eyes. "Never mind. It's complicated."

Ishibashi narrowed his eyes. "Your family was the enemy of Marcus Today?"

"No!" Alex exclaimed. "No, not at all. I loved him. He was—he was like a father. . . ." He stopped, overwhelmed. He didn't have the emotional stamina left to explain further, except to add, "My brother is my enemy." The lifeless words hit the rock walls with a dull thud. Alex dropped his gaze.

Ishibashi nodded. "I see. I am sorry." He was silent for a moment as a wave of pain washed over his face, and then his countenance cleared and he held out the mass of broken pieces. "This will help you fix the tube?"

Alex reached out, and Ishibashi poured them into his hands.

"Thank you," Alex said. "Truly." He hoped the scientist knew he meant it.

Ishibashi's lips curved into a sympathetic smile. He put a hand on Alex's arm, nodded, and then disappeared once more, leaving Alex to his thoughts.

» » « «

When the sky grew lighter and the lightning faded, and the others headed to the shore to work on the ship, Alex darted out into the wind and rain with a woven bag full of tools, supplies, and the bits and pieces of the control panel that Ishibashi had given him. He made his way across the rocky terrain and slipped inside the tube, which offered a bit of shelter from the elements. Setting the bag down, he looked everything over carefully. The tube was in rough shape.

The entire unit slanted fifteen degrees or so in one direction—enough that Alex couldn't stand up straight in it without his head brushing the glass wall. He stepped outside and pressed his hands against it, trying to push it back the way it was supposed to be, but it didn't move. He pushed the tube harder, but nothing happened. Finally he slammed his shoulder into it with all his might.

It didn't budge. Alex stepped back to catch his breath, and then he moved around the circumference of the tube and saw that years of constant wind had forced sand and debris to build up under one side, causing the tilt. He scraped at the base of the tube with his hands, then thought the better of that and pulled a long metal bar with a flat end from the bag and began chipping at the refuse. It was packed so tightly that it seemed practically petrified. Alex worked at it with all of his strength until a large chunk of debris cracked loose. He poked and prodded, trying to dig all the way to the root of the problem, and finally he dislodged the entire wedge enough to get a decent grasp on it with his fingers. He set down the tool, gripped the edge, and yanked it out. The tube groaned and settled into place with a satisfying thud.

A few moments in the rain had the block of particles disintegrating in Alex's hand. He tossed it aside. It crumbled and the wind picked up the pieces and sent them out to sea. Alex wiped his hands on his pants and stepped back inside the tube. It was slightly wobbly, but level for the most part. He jumped up and down a bit, making sure it was stable, and felt it settle even farther into place. Satisfied, Alex got on his knees and began scraping up the moss on the floor, pocketing the green bits to use later for components.

When it was fairly clean, he stepped out once more and began collecting rocks and dragging them over to the base of the tube. He propped them up against the sides in order to hold the tube in place and act as a barrier to block further debris from working its way underneath.

"Now for the hard part," he muttered, looking at the broken panel. He dug inside the bag and pulled out some of the pieces Ishibashi had given him. He looked at them. He studied the panel. He looked at the pieces again, hesitated, picked up one, and pressed it into a hole. It fell through and clattered to the floor.

Alex picked it up and stared some more. He hadn't felt this lost on a project in a long time. Clearly the mechanics of the tube system were beyond Alex's abilities, at least without some sort of guide. "Add *Repair Your Tube in Seconds!* to the list of books I need to find in Mr. Today's messy library," he muttered. And then his heart sank as he remembered he might never get back there. He sighed, completely discouraged. "Simber," he groaned. "Help. Get us out of here!"

Over the course of the hour of calm, Alex tried plugging every piece into the panel in a variety of combinations. He used tools and supplies from Ishibashi to attempt to secure the controls in place. He imagined what magical incantations Mr. Today might have come up with to make the thing work. He even managed to find the piece that looked like the most important directional button, and he got it to fit partially in the space where he thought it should go. But when he pressed it, nothing happened.

It was no use. The tube was broken beyond repair.

He kept trying, barely noticing the worsening storm until the sky grew too dark for him to see clearly. He looked up just in time to see a big scrubby bush flying through the air straight at him. Alex covered his face and let out a gasp as it slammed into the side of the tube, then bounced around it, out of sight.

Alex opened his eyes. He had to get to the shelter. He took one last look at the control panel, which now resembled something Carina's young son Seth might create—a pile of junk all stuck together—and shook his head. This tube would never work again. Eyeing the storm, he hoisted the bag to his shoulder, took a breath, and dashed out into it. The wind nearly took him away, so he bent down and pressed forward, shielding his face from the blowing bits of dirt and brush and the thick waves of rain, until finally he made it back to the shelter. He staggered past Florence and ducked inside, the wind howling behind him.

When he lifted his head, he saw the Artiméans awaiting him with hopeful faces. Alex, streaming wet, took one look at them, sighed, and shook his head. "There's no fixing it," he said. "Maybe Ms. Morning or Mr. Appleblossom would know what to do if they were here, but they're not. I tried everything I could think of."

Fear returned to their eyes. Another hope dashed.

"I'm sorry," Alex said.

"But what—" Crow began.

Alex interrupted. "We keep working on the ship until Simber comes," he said. He looked from one dejected face to the next. "Please, just focus on the ship, and find useful things to do during the times we're stuck inside. Got it?" His words came out sharper than he intended, but he couldn't stand to hear another person ask what they'd do if Simber didn't come back. He wiped the rain and dirt from his eyes, and added with false surety, "He's coming back."

The murmurs began anew.

LISA McMANN

Something about this situation reminded Alex of when Artimé was lost, and people were getting restless and angry. Only back then he'd had his silent partner to lean on. She was here now, but there was no leaning. She was among the first to turn away.

One by one his friends walked off, leaving Alex to brood alone.

The Art of
Rebuilding

With such a limited amount of time each day to scavenge the other wrecks, shipbuilding was slow. Florence could work longer than the others in the gale-force winds each day, but not much—it didn't take very many minutes for the wind to be so furious that it would rip material and tools right out of her hands and carry them skittering across the rocky ground, no matter how hard she tried to hold on.

After the first few days of waiting just a little too long to pack up the excess material only to lose it to the wind, Florence, Copper, and Sky began to pay careful attention to the storm's warning signs. Florence and Copper instructed the scavengers to gather up the extra material before it was too late and carry into the shelter each day when the hurricane returned. And they used the time in the shelter to construct the necessary pieces for the next day.

The scavengers had a variety of other things to keep them busy as well when they were forced inside the stone structure. Captain Ahab needed attention after his injuries, so Ms. Octavia did what she could to help him hear once more, going so far as to take his head apart and clean it out to see if that would help him make a bit more sense. Inside she found quite a lot of cobwebs, a tiny mouse that was slightly larger than Kitten, three honeybees, and a rather delicate butterfly cocoon attached to a twig. Everyone was quite sure these items must have contributed to the statue's increasing dementia. Ms. Octavia also found some pieces of Ahab's broken ear inside, which was definitely causing the rattling sound.

They placed the cocoon in a jar in the greenhouse where Ishibashi, Ito, and Sato could watch for the butterfly to appear, and they shooed the honeybees in that direction as well, to the scientists' great delight. They let the mouse run about through the cave, where it chased Kitten and pounced on her a little too rambunctiously, causing Kitten's porcelain tail to get a chip in it. Luckily, Ms. Octavia fixed Kitten immediately, and then she herded the little mouse into one of the unused nooks and gave it some food and materials for nest making, which kept it busy from that point on.

Once Ahab's head was put back together and reattached, he felt better than he had in a long time, and he began to help with the ship's reconstruction, choosing the grand task of making a new helm from chunks of driftwood. Fox delivered some giant auger shells to the shelter, courtesy of Spike, who had batted them ashore with her tail. Ahab used the shells for the wheel's spindles, which gave it an exotic look.

Henry and Crow spent part of their indoor time helping Alex with spell components and assisting Copper with ship parts. But Henry often snuck away from the others and tagged along after Ishibashi, learning about the greenhouse that Mr. Today had helped create, and talking to the little man about scientific things.

Samheed, Lani, and Alex collected moss and pebbles every chance they could get to try to create new magical spells.

Ishibashi was gracious enough to let them go through the storage room as well as his personal collection of strange items that he'd picked up from wreckages over the years. There they found a large bucket of something called rubber cement, which Alex determined was perfect to help seal and preserve the ship—once he added a little magic, of course. He and the others went to work rolling bits of the rubber cement into tiny component-size balls so they'd be ready as soon as Florence and Copper finished the repairs. And while he worked, Alex thought and thought about how to construct the flying carpet component. After a few failed attempts at creating something viable with the moss he'd collected, he came to the conclusion that there was no way to make the moss dense enough without a loom to weave it. And that was definitely one thing Ishibashi didn't have.

One evening, Alex found a private nook, sat down, and rested his head against the wall in defeat. It was almost harder to create things here on this barren island than it was in Quill, where things were outlawed. At least there he'd have chicken bones to whittle into a makeshift loom. Here he only had random junk to work with, and the only things in abundance were moss and rocks.

Sky walked past the nook and hesitated when she caught sight of him. A shadow passed over her face and she nearly continued on. But instead she asked gruffly, "Everything okay?"

Alex turned to look at her. He shrugged. "Not really," he said, surprising himself with the confession. He'd been increasingly positive in front of the team.

Sky knit her brows. "What's wrong?"

Alex looked away, embarrassed. "Nothing. I don't know why I said that."

"Oh." She shuffled her feet, contemplating her plan of escape from the awkwardness, when he spoke again.

"It's fine really. I'm just frustrated," he muttered. "I can't create the flying carpet component without a loom, so if you happen to find one anywhere . . ." He shrugged again and his face got warm. "Stupid, I know. Never mind. I'm just in a weird funk. I'll just . . . yeah. I think I'm tired. I'll figure something out."

"Yeah. Okay," Sky mumbled. She frowned at the floor, and then turned and slipped away.

Alex watched her go, and then shook his head. "Stupid," he muttered.

» » « «

By the end of a week, the Artiméans had grown accustomed to the schedule, and their days began running quite smoothly. During the hour or so of calm each day when Alex was outside, diving and pulling things from shipwrecks, he didn't have time to think about much besides the task at hand. But when he was in the rock shelter, he had plenty of time to think about how senseless all this ship repair was without Simber there to get them safely on board.

Where was he? Why wasn't he back yet? Were they so far from home that it would take him this many days to make a round trip?

Alex assumed that the cat's keen eyes would have no trouble spotting the ship on the shore of this island, in spite of the raging storm, but what if Alex and the others had actually floated much farther off course than Simber expected? What if Simber couldn't find them and was just flying aimlessly over the ocean? Or worse . . . what if something had happened to him? There was a time not long ago when Alex had foolishly thought Simber invincible. But he knew better now.

Ishibashi, Ito, and Sato were ever gracious, giving the

LISA McMANN

visitors plenty of space and privacy. But sometimes in the evenings, Ishibashi joined them around the fire.

"I am hungry for your stories," he said. "Do you have any?"

Fox and Kitten had plenty, and with Simber gone, Fox could tell them without fear of reproach. The other Artiméans shared stories from their trip to the Island of Legends, much to Ishibashi's delight. "A living-crab island," he marveled again and again. "I can hardly believe it."

Something Ishibashi had said the first day they met stuck with Sky, and one night, before he could ask for stories, she said to him, "Tell us a shipwreck story. When did all the wrecks happen? Have you explored them?"

"Yeah," said Crow. "What about the vehicles that are all underwater? Where did they come from?"

Ishibashi pursed his lips. He glanced down at his wrinkled old hands. "Where? That is a question indeed."

The Artiméans leaned in, and Florence poked her head inside the shelter to listen as well.

Ishibashi pondered for a long moment, his face troubled. "I am reluctant to say," he hedged. "I do not know exactly where the ship came from. There were no people on board when it

LISA McMANN

wrecked. It was . . ." He seemed to struggle for the right word. "Abandoned," he said finally.

"No one on board?" breathed Crow. "You saw it happen?"

"*Hai.* I did."

"So they must have jumped like we did," Henry whispered. He turned back to Ishibashi. "What else do you know?"

"Very little," Ishibashi replied. "Ah, but I will tell you about the recent visitor who escaped," he went on, as if he were trying to change the subject.

"That's actually what I was going to ask about," Sky said. "You said he escaped?"

"She," Ishibashi said with a small smile. "A young woman. Like you."

Sky and Lani exchanged glances. "Was she alone?"

"Yes," Ishibashi said. "In a sailboat. She stayed only three days to repair it. A very nice girl. Quiet, intent on the task, and anxious to leave. I tried to tell her it wasn't safe, but she said she had to get back to—" He faltered.

"Back to where?" asked Fox, who lay at Ishibashi's side.

"Back to—" Ishibashi looked wildly around at the group, his smile gone. "I'm sorry," he whispered. "I have said too

LISA McMANN

much. I forget sometimes. . . ." He shook his head and feebly rose to his feet. "Old age. I must rest now."

Sky jumped to help him, but he smiled weakly and waved her off, then tottered to his room. When he had disappeared, Florence whispered loudly from the doorway, "What just happened?"

"He forgot where the girl wanted to go," Alex said.

"I don't think he forgot," Samheed said, eyes narrowed. "Not the way he was acting. I think he didn't want to talk about it."

Lani frowned. "There are only six places to go back to. How does anyone forget that?"

"He seemed rather elusive," Ms. Octavia agreed.

"Mewmewmew," said Kitten.

Fox nodded at her. "True," he said. "Ninety-six big ones. That's old enough to forget things."

"I don't know," Alex said. "Whatever. It doesn't matter. What matters is that the girl made it out of here. Just like we're going to do."

He wanted to believe it. But the girl was a single person in a sailboat. He had a whole zoo full of people and creatures and statues, plus a giant ship to move. The task seemed insur-mountable, yet he continued to mask his worry in front of the others. "Simber will be here any time now. And then we're out of this wretched place."

Sky shot him a look, and Alex hurriedly turned away, know-ing she didn't believe a word of it.

A Second Chance

Progress outside on the ship was slow and purposeful. Inside, things were moving along at a quicker pace. Soon there was a backlog of material assembled and ready to repair the ship, and every day fewer scavengers were needed and more hands were on deck to patch things.

But still there was no Simber.

Alex buried himself in tasks to keep his mind occupied. Finally finished rolling preserve spell components, Alex set them aside. He would instill them with magic when his mind was fresh and he could concentrate. Instead he turned to his next indoor task. The moss.

He stared at the huge fluffy pile that had been faithfully added to daily by the Artiméans, waiting for when Alex was ready to make the flying carpet components. Little did the castaways know the mage was losing sleep at night, silently begging Simber to hurry so he didn't have to figure out how to accomplish this impossible task. Going back to try to fix the tube again seemed like a less bleak option at this point.

He began to pull the moss apart and twist it into strands—perhaps braiding them would work, he thought. But try as he might, he couldn't get the fragile material to braid tightly enough, and inevitably he ended up with a carpet that wasn't strong enough to carry Fox, much less a human.

Still, he kept up the farce, declaring he was nearly there with the design. "Just a few tiny kinks to work out," he said whenever anyone asked about the progress. He even enlisted help from Ms. Octavia, but to no avail. Without a loom, she had nothing to offer.

After a few days with no progress, Alex knew he'd have to

LISA McMANN

confess the truth. He decided to go back to the drawing board one last time before breaking the news. But when he entered the nook where the moss awaited him, he saw something else sitting next to it.

A tiny, makeshift loom.

Alex looked all around, wondering who had created it, but everyone was busy with her own tasks. He wasted no time searching for the responsible party, and instead grabbed a handful of moss threads and got to work, fumbling as he tried to get used to the small size. Besides, he had an idea of who was responsible. And it wasn't Ms. Octavia.

Late into the evening he stayed bent over the machine, amazed at the careful, beautiful construction made mostly from pieces of absolute junk. Only a true visionary could have imagined the final project with the variety of items contained in it: two auger shells left over from making the captain's wheel, an old carpenter's ruler broken into pieces, gears that looked like they came from a clock, a few pieces of metal, some driftwood, a number of thin sticks that were carefully whittled and completely smooth, and a length of gold chain cut into sections.

After a dozen attempts and countless tiny adjustments to the loom and to the thickness of the moss threads, and a hundred restarts due to Alex's own clumsy hands, Alex finally had a component prototype that he thought would work. Excited, he quickly instilled magic into it, and with fingers crossed, he cast it upon the ground. The tiny woven bit of moss expanded into a thick carpet. Alex sat upon it and commanded, "To the greenhouse!"

The carpet lifted him off the ground and moved him out of the nook, flew a short distance, and then disappeared into thin air. Alex fell to the floor with a thud. "Oof," he said.

He heard a soft laugh from the nearby sleeping room, but he didn't care—the carpet had carried him! The prototype was a success. The magic needed a little tweaking to make the carpet fly longer, and Alex had to figure out how to weave faster so it didn't take him a million years to make enough for everyone, but those were easy tasks compared to creating the prototype. What a relief!

He got to his feet and went back to the room with the moss—there was no time to sleep when things were going well.

It was only a few minutes later when a shadow fell over the loom. Alex looked up. It was Sky, her hair tousled, sleep in her eyes.

"You did it," she said.

"Thanks to you," Alex said. "I don't know how you did this, but it works."

"I'm sorry it's so small."

"No—really. It's perfect. It's my fingers that are too big." He pointed to the gold chain links. "Sky . . . please tell me this isn't the bracelet from your mother."

Sky smiled, ignoring the question, and sat down next to him. "Here," she said, reaching for the loom. "Let me show you a few tricks that can help you go faster."

The nearness of her after so long was almost overwhelming. Alex didn't dare react for fear of Sky coming to her senses and leaving. Maybe she was sleepwalking. Or maybe she was just ready to forgive him. Alex tried to focus on what she was saying, but he could barely hear her over the pounding of his pulse.

"Now you try," she said, sliding the loom in front of him.

Alex frowned as he leaned over the loom. The wind howled

outside, but he'd grown so used to the near-constant storm that he didn't hear it. He stared, unseeing, forcing himself to think of something other than Sky as he worked the machine. And of course the only other thing consuming his thoughts of late was Simber.

His anxiety returned, and he fumbled with the threads. After a moment of struggle as he tried to fix his mistakes, Sky uttered a low "Hmm."

Alex looked up. "I'll start over."

Sky was giving him that knowing look. She could always tell when he was preoccupied. "Mage problems again?" she asked softly.

It was a tense subject between the two, or at least it felt that way to Alex. He cringed. "Sorry." He looked at the perfect little green carpet that she had constructed. "Can you show me one more time?"

He reached for some moss. Sky took half of it from him, worked it into threads, secured them on the loom, and demonstrated once more how to handle the loom so that Alex's fingers wouldn't get in the way. Then she took his hands and placed them into position, showing him how to do it himself.

LISA McMANN

At her soft touch, Alex winced. He wanted to slip his fingers between hers. Instead he swallowed hard and nodded, though his mind was lost once more.

He began fresh, but this time his moss fell apart. He picked it up and struggled again to weave. "I swear I did this all by myself once," Alex said.

Sky chuckled. "Yes, and it only took you what, seven hours? Just think—with my help, you might be able to cut it down to a couple."

Alex made a face, but knew she was right.

After a moment of watching him, Sky nudged him and leaned closer. "You're really not very good at this, Alex," she whispered, her orange eyes mischievous. "And I thought you were good at everything."

Alex winced. "Clearly I have a looming weakness."

Sky snorted, and Alex reluctantly grinned.

"I have a few other weaknesses too," he said. "You might have noticed."

Sky smiled. She rested her hand on Alex's knee for a brief moment. "I won't tell the enemy." She tilted her head and held his gaze.

Alex pressed his lips together, and then the words he'd held in for so long finally tumbled out. "I'm sorry, Sky," he said. "I really am. I'm sorry I didn't talk to you about what was happening . . . you know, with me and being the head mage and everything. That wasn't fair. I was wrong to treat you like that."

"Thank you. I accept your apology," Sky said.

"I miss . . ." His chest ached. "I miss the way we used to talk."

"Me too," Sky said. "I miss it a lot. Shall we start doing that again?"

Alex laughed and nodded. "Yes, I'd like that."

"Great," said Sky. She sat up straight and slapped the floor next to the loom. "Now pay attention and learn how to weave your dumb carpets faster. I don't have all night for you, you know." She grinned and shoved a pile of moss at Alex. "And stop worrying about Simber."

"How did you—"

"Please, Alex. I just know. And I get how your mind works. When it's stuck on something, it won't let go. I've seen you in action, remember?"

"Do I ever," Alex muttered.

"Simber's fine. He's probably taking care of whatever problem Ms. Morning was having. She hasn't sent any more seek spells, so I take that as a sign that all is clear. I'm sure Simber will turn up eventually. But even if he doesn't, you can handle this without him. And you know what? I think you need to."

"Need to?"

"You need to handle our escape without counting on Simber to save us, Alex. The endless waiting for Simber is just making everyone more anxious. We need a definitive plan."

Alex closed his eyes, a pained expression on his face. Eventually he sighed. "You're probably right."

"Of course I am."

As he sat there contemplating the problem in a new light, Sky squeezed his arm. "I'm going to bed. You should too. We can work on this tomorrow."

She slipped away, and Alex felt a great weight lifting off his heart.

Everything always felt so much better with Sky.

Henry Helps Out

At first, when Henry began following Ishibashi around, Crow tagged along, but he soon grew bored with the greenhouse, preferring to work on less delicate things like cutting wood and pounding nails. Henry, on the other hand, couldn't get enough of his time with the scientist. He longed to spend all of his time in the greenhouse with Ishibashi, learning about the healing nature of plants, and how to breed them to make new strains.

Before the Artiméans arrived, Ishibashi had been working on creating a new fruit and vegetable combination he called sweet applecorn, which grew in oblong pods on a stalk with a tuft of bright red leaves at the top. Ishibashi took a knife and sliced off one of the pods, then peeled back the edible husk, revealing a red-and-yellow-checkerboard vegi-fruit inside. He chopped it up and put it into a bowl, added a little bit of fresh diced onion, a few drops of avocado oil, and a squeeze of lime juice, and presented it to Henry, who declared it his new favorite food.

Having no paper to write on, Henry could only take notes mentally and hope that he remembered everything he learned. Before bed he repeated recipes and formulas to himself so they would stick in his brain better.

One morning after the hour of calm was over and the Artiméans had brought the day's scavenged leftovers into the shelter, Henry dried off and made his way as usual to the greenhouse to find Ishibashi. The old scientist was there like always, puttering around the plantings. On the floor was a large container that Henry had never seen before. He dropped to his haunches next to it and peered in. It was filled with water and a slimy-looking substance that glowed fluorescent blue. "Ishibashi-san," said Henry, "what is this?"

"Seaweed," said the old man, not looking up. He crouched on the ground, watering some plants very carefully. He counted out the drops of water under his breath. "Also known as breakfast, for some. But do not taste it."

Henry crinkled up his nose. "I won't. Do you guys eat this?"

"*Hai.*" Ishibashi moved to the next plant. "It grows only on the leeward side of the island, where your whale takes shelter in the cove. She is a beautiful creature. I spoke to her today as I was out collecting the seaweed."

Henry sniffed. It smelled briny, but not terrible. "Do you like this stuff?"

"Not really. Ito and Sato eat it as a scientific experiment. But it can be dangerous."

"What's the experiment?"

Ishibashi didn't answer for a moment, concentrating on his plants and silently counting drops. "Life," he said solemnly, looking up.

Henry felt a shiver go down his spine. He could tell by the way Ishibashi spoke that this was a precious secret not to be

LISA McMANN

233 « Island of Shipwrecks

shared. And as much as he wanted to know everything, he dared not ask more.

But he couldn't forget it.

Every day thereafter, while Alex and the others worked on spell components, Henry made his way to the greenhouse. Ishibashi taught him about each plant: how to identify it, what its special properties were, and how it could be used to heal cuts and bruises or to ease pain. Henry recognized a few of the plants that were also native to Artimé.

He pointed them out. "I've seen these before."

"They came from Marcus Today," Ishibashi said. "He brought them in the tube." The scientist turned to Henry. "I see Alex-san has given up on fixing it?"

"Yes," Henry said. "He tried, but it's no use."

Ishibashi nodded. "That was my fear. I'm sorry. This island isn't kind to anything or anyone."

He handed Henry some cuttings of foreign plants. "These are for you to experiment with. See what magic you can do to make them even stronger. If you are working hard it will help to keep Mage Alex-san from giving you angry looks," he said with a toothless grin.

Henry laughed. "Alex doesn't care that I'm here. He knows I'm learning things. I'm pretty much the best healer we have in Artimé," he said with a bit of a swagger. "And now, thanks to you, I'll be even stronger." His face clouded. "If we ever get back there, anyway."

The Glowing Seaweed

Every now and then, Henry found himself looking at the seaweed, wondering what made it shine so bright. Wondering what Ishibashi meant when he said it was an experiment on life.

Henry thought he knew, though. Ishibashi was ninety-six years old, yet he was as spry as somebody a third of that age. And Ito was one hundred and ten! Henry didn't know anyone who had ever lived to be that old. Not even in the Ancients Sector. There was no reason in Quill to keep people living that long—they weren't useful. Yet . . . He looked at the three old scientists hard at work in different parts of the greenhouse, creating new strains of plants and doing experiments with the material they had. They were extremely useful people, and they actually seemed like they enjoyed living here on this horrible stormy island. Just like the Unwanteds, they'd found the creative things they did best, and they'd gone to work doing them.

"Once we get our ship working again, do you and Ito-san and Sato-san want to come with us?" Henry asked. "Artimé is so beautiful and sunny, and it's filled with magic and a mansion and a jungle and tons of plants. And it hardly ever storms." He hesitated, then added, "It wouldn't be any trouble. Everyone is welcome in Artimé."

Ishibashi paused in his work, his face troubling over, but he didn't lift his gaze. After a moment he asked, his tone careful and measured, "Artimé is one of the islands, isn't it?"

Henry laughed. "Of course. What else would it be? That big block of land that doesn't exist?"

Ishibashi chuckled uneasily. "Big block of land? What do you mean?"

"I'll show you," Henry said, hopping off his stool. "Be right back."

LISA McMANN

Ishibashi looked over his shoulder, watching the boy go. He resumed working, but his face didn't lose the troubled expression.

Henry found Lani in the entry room of the shelter, spreading out a large pile of wet moss on the floor so it would dry more quickly.

"I need your map," he said to his sister. "Just for a minute."

Lani scowled. "Why?" She was tired of the storms, and nearly everything set her on edge.

"I just want to show it to Ishibashi-san. Come on." He jiggled a bit, trying not to reveal his impatience. "Please."

Lani rolled her eyes. She reached into her pocket and pulled out the map she'd nearly destroyed. "Here," she said, handing it to him. "Be careful. It's starting to fall apart."

"Thanks," Henry said. He took it and dashed back to the greenhouse to Ishibashi's side.

Ishibashi narrowed his eyes as Henry carefully unfolded the paper, revealing the burned corners.

"It's a map. See? Artimé and Quill make up this one," Henry said, pointing to the center island. "And this one over here," he said, pointing to the easternmost island, farthest from the fake mass of land, "is your island."

"I see." Ishibashi studied the map for a very long time. "And what about this land?" Ishibashi asked, pointing to the large piece. "Have you ever been here?"

"It doesn't exist," Henry said. "We tried to get there, but the sea swallowed us and spun us around the bottom of the world, and we ended up here."

Ishibashi stared at Henry. "What a horrible journey that must have been," he said softly, and reached for the map. "May I have a closer look?"

Henry nodded and held out the map. Ishibashi took it and held it close to his face. It shook in the old scientist's hands. "Where did you get this, Henry-san?" he asked gently—so gently that it made Henry look up in surprise. There was pain in the old man's eyes.

"My sister—she found it in a book that washed ashore on Artimé after an air vessel fell out of the sky," Henry said, puzzled. "Why are you sad? Don't you want to come to Artimé with us? It's a very happy place."

Ishibashi sighed. Then he smiled ruefully, collecting his feelings and hiding them once more, and patted Henry on the shoulder. "Did all of your family grow up on your island? Your parents, too?"

"Yes," said Henry.

"Your people—is it the same for them? All born on your island?"

"Except for Crow and Sky and Copper. They came from Warbler, this one here," he said, pointing to the island on the map. He looked up, puzzled. "Which island did you come from, Ishibashi-san?"

The old man closed his eyes for a long moment. When he opened them, he said, "It has been so long that I do not remember."

Henry thought that was ridiculous—how could anyone not remember which island he came from? But he knew it would be rude to say so. Instead he said, "I think you would like Artimé."

Ishibashi handed the map back to Henry. "Life is very complicated," he said with a little laugh. "Filled with dreams and adventures, and disasters and broken hearts, too."

Henry tilted his head, puzzled. "I don't get it."

The old scientist turned back to his work. "I am most grateful for your kind offer, Henry-san," he said, "and so are Sato and Ito. But our home is here. Our work is here," he said. "And our precious machines, our equipment, everything we dedicated our lives to is right out there, half-buried in the sea. We could never leave it behind."

He hesitated, glancing at the map, and then looked away and dug his hands into the dirt around a plant. "This is our life, now. There is no one left to search for . . ." He trailed off and hunched over, focusing intently on the task before him.

Henry nodded sadly. "I understand," he said, even though he didn't. He got the feeling that Ishibashi didn't want to talk about it anymore.

After a minute, standing there in a somewhat awkward silence, Henry folded up the map and said, "I'm glad you got your toolbox back, at least." He pointed at the crate, which Florence had delivered to the shelter the day after they arrived. "That's good, right?"

But before the scientist could respond, they heard a

LISA McMANN

commotion in the shelter. Henry ran to the doorway and peered out to see what was happening.

Fox and Kitten came racing toward the greenhouse, Fox calling Henry's name. "Henry! Henry! Kitten has found a very dear important friend who is hurt! Do you have any medicine?"

Henry rushed toward them. "What? A friend? Hurt? What?" Ishibashi followed.

"Mewmewmew!" cried Kitten.

Fox's back end shook with excitement. "She says her very very good friend Sea Turtle has been struck savagely by a flying piece of driftwood—not me, of course—and now the sea turtle is dying!"

"Where?"

"Near the entrance to the shelter!"

Henry and Ishibashi ran through the stony rooms, past the group working on spells, dodging Samheed, who was testing out a very-slow-moving magic flying carpet, and out the doorway into the storm. Without hesitation, Ishibashi hoisted the sea turtle in his arms and staggered back inside.

"Back to the greenhouse," Ishibashi said. "Let's hurry."

Henry helped him carry the turtle to the greenhouse,

where they set it carefully on the floor on its back. Fox and Kitten crowded around. Ishibashi crouched next to the turtle and carefully checked it over. It seemed to be unconscious . . . or quite possibly dead.

"Henry-san," Ishibashi said quietly, "fetch me a bit of the seaweed. Just a pinch."

Henry jumped to his feet and rushed over to the tub where the glowing blue seaweed floated. He reached in carefully and pulled off a tiny bit, and raced back to Ishibashi.

"Slip the seaweed into the side of its mouth and massage it in the cheek," Ishibashi instructed, holding the turtle's head. "Careful of the beak."

Henry did as he was told.

Fox, Kitten, Henry, and Ishibashi all leaned forward, watching intently.

Nothing happened. The turtle lay still and lifeless as before. Then, with a small wheezing sound, its mouth opened, and then its eyes. Soon its flippers began to wave in the air.

Ishibashi rolled the turtle over, flippers down this time. It stood, then walked around slowly, unbothered by Fox and Kitten who raced around it, talking and mewing at top speed.

LISA McMANN

Henry couldn't believe it. The sea turtle was healed. "Wow," he breathed. He looked at Ishibashi, thinking of all the people and creatures he could heal with one little clump of that seaweed.

"*Hai*," whispered Ishibashi. "We have a little magic of our own. The problem is that we do not know the long-term effects of even a small amount. Will the sea turtle now be invincible from death? Will he live forever? Or could he die tomorrow of some other ailment or injury? We don't know."

Henry looked at the man, wide-eyed. "Is that why you are so old, Ishibashi-san?"

The man smiled, amused. "Yes, Henry-san. That is the reason." He watched the turtle walk out of the room, Fox and Kitten on its heels, and continued. "Once we discovered the seaweed's power, we three scientists began experimenting. Ito-san, the oldest, eats a small bit every day. Sato-san only takes a bite when injured or ill. And I ate one bite thirty-three years ago, and nothing since." He gave Henry a solemn look. "Clearly we are all doing well for our ages as a result. But now we worry—what if we will never die?"

Henry thought about that. "Would that be a bad thing?"

Ishibashi nodded. "For me, yes. I would not want to go on and on forever. Would you? Think about it."

With that, the old man went back to his work, leaving Henry to ponder.

After a while, Henry found Ishibashi again. "So, um, where did you say I could find some of that seaweed? The cove on the other side of the island? Is it all right if I . . . I mean, since I'm the main healer person in Artimé and all . . . ?"

Ishibashi smiled. "Have you thought about whether you would want to live forever?"

"I have," Henry said.

"And what conclusion did you come to?"

Henry looked at the man and spoke truthfully. "I don't know. I would have to think about it a lot more."

Ishibashi nodded. "As would everyone, yes?"

Henry nodded solemnly.

Ishibashi clasped his hands in front of him, seemingly satisfied with Henry's answer. "I would never forbid you to have it, Henry-san. I will give you some myself. But you have to understand—this seaweed is both wonderful and very, very

LISA McMANN

dangerous. Its power is great, and it must not fall into the wrong hands. In fact, you must tell no one about it."

Henry's eyes widened. He nodded.

"Most of all," Ishibashi continued in a voice so low Henry could scarcely hear him, "despite what I have told you about our experiments, you must never, ever use it on humans without their full understanding and consent."

Aaron Strikes Oil

Sir," Liam began from the doorway of Aaron's office, "there's a bit of a problem. The barbed-wire ceiling over Quill has been coming down with the wall, and it's resting on the tops of the houses. No one knows what to do with it."

Aaron frowned at the contraption in front of him. "Where's Gondoleery? Make her take care of it."

"I don't know, High Priest. I haven't seen her in weeks. I'm a little concerned that she's—"

A spring exploded from the middle of the contraption, hit the ceiling, and dropped to the floor halfway across the room.

LISA McMANN

Aaron sighed. "Go away, Liam," he grumbled, not looking up.

Liam opened his mouth to say more, but it was no use. "I'll be in my room," he muttered as he left.

As it turned out, building an oil press was much more complicated than Aaron ever expected it to be. After weeks of focusing all his energy on finding the proper pieces he needed, and then pounding them into shape or cutting them to size or curling them into delicate metal links by hand and attaching them together to make a chain, he barely even noticed the enormous wall crumbling outside his window. And he gave little thought to the new, unprotected view of the sea. For today, finally, Aaron was ready to attach the last piece of the contraption to see if the thing actually worked.

He picked up the crank and held it to the light so that the sun shone through the square hole he'd fashioned on one end. It was almost perfect . . . but not quite. He strapped it to his desk and gave it one final pound with a mallet to straighten it. Then he picked it up once more, gave it a hard look, and slipped the end with the square hole over the rod that poked out of one side of the machine. He wiggled the crank onto the squared portion of the rod until it grabbed hold.

Carefully Aaron turned the crank, scrutinizing the machine's many intricate parts, checking each piece of it to make sure it all moved together just as he'd pictured it. And it did. The synchronicity of it was the most beautiful thing he'd ever seen—in Quill, anyway. His mind briefly wandered to Artimé, where beauty was everywhere. Something like this might be commonplace there, but here in Quill, it was quite spectacular, and most importantly, Aaron had created it himself.

He frowned. He didn't like the word "created." It seemed too much like an Unwanted word. He'd *built* it himself. That was more like it. It sounded a bit more Quillitary-ish. He pushed aside the nagging thought that the two words were very similar, and returned his attention to the workings of the machine.

When he was satisfied that the gears and cranks and chains and presses were all working properly, he went to one of the sacks on the floor and pulled out a large handful of cashews, which had been stripped of their poisonous fruit by

LISA McMANN

249 « Island of Shipwrecks

a few Necessaries in the Ancients Sector who were scheduled to die soon anyway.

Aaron carried the nuts to one end of the contraption and loaded them into the hopper—a metal box with a small hole at the bottom. The nuts dropped through the hole, went down a chute, and landed neatly on a conveyor belt. Aaron turned the crank, which made the conveyor belt move so that the nuts coming out of the chute landed a few inches apart from each other. From the belt, the nuts dropped into a circular container with a mesh bottom and a thick metal lid. The lid dropped on top of a few nuts and pressed down. Aaron turned the crank harder, intently watching the circular container as the nuts were smashed to a pulp. After a long minute, a small, cloudy drop of liquid fell onto the desk below.

Aaron stared at the drop. He let go of the crank and rushed over to the other side of the desk to look at it more closely. He reached his finger out to wipe it up, and gently rubbed it between his finger and thumb. It was silky smooth.

"It works!" he cried. "It works! Liam, come and see!"

Aaron heard feet pounding on the stairs and sliding in the hallway, and soon a wild-haired Liam, who looked like he'd been grabbing a quick nap, poked his head in the doorway of Aaron's office.

"Come in, come in," Aaron said impatiently. "You have to see this."

Liam came closer.

Aaron pulled the cashew pulp out of the circular mesh container and popped it into his mouth. "Hmm," he said, chewing. The nuts tasted like dirt, but they were still edible. Another bonus! He'd feed the remains of his project to the Necessaries, and there would be no waste.

"Now watch," he said. He turned the crank. The next nut dropped out of the hopper, went down the chute, and landed on the conveyor belt. And then the next one did the same. They moved along until one by one they were deposited into the mesh container. Aaron kept cranking. The thick metal lid dropped down on top of the nuts and pressed down hard.

"Watch over there!" Aaron cried, pointing.

Liam watched.

This time a larger cloudy drop of oil splattered onto the desk below.

"Touch it," Aaron commanded.

Liam obeyed. His hand darted out and he swiped at the drop of oil. He held it to his nose and inhaled. "It's great!" he exclaimed, not sure what he was actually supposed to be feeling.

"Yes, I know! It's perfect!"

Liam nearly began to laugh, somehow overjoyed by Aaron's enthusiasm. He'd never seen the high priest so . . . so passionate about something before. "Absolutely perfect," Liam said, beaming. "You did it!"

Aaron grinned back. It felt so good. He'd done it! He'd seen a picture in his head, and he'd built each and every part of it himself, and now here it was, running smoothly and perfectly right before his eyes. After weeks of hard work, he finally had something to show for it. His insides were alive. Success! It felt . . . it felt . . .

The smile faded from Aaron's face. It *felt*.

Liam noticed, of course. "What's wrong?"

Aaron stared at Liam, wild-eyed, quickly controlling his expression like he'd always done—or always tried to do, at least in the presence of others. "Nothing," he said. He dropped his eyes, pretending to be checking something.

Liam bit his lip, uncertain as to what was happening, but he thought he knew. He felt a strange wave of fatherly warmth come over him for the troubled young man, and even though he knew he could be punished for it, he said softly, "You built a terrific machine, Aaron. It's okay to be proud of it."

In the past, Aaron might have sent such an insolent person to the Ancients Sector. But something uncontrollable inside him longed for Liam to be right.

The high priest swallowed hard and didn't look up. When he spoke, his voice was thick. "Help me move this contraption to Justine's old meeting room. Then round up a team of guards to run the crank round the clock. The sooner we can press a few barrels of oil, the sooner we can team up with the Quillitary. And finally we'll be able to take over Artimé."

LISA McMANN

Slowly but Surely

During the hurricane hours, Alex abandoned the loom since Sky was so much faster at making the flying carpet components, and instead he went back to the preserve spell components, which would seal the new material to the existing ship and keep the vessel from taking on water. It would also help prevent the ship from breaking up again. Alex wished more than once that he'd thought to use the preserve spell on the ship before sailing it. Most often he thought it late at night, when his shoulders and head ached from concentrating so hard on instilling the rubber cement balls with magic. It was a painstaking job.

LISA McMANN

Little by little during the short time each day that the Artiméans could work outside, the ship became whole again. It was quite an odd sight, like a patchwork quilt, with pieces of a dozen different ships holding the original ship together. Each shipwreck they borrowed from had its own unique style, color, and materials. And while most of the wrecks had few treasures left inside, the Artiméans occasionally scored something useful. From the ship that had carried the military vehicles, Crow found a case of frying pans and dozens of mess kits and utensils. From a different wreck, Sky and Ms. Octavia recovered a crate full of fabric and sewing supplies. And when Florence had a free moment to spare, she went after the giant instrument that Alex had spotted just outside the scientists' shipwreck. She wrestled it to shore and dragged it back to the shelter for Ishibashi, Ito, and Sato, whose eyes shone with gratitude.

Soon Florence and Copper had all the repair pieces attached to the ship, including a beautiful glass porthole they used to fill the hole that came from their trip around the world, giving them a window to the sea. When everything was secured, Florence, Ms. Octavia, and Alex began the slow but satisfying job of preserving the ship, going over it inch by inch to be sure there would be no leaks.

Samheed and Lani helped make moss threads so Sky could weave them into magic carpet components. She made dozens of them, for no one was exactly sure how far the carpets would be able to fly—or if the storm would hinder them at all. Sam and Lani began instilling the magic into each one.

As their tasks wound down on the Island of Shipwrecks, everyone became increasingly restless. Alex knew Sky had been right. They couldn't wait for Simber forever. He felt Artimé tugging at him. And here was his chance to prove that he didn't need Simber around to lead his people safely home.

When the Artiméans had gathered that evening, Alex stood up. "Everyone," he said, "the ship is ready, and our time for departure has come. Our beloved Artimé needs us, and we need her. We simply can't wait for Simber any longer." He glanced at Sky, who gave him an encouraging nod. "We have to go for it without him."

The Artiméans looked at one another, murmuring, their faces alive and animated with the news. It would be a huge challenge to battle the hurricane without Simber. But they were all anxious to go home.

Alex watched their reaction, the clutch of fear loosening in his chest as he saw their nodding heads and heard their excited whispers. He took a deep breath. "So we're in agreement, then? Who's with me?"

"I'm with you, Alex," Florence called from the doorway. Lani, Sky, and Samheed stood up. "We're with you," they said. And in seconds, the entire crew of the pirate ship was on their feet, shouting, "We're with you, Alex!" From their midst, a cheer rose up. The Artiméans were going home.

On what looked to be the Artiméans last day on the Island of Shipwrecks, Ishibashi, Ito, and Sato took Henry aside. With great reverence, they presented Henry with a box of seeds.

Henry looked inside it, and his face lit up.

"You, greenhouse!" Sato said proudly.

"Oh, thank you, Sato-san!" said Henry. "I will build my own magical greenhouse, I promise."

Ishibashi handed him a small container of the glowing

seaweed. "Remember, the bad can be greater than the good," he reminded Henry. "But the good is worth having. Choose wisely and be thoughtful, Henry-san. Most of all, remember what I said. Understanding and consent."

Henry nodded solemnly. "I will remember. I promise. Thank you for everything, Ishibashi-san." He slipped the container of seaweed into the inner pocket of his component vest and placed the seeds in the outer pocket, leaving room to replenish the remaining ones with all the new components the others had made during their time here. He looked up at the old man. "I will never forget you as long as I live." He reached out and hugged the little man.

"The same is true for me," Ishibashi said, patting Henry on the back. There was a hint of sadness in his voice.

That night, Alex gathered everyone together around the fire, and as the wind howled, he explained the plan for the next morning.

"As soon as the storm dies down," he said, "Lani, would you please run to the lagoon and tell Spike to make a break for the open sea? I want her to swim without stopping all the way around to the south side of the island—the side the ship is on—and continue straight out from there to beyond the storm's circumference. Tell her not to stop fighting the current until there's sunshine overhead and she can swim freely. We will meet her there."

"Got it," Lani said.

"Good. Once you've spoken to Spike, meet us on the ship side of the island. Squirrelicorns, once I use the transport spell, I want you to fly up high and watch for the ship to appear. As soon as you spot it, come back down and point us in the right direction. Then three of you take Captain Ahab, and the other three take Copper to the ship."

"Three, sir?" asked a squirrelicorn. "We can do it with two."

"I don't want to risk it. It's going to be a long flight for you as it is, and with the winds, I want to make sure you have more than enough power to fight through it and get Ahab and Copper there safely."

"Sir, yes, sir!" said the squirrelicorns in unison.

Alex sought out Copper. "Are you comfortable with that?"

"I prefer it to a flying carpet," Copper said with a smile. "The squirrelicorns have served me well. Thank you, Alex."

"Captain?"

"Aye," said the captain, sounding a bit saner than he ever had before. "Anything to feel the sea beneath my leg again."

"Great," Alex said. "So that leaves the rest of us to get to the ship using the magic carpets."

Sky and Crow looked at each other nervously.

"Sam and Lani and I have been testing them," Alex said. He turned to Samheed. "Will you demonstrate, please?"

Samheed got up and took out a small square of green from his component vest. He threw it to the floor of the shelter, where it grew into a large square, and sat on it. "Across the room," he commanded.

The carpet lifted Samheed several feet off the ground and slowly transported him, then dumped him off rather unceremoniously at the other end of the room. "Oof," he said. He got up and dusted off his pants. "We're still fine-tuning it," he said, "and we don't have a permanent version figured out yet, but it does the job we need it to do for now, which is getting us to the ship."

"Our longest flight lasted about ten minutes before the carpet collapsed and disappeared," Lani said. "Just make sure you tell it where you want it to go as soon as you are settled on it. You're going to need every minute of spell time."

Florence cleared her throat from the doorway. "Alex," she said, looking down at her large body, "I'm not sure . . . I mean, how exactly . . . ?"

Alex nodded. "I know. It's a risk because we don't know how many carpets it will take to lift you, and we don't have enough components to do a test run. We'll have to figure it out on the spot in the morning."

"But what if it doesn't work?" Ms. Octavia asked, alarmed. "We can't leave without Florence."

"We won't," Alex said. "There has to be another way. Florence, you'd be able to walk out to a point beyond the storm, right?"

"Sure," Florence replied, "but I don't think Spike can lift me all the way to the surface. Don't worry, though, Octavia—it's not ideal, but I can walk all the way to Artimé if I have to. It just might take a month."

"All right," Ms. Octavia said, "but don't forget about that eel, and no one knows what other creatures live underwater. If something happens to you, how will we find out? I don't like that plan at all."

LISA McMANN

"We'll get her to the ship," Alex promised. But Ms. Octavia's reminder made him nervous.

Sky couldn't hide her concern. "Alex, I don't think Crow and I can command a magic carpet. We're not good with that stuff. Not good enough, anyway, to try and control something like this, with all the rain and wind and . . . well, I'm worried about it. I don't think it's safe for us."

Alex smiled. "I'm sorry you're worried—I was getting to that. Samheed and I tested a carpet with both of us sitting on it, and it carried us fine. It just goes a little slower. So you and Crow can each ride along with someone else if you feel more comfortable."

Sky let out a nervous breath. "Yes, please."

"You can ride with me if you want," Alex said. His eyes held hers, and he willed her not to look away.

Everyone around them had witnessed the tension between them throughout the entire journey, whether they wanted to or not, and now they sat silent, watching.

Sky pressed her lips together and swallowed hard. "All right. That sounds fine," she said.

"Good," said Alex softly. He smiled again and straightened

up, addressing the group once more. "And, Crow, you can go with Samheed or Lani."

Crow eyed them both. "Lani, please," he said.

Samheed pretended to be offended. "What, you don't trust me?"

"Not as much as I trust her," he said, pointing to Lani.

"Good choice," Lani said, poking Samheed with her elbow.

"I guess Fox and Kitten are stuck with me," Samheed said.

Fox gave Samheed a wary look, but Kitten seemed pleased.

Alex wrapped up the meeting with a few more details about the next day's plan, then dismissed everyone to tidy up the shelter and prepare for the hasty departure in the morning.

Late that night, when Alex had finished inspecting the shelter to make sure they were leaving Ishibashi's home in perfect shape, he found Sky hunched over the loom.

He leaned over next to her. "What are you doing?" he whispered.

She looked up, weary. "Oh, hi. I thought I'd try and make a few more magic carpet components in case we need them for Florence. Can you instill them with magic or are you too tired?"

LISA McMANN

Alex flopped down next to her, exhausted. "I'm not too tired."

He picked up a component and held it, closed his eyes, and pictured the job the carpet was supposed to do. *Fly*, he thought, over and over. *Fly, fly, fly.*

Once the magic took hold, Alex placed the component inside his vest pocket and picked up another one. *Fly, fly, fly.*

He did this for each of the components. Finally there was only one left.

Fly, fly, fly, he thought. *To the sky. Sky. Sky.*

Sky.

When he opened his eyes and placed the last instilled component inside his pocket, he saw that Sky was watching him, a curious look on her face.

"What's up?" he asked.

"What do you think about when you close your eyes?" she asked.

Alex looked at her, her silky orange eyes catching light from the fire, her hair falling against her cheek, her lips soft and full.

"You really want to know?"

She nodded. "Yeah."

"I think about you," he said.

Aaron Ventures Out

Aaron watched over the oil press workers more intensely than he'd watched over anything in his entire life.

"Crank it harder," he instructed, hovering over the guards. "For the best results, you have to twist your wrist just so as you do it."

The guards complied with all of the high priest's whims, even when they changed from hour to hour, or minute to minute. It was clear the high priest was quite possessive of his masterpiece—so possessive that he hardly ever left the conference room where the machine now sat. He even slept

LISA McMANN

in snatches in the corner, surrounded by empty barrels.

Sometimes Aaron took a turn at the crank when he was feeling angsty, just to remind the workers that he was the best at it. And sometimes he'd kick them out completely and take an entire shift, which is exactly what happened each time the oil neared the fill line inside a barrel. There was something so rewarding about pressing the last possible drop of oil into a barrel and sealing the top.

One barrel of oil probably would be enough to impress General Blair, Aaron knew. But two—two would blow him away. Unlike the watered-down chicken fat that the Quillitary had been using for years, this viscous oil would last a very long time. The desert heat wouldn't make it evaporate, and the vehicles wouldn't need much of it at all to get their engines working smoothly. Still, Aaron wanted to impress the general so much that he'd have no hesitation in giving Aaron a key role in their plan of attack on Artimé.

Finally the moment came when the second barrel could hold not one more drop. Aaron carefully placed the lid on top and sealed it. He commanded his guards to load the barrels of oil into the back of a Quillitary vehicle.

As they did so, Aaron watched like a hawk over their every move out the door and to the vehicle. Just as they were finished, Liam strode up the driveway from Quill and joined the high priest.

The governor looked at Aaron. "All finished with the oil, then?"

"For now, at least," Aaron said. He squinted in the sunlight, which seemed all the brighter without Quill's wall, and looked around. It had been weeks since he'd gone outside. The enormous wall was completely toppled as far as he could see in both directions, and the rubble had been pushed down the hill and smoothed out all the way to the edge of the sea. It looked rugged, and actually rather nice. And while Aaron had hardly noticed the outside work because of his other preoccupation, he now felt terribly exposed.

"The breeze is pleasant," Liam said. "It's much cooler now, don't you think?"

Aaron's heart palpitated. "I suppose," he said.

"Have you been down by the water yet?"

"No."

Liam glanced nervously at Aaron. "It's nice. The water is warm.

It's all right for bathing, but it tastes terrible. Word is that you can actually eat the, ah, the animals that live in the sea—do you know anything about that? Gondoleery was telling people about the sea animals when she was hanging around by the amphitheater the other day. She and Governor Strang took groups to the water to show them how to catch the, ah, the food."

"Fish," Aaron muttered. "They're called fish."

"Ah, yes, right—fish. I wasn't familiar. With the name for them, I mean." Liam clasped his hands in front of him. "So anyway, people seem to like the water once they get over the fright of seeing it everywhere."

"Hmm," Aaron said. He wondered if he'd ever get over the fright of it.

"It's making you look good."

"The fish?"

"No, the wall coming down."

"Is it?" Aaron looked at Liam.

"Yes, indeed," Liam said. "Quite good."

"And are Gondoleery and Strang also doing what they're supposed to be doing, helping the Wanteds get angry about Artimé's attack on Secretary?"

Liam opened his mouth, and then closed it. "That . . . ? I don't know. I hadn't seen Gondoleery for weeks as I mentioned to you some time ago, and then out of nowhere she appeared in the commons, looking quite, ah, quite normal for once, actually."

Aaron didn't much care to discuss Gondoleery's appearance. She was disturbing from the inside, and that was all that mattered. It was less stressful not to think about her at all. He stared at the sparkling sea and sucked in a breath, then blew it out slowly and glanced at the jalopy, loaded with the oil barrels, the driver waiting patiently in the front seat. "I suppose I should go down to the water at least once," he said.

"If I may be so bold, I'd say I advise it, based on the positive reaction Gondoleery is getting from the Wanteds. They seem quite supportive of her and her recent interactions with the people. If you understand my meaning." Liam had tried several times to make Aaron aware of Gondoleery's sneaky ways, but he couldn't force the high priest to listen, and he didn't have any real proof that Gondoleery was a threat—only what Eva had suggested and what little bit Liam had seen of her strange practices.

But Aaron seemed eternally thick-headed when it came to

LISA McMANN

Gondoleery. And if it became clear that Liam was mistaken about her, Aaron might turn against him. He had to be very careful about what he said.

"Come along, then," Aaron said. He glanced this way and that to make sure there weren't throngs of Quillens about, watching him, and then he strode across the driveway to the rocks and rubble. He walked carefully from piece to piece, all the way down to where the sea lapped at them. Liam followed close behind.

"It has a different sound to it," Aaron said after a while. "Doesn't it?"

"Oh, yes," Liam said, though he didn't have a clue what Aaron meant.

"Not disturbing," Aaron said.

"No, not at all. Peaceful, even."

Aaron liked that. "Peaceful." He strained his eyes westward, looking at the vastness of it all—the sea, the sky. He'd seen it before, of course, but never at a time when he wasn't filled with panic, so it looked somehow less frightening now. "Not much out there." He dipped his hand into the water and let the liquid drip out between his fingers.

"No," Liam said. "And if there *was* something, we'd see it from quite far away, I should think. We'd have plenty of time to prepare for whatever it was."

Aaron nodded and dried his hand on his pants, keeping his eyes trained on the horizon. Every now and then he thought he saw a bump or two far away, but then the bumps would waver and almost disappear, though one seemed to be quite consistent. He stared at it until his eyes watered. Closing them for a moment, Aaron imagined himself sitting and relaxing on the rocks by the water. It seemed like it could be very pleasant here, as long as Quill wasn't about to be attacked from all sides.

Soon the moment of peace passed, and he grew anxious again.

"All right, well, that's enough of that." He turned and started hiking up the rocky bank toward the palace. As he climbed, his mind replayed the conversation. Something was stuck in his craw and he couldn't seem to get beyond it.

When they reached the driveway once more, Aaron turned to Liam. "What do you suppose Gondoleery is up to?"

Liam's heart skipped a beat. "I don't know, sir, but I'm not certain that I trust her to be fully, ah, supportive of you. I might be wrong, though."

LISA McMANN

Aaron scowled, remembering the bolt of fire she'd hit Meghan with. "I don't trust her either. She's sneaky and dangerous. Don't be afraid to speak up if you notice anything amiss, all right, Governor? But I'm betting on us. Once we get a plan in place with General Blair, we'll have the full support of the Quillitary, and we'll no longer have a need for her. I'm thinking it'll soon be time to send Governor Rattrapp back to the Ancients Sector. Her usefulness to me has quite run out."

Liam nodded. "That might solve some problems," he said lightly. The biggest problem of all was more like it. It wouldn't fix everything, but . . .

As always, Liam kept his thoughts to himself. It was an interesting tightrope to walk, he mused, and his respect for the dearly departed Eva Fathom continued to grow. He was actually a little afraid of being able to fill her shoes. He just couldn't mess this up. Not for Artimé, not for Claire, and certainly not for Meghan, who was the only one who seemed to believe in him. At least for now.

The pressure was blinding.

Aaron Scores

The trip to the Quillitary was slow and labored due to the extra weight of the barrels, and for a time Aaron feared they wouldn't make it. He was tempted to pour a bit of the oil into their jalopy's engine to ensure their arrival, but after having topped off the barrels so perfectly, Aaron didn't want to dip into the precious liquid until the general had seen it.

As they puttered along, Aaron took in the new, somewhat shocking view of the sea the entire way. The Quillitary and Necessaries had done a decent job smoothing out the rubble, spreading it from the side of the road, down the slope, and to

LISA McMANN

the shore. Aaron had to admit the work was quite impressive. It was strange how quickly he was growing accustomed to seeing the water all around.

When they finally arrived inside the Quillitary grounds, Aaron, Liam, and the driver wrestled the barrels of oil from the vehicle. Aaron sent the driver away to wait for them while one of the Quillitary soldiers went to get General Blair.

As they waited, Aaron looked around. The Quillitary grounds remained enclosed with walls on all sides—only the gate provided access, as before. Aaron scratched his head, wondering about it, but soon General Blair came striding toward them. Aaron put the thought aside and stood tall, extending his hand in greeting.

The general eyed the barrels. "What's this?" he asked.

"It's the oil I promised you for your vehicles," Aaron said. "Would you like to have a look?"

"Humph," the general said.

Aaron took that to mean yes, so he unfastened the lid of one of the barrels and lifted it, letting the excess oil drip back in.

General Blair dipped his finger into the liquid and withdrew it. He rubbed the oil between his thumb and finger and studied the residue. He put his thumb to his nose and sniffed, then held his hand out in front of him, regarding the oil once more.

"Does it work?" he asked.

Aaron blinked. He hadn't actually done a test. Liam shifted uncomfortably next to him, and Aaron blurted out, "Of course it works."

"Let's see, then." The general looked around the yard and chose one of the vehicles that seemed to be in good shape.

Aaron, who had forgotten to bring along a smaller can in which to transport the oil, looked around the yard for something he could use. He found a rusty pail, shook out the dust, and dipped it into the barrel, careful not to make it overflow.

Cupping his hand under the pail to catch every precious drop, Aaron walked over to the vehicle. The general lifted the hood and propped it open, and then he stood back and folded his arms across his chest.

Aaron looked over all the different parts of the engine, trying to figure out what each was for, and trying to locate the right spot for the oil without giving away his ignorance. After careful examination, Aaron determined that there were only three possible parts into which he could pour liquid. He

LISA McMANN

eliminated one of them immediately, and then blindly chose from the other two, unscrewed the cap, and peered inside. He couldn't see anything, but it smelled faintly like chicken grease.

Feeling quite sure he'd found the right spot, he first crawled under the vehicle, looked around for a way to remove the existing grease, unscrewed a cap below the tank, and drained the liquid that was in there. When the container was empty, he closed the drain, slid out, and poured his cashew oil into it. He screwed the cap on and dropped the hood with a startling clang, then went to the driver's seat to see if he could get the vehicle to start. He'd never done that before, either, but he'd watched how it was done on several occasions and he felt pretty comfortable giving it a try. He glanced at Liam, who was doing a terrible job of hiding his anxiety, and turned the key that sat in the ignition.

The vehicle choked and sputtered.

Aaron quickly turned it off. He pumped a pedal on the floor as he'd seen his drivers do on occasion, and then he turned the ignition once more.

The vehicle screeched, protested, and died on its own.

Aaron didn't know what to do. Sweat dripped from his

temples and down his cheeks. He leaned back in the seat, craning his neck to look at the pedals on the floor, and tried pumping a different one. Then he took a deep breath and turned the ignition once more.

This time the vehicle sputtered and roared with life.

Aaron bit his lip to hide his glee and held his breath, wishing for his luck to hold as the roar settled to a smooth purr. After a minute, Aaron looked up and saw that a few of the Quillitary soldiers had gathered around to see what was happening. He could hear their comments about the bright sound and the smooth chug of the engine, which confirmed what he already knew to be true—that Quillitary vehicles had never sounded so steady before.

Leaving it running, Aaron stepped out so that the general could take it for a test drive, and he watched as the man rode around the yard in a circle. A moment later the general got out and instructed one of his soldiers to take it for a ride up to the palace and back at top speed to see how fast it would go now.

As the vehicle sped out of the grounds and onto the main road, Aaron, Liam, and the general jogged after it for a few yards, watching it leave a huge cloud of dust in its wake.

"Not bad, High Priest," General Blair said. He looked at Aaron. "Maybe you're useful after all." He turned and walked toward his house, laughing to himself as if he'd just made a mean joke. After a few steps, he turned and looked at the high priest and governor. "Well, come on, then! Let's plot the demise of Artimé."

The War Room

Gomeral Blair invited Aaron and Liam to sit around the table in his house. Spread across it were half a dozen little black instruments with bits of rusty barbed wire attached.

"What are these?" Aaron asked.

"I'm not sure," General Blair said. "They came off the top of the wall in different places. I've never seen anything like them before."

Liam picked one up and turned it in his hand, and then his mouth went dry. He knew what they were. Eva had told him about the screens in Mr. Today's—now Alex's—office

LISA McMANN

that constantly showed different parts of Quill. These were the magical cameras. He set the piece down. "Looks like a piece of junk to me."

The general shot Liam a curious look, and then shrugged. "Maybe," he said.

"What did you end up doing with the barbed wire, by the way?" Liam asked, trying to change the subject.

"My soldiers are cutting it up and stacking the pieces here in the Quillitary grounds. We'll use it for weapons eventually."

Aaron nodded. "Resourceful," he said. "Really smart."

"Of course it is," said General Blair, his face clearly showing signs of annoyance. "Well, then, let's discuss. We'll begin with everything that went wrong in the initial battle with Artimé."

"Good idea," offered Aaron. He was really out of his element now, yet couldn't seem to stop commenting. "Go ahead."

"If you'll keep quiet," General Blair muttered.

"I will," Aaron said. "Continue. Please."

The general cleared his throat. "First, they saw us coming from a mile away," he said. "And our approach was ridiculously slow."

"But that little problem is fixed now, isn't it?" Aaron asked smugly. He pointed out the window at the soldier who had already driven to the palace and back, and was now getting out of the vehicle.

General Blair ignored him. "We're removing the wall, which was the main hindrance and cause of our initial loss. And we're working to smooth out the terrain so that the rubble is something our vehicles can drive over if necessary. And while my Quillitary is doing that painstaking job, they are also preparing for the battle by using the rubble as a physical training device. Soon they'll be perfectly nimble and able to run at top speed over the rocks anywhere in Quill and Artimé."

"That sounds extraordinarily wise," Aaron said, trying to sound wise himself, but not doing a very good job bluffing his way through all things Quillitary. He tapped a finger to his chin. "And what about weapons? Besides the potential new ones made of wire, I mean?"

General Blair narrowed his eyes. "There's nothing wrong with our weapons."

Aaron glanced sidelong at Liam, who didn't return the look. "Nothing wrong with the weapons?" Aaron repeated, trying not to sound too incredulous. What was the general thinking? The weapons were a mess of rusty scrap metal from ages past, and a few guns with almost no bullets left. "It seems like excellent weaponry might be an important factor when fighting against magic."

Aaron thought about the sack of magical components that Liam had stolen from Artimé and nearly mentioned them as a potential surprise attack weapon, but then thought the better of it. Instead he added more generically, "Magic itself might not be a bad idea, either."

The general leaned forward, the scar at his throat pulsing. "Is that what you think?" he asked. "Magic is for Unwanteds who deserve to die. There's nothing wrong with our weapons," he said again. "And even if there was, it's not your worry. Got it, High Priest?"

Aaron didn't like the general's tone. They were supposed to be a team now, but the general still seemed to be running everything. It was unsettling, but Aaron didn't know what to do about it. "Fine," he said, frustrated. "What'll *I* worry about, then?"

The general glared at Aaron. "You'll worry about getting your weak little self back to the palace," he said. "You'll make

LISA McMANN

me some more oil. And you'll stay out of my way. That's how this team is going to work."

Aaron narrowed his eyes and set his jaw. He hated General Blair now more than ever. But he needed General Blair. Now more than ever.

When Aaron held his tongue, the general smiled. "Good. I'm glad we've reached an understanding." He stood up, signaling the end of the meeting. Reluctantly Aaron and Liam stood too, Aaron fuming over the shoddy treatment, but unable to do anything about it. General Blair ushered them roughly to the door with a final, ominous warning: "Prepare to secure the palace, locking yourselves inside. I'll send soldiers when the time comes. We attack in four days."

A Messy Escape

LISA McMANN

After adding magic to the extra magic carpet components Sky had made, Alex's ability to concentrate was spent. But even as tired as he was, he tossed and turned all night, knowing that the morning could potentially bring disaster. What if he transported the ship too far away? What if the Artiméans couldn't reach it with their flying carpets before the spells wore off and everyone crashed into the sea? What if Spike couldn't swim out of the grasp of the rough undertow, or Florence was too heavy for the carpets, or the wind was too strong and swept them up into the sky? What if Alex couldn't get to sleep tonight, leaving him without the proper concentration in the morning to transport the ship?

And where was Simber? Alex had been tempted multiple times to send a seek spell to Artimé, but he didn't want anyone to worry or think there was trouble here—especially if it was trouble *there* that was keeping Simber away. So he refrained. But now, thinking of all the things that could go wrong, Alex wondered if he'd made a mistake by listening to Sky and trying to handle this escape without the giant beast.

But then again, everyone was beyond restless. The rain was driving them mad. There was no way they could stay here indefinitely. Florence and Sky were both right—they didn't need Simber. They could do this.

"It still wouldn't hurt if you showed up, you know," Alex muttered. He rolled over and tried anew to sleep. But there was always so much to worry about. At least he didn't have Sky on his mind constantly.

Yeah, right. But thankfully she didn't seem to be as miserable without him as he was without her. And they were working at becoming friends again, so that was good, wasn't it? It would have to be enough.

285 « Island of Shipwrecks

LISA McMANN

Finally Alex fell into a deep sleep. And when he woke up, it was very nearly time to go.

With the hour of calm fast approaching, the Artiméans said hasty good-byes and thanks to Ishibashi, Ito, and Sato, who offered them a crate of food to store on the ship to keep them from starving on the way home. Soon Florence announced that the storm was lessening, so they all filed outside, hopefully for the last time.

"You all know what to do," Alex said, knowing there was no time for a lengthy announcement. "Teamwork. Let's go! See you all safely on board within the hour."

With that, Lani peeled off from the group and sprinted to the leeward side of the island to give Spike her instructions. The others quickly made their way to the shore where the ship sat. It was not pristine and polished as it had once been, but hopefully with a bit of magic and a little luck, it was sound and functional. They'd find out soon enough.

Alex didn't waste any time. "Squirrelicorns, to the sky!" he cried. "Everybody else stand back and be ready with your carpet components. You have about ten minutes of flying time to make it all the way to the ship before the spell wears off, so don't waste a second."

Florence hoisted the crate of food to the main deck and stood back as Alex patted the ship's side. "Everybody ready?" he called out.

"You can do it, Alex," Florence said. "Just like last time. You've got the touch."

Alex grinned. Her confidence in him erased some of his jitters. "Okay, here goes," he said, glancing one more time at the spot he'd been envisioning for days—the spot where the sunlight made the waves sparkle beyond the oppressive weight of the storm.

He let his hand rest on the side of the ship and closed his eyes, feeling the light rain against his cheek, and the wind, steady but not overpowering. Thunder rumbled in the distance. Alex cleared his mind of everything except that spot in the sunshine. He concentrated on it, picturing the ship sailing there, outside the realm of crashing waves and under the clear skies and warm sun. He could feel peace come over him, and when he was ready, he whispered, "Transport."

In a flash, the ship disappeared. Alex opened his eyes and

put his hand to his forehead, squinting to watch for it. It would be hard to see from this distance, but hopefully not impossible.

"Does anybody see it?" Alex called anxiously.

The others were straining to find it too, but so far no one had spotted it. Not even Florence from her height.

Alex looked up. "Squirrelicorns?" he called. "Anything?"

Florence signaled everyone to be ready to throw their carpet components down.

After an agonizing minute of silence as the squirrelicorns glided in a circle overhead, one of them nosedived toward the ground and swooped in front of Alex. "It's in the water, but on the opposite side of the island, sir!"

"Drat!" muttered Alex. "There always has to be some problem." He looked in the other direction, but couldn't see over the rock shelter. "Is it clear of the storm, at least?"

"It looks to be, sir! Enjoying open water, nice and calm."

"And not sinking?"

"It doesn't appear to be."

"At least there's that." Alex looked at the others, rapidly reassessing the situation. "Change of plans. Let's save the spells for now and run to the other side of the island. Then cast your components and go—you're on your own! There's no time to waste."

The Artiméans made a frantic dash for the other side of the island while the precious minutes of the hour of calm ticked away. Alex followed the others, hanging back with Florence, who was trying to help Captain Ahab maneuver over the rocky ground more quickly.

When they'd made it halfway to the other side and it was clear that Captain Ahab could move no faster on his wooden leg, Alex called out to the squirrelicorns. "Three of you take Captain Ahab now, will you, so he doesn't get left behind?"

Three squirrelicorns soared down and quickly picked up the captain, allowing Alex and Florence to try to catch up to the others. While they ran, they caught glimpses of the squirrelicorns swaying through the wind as they carried the statue out over the waves, heading toward a dot on the horizon that Alex could just barely see. The other three squirrelicorns flew down to fetch Copper and carry her away.

Just as Alex and Florence reached the other side, Samheed threw down his carpet. It expanded. He sat on it and gathered Fox and Kitten on board. "To the ship," he commanded.

His carpet lifted him several feet above the waves and puttered toward the ship. Alex watched intently, hoping the wind would stay quiet enough not to upset the carpet and knock them to the sea.

Lani went next. "Come on, Crow!" she said. She threw down her carpet, and when it expanded, she sat down and patted the space in front of her. Crow hopped onto the spot and soon they were off, following Samheed. They tipped a bit, but both hung on tightly to the sides of the carpet, and it righted itself again.

Henry followed, flying solo, and soon overtook Lani and Crow.

Octavia threw her component down, climbed on, and whisked away, leaving Sky, Alex, and Florence on the island.

"So far so good," Florence said, gathering her components. "Sky, keep your eyes on the ship and let us know if anybody fails to make it. Let's get mine started, Alex."

It was nearing the halfway point in the hour of calm, and there was no time to lose. Alex and Florence marked off an area on the rocks and began throwing magic carpets down at breakneck speed, overlapping them slightly for more stability, five across and six deep. Florence sat down on them, trying to spread her weight evenly over the thirty carpets. "I sure hope this works," she muttered.

"Go!" Alex said. "Hurry!"

"To the ship!" cried Florence.

Sky and Alex held their breath.

The magic carpets strained and wiggled beneath the warrior. The ones around the edges lifted her up an inch, maybe two . . . now three . . . but the ones in the middle didn't budge.

"Come on," Sky pleaded.

"You can do it, Florence," Alex said. "Lie flat on your back! That might help the ones under your—you know what."

Florence shot Alex a look, but did what he suggested. All the carpets rose a bit with Florence lying stiffly on top, and then lifted a little higher and began to move toward the ship, just barely clearing the rocks and shipwrecks that jutted up above the waves. She was moving very slowly.

Sky gripped Alex's arm. "If she doesn't speed up, she's not going to make it, is she?"

Alex shook his head. "I don't know." He glanced into the distance, looking at all the dots in the sky and counting them.

LISA McMANN

"Everybody's still flying," he said. A few of the dots bounced around a bit in the air with the wind. Florence's ride continued steadily, but very slowly.

"Alex," Florence called out. "I don't think this is going to work."

"Think positive, Florence!" Alex called out in desperation. "You can do it!"

Sky looked at Alex. "Can you send a few more carpets out to go under her?" Do you have extras?"

"A few," Alex said. "We already used some of the ones you made last night." Alex rummaged in his vest pocket and grabbed four carpet components.

"Florence, catch!" he called out. He tossed the four components to Florence, and she caught them. Soon she had a second small layer of carpets under her center of gravity.

"I think that helped a little," Sky said. "Maybe."

Thunder rumbled, a little louder than before, and a gust of wind blew Sky's hair across her face.

"Storm's picking up. We should go," Sky said.

Alex strained his neck, looking at the darkening skies, and worrying over Florence, whose journey was frustratingly slow.

He turned to Sky. "Okay. But there's one more thing I forgot to do before we go. I think I have just enough time. Wait here and keep an eye on Florence—I don't want you to get hurt."

"What?" cried Sky. "Alex, don't be crazy—what are you doing?"

"I'll be right back," Alex promised, and with that, he dashed off at a mad pace, back to the windward side of the island, leaving Sky standing on the shore alone.

LISA McMANN

A Reckless Parting Gift

Clearly Alex had lost his mind, and he knew it. Yet he ran as fast as he could to the other side of the island, past bewildered Ito and Sato who were collecting moss during the hour of calm. "Stay back!" he said to them, and ran straight into the water. As soon as he was deep enough, he dove and swam with all his might to the scientists' ship.

When he reached it, he surfaced and pressed his hand against the part of the stern that stood above the water. He took a moment to catch his breath, staring intently at the shore in the exact spot where the pirate ship had stood for weeks.

A flash of lightning cracked the sky, startling him, and he knew he had to get back to Sky before the storm grew worse. He forced himself to focus, thinking only of the newly empty stretch of land nearby. Now that the pirate ship was out of the way, he could finally do something for the scientists who had been so hospitable to them all this time.

When Alex had eliminated all other stresses from his mind, he closed his eyes, picturing the cleared section of the island, and whispered, "Transport."

As soon as he could feel the ship no longer, he opened his eyes. And there, perfectly placed on the shore, sat the almost pristine craft, marred only by the long, angry gash in its side. Water, fish, and mud streamed from it.

With a triumphant shout, Alex struck out toward the island once more, feeling the sea churning and pulling beneath him. He ran onto the shore and sped toward the other side of the island, past the shelter where Ishibashi was just coming out.

"I left you a present!" Alex shouted. "Go look!"

Ishibashi stared at Alex as the boy ran past, and then heard the shouts from Ito and Sato and hurried toward the recovered ship.

LISA McMANN

With all his heart, Alex wished he could see the scientists' reactions when they found their ship and all the equipment still inside. But he didn't have time. He pressed on toward Sky, who had followed after him a short distance and waited anxiously for him to return.

"Alex!" she shouted when she caught sight of him once more. "Hurry!"

Alex's legs and lungs burned as he ran and jumped over the rocky terrain. As he went, he fished around in his pocket for his magic carpet component so they could take off. But by the time he reached Sky, he still hadn't found it.

"Florence is in trouble," Sky said, grabbing his arm. "Look!"

Alex stared. In his urgency to do something good for the scientists, he'd almost forgotten about Florence and her low ride across the water. "Blast it," he muttered, spotting her. She was so low that waves splashed against her sides.

Sky gripped his arm. "It's been almost ten minutes already and she's not halfway there. She's not going to make it! What are we going to do?"

Alex turned his pockets inside out, searching madly for components, and then stared at Sky. "Do you have it?"

"Have what?"

"The carpet component for us—I don't have it!"

"I gave them all to you last night!" Sky said. "Why would I—? No, I'm sure you have them. I don't have any." She whipped her head toward the sea to look at the ship, as if that would bring it closer. "Alex! Tell me you have it!"

Alex's lungs contracted. He felt light-headed. "I must have used them all for Florence," he whispered.

Sky stared. She yanked his arm, pulling him so they stood face to face. "Alex," she said in a sickly calm voice, her fingers digging into his skin, "my mother and brother are on that ship. They will freak out if I don't get there."

"I know, I know. I'm thinking." He couldn't look at her. "Maybe I lost it in the water," he muttered, turning to look over his shoulder. It would be useless to search for it in the churning waves.

"Alex," Sky said, shaking him. "What are we going to do? And what about Florence? She's going down!"

Alex drew in a breath. "We'll make another component. We have to."

"There's no time for that!" Sky cried. "The moss needs

LISA McMANN

to dry, the loom is in the shelter—and the storm is getting stronger. Plus one component won't help save Florence!" She looked around wildly and gripped her head in frustration. "Where's Spike?" she asked, knowing full well that Spike was probably waiting exactly where Lani had told her to go, on the opposite side of the storm's circumference.

"Florence will be okay," Alex said, though the thought of her plummeting to the bottom of the sea gave him a stomachache. "She will. She said she will."

"But what about us? How will our friends know what happened? They'll think we drowned, Alex—we have to do something. *Now*."

"Maybe the squirrelicorns will come back for us," Alex said, but wasn't at all confident about it—the squirrelicorns always waited for orders from him or Florence, and neither were there to give them. Alex could hardly stand hearing Sky's pleas—he didn't know what to do. There was nothing he *could* do, not now at least. The thunder crashed and the sea churned as the wind began to howl once more. Sky and Alex looked at each other, and at Florence, who barely skimmed the waves now, three quarters of the way to the ship.

When all seemed lost, a shout rose up on a wind gust behind them. Alex and Sky turned to see Ishibashi running full speed toward them, screaming at the top of his lungs and waving his hands wildly as if his life depended on it. For right behind him, flying low over the rocky island, was an enormous, roaring, stone cheetah.

To the Rescue

The giant cat soared over Ishibashi's head. "Sprrread aparrrt and grrrab on to my wings!" he called out to Alex and Sky, and without hesitating, the two dashed in opposite directions. As the cat flew between them, they jumped into the air and grabbed on to the tips of his wings. Simber flipped them up and held steady while they scrambled to his back. They soared out over the water toward the ship.

Sky had the good sense to wave to Ishibashi, trying to let him know that the strange creature was a friend, not a foe, but the little man kept yelling. Eventually he gave up and just stood there, watching them go. He grew smaller as Simber flew.

"That was pretty good timing, Sim," Alex shouted over the storm, hanging on tightly as the wind grew to near-hurricane strength. "Nothing like waiting until the last second."

Simber growled in laughter. "This isn't overrr yet," he said. "Both of you need to move off my back and onto the base of my wings forrr a few minutes."

Sky and Alex obeyed, sliding their grip a little at a time as they inched in opposite directions.

"Arrre you hanging on all rrright?" he asked Sky, who hadn't had as much experience riding on Simber's back as Alex had.

"B-b-barely," Sky said, her teeth chattering as she moved up and down with the flap of Simber's wings. "But there's no way I'm letting go."

"Good," Simber replied.

They closed in on Florence, who was almost completely submerged now. It was amazing that the carpets had kept going this long—Florence was clearly trying every magic spell she could think of to help sustain them, but they were sinking fast. And the ship wasn't far off. Alex could see everybody lined up at the railing, cheering at the sight of Simber and watching the rescue.

"Wherrre's Spike?" asked Simber.

"We sent her to the other side of the island by mistake," Alex shouted over the rumble of thunder. "It's a long story."

"So we'rrre going to have to do this without herrr, then," Simber said. "Sky, Alex, be rrready. We'rrre heading underrr waterrr. Just flatten out on top of my wings and hang on, that's all you have to do. Hold yourrr brrreath and don't let go."

"Got it!" Sky yelled.

"Me too," called out Alex.

"Herrre we go!"

The two took giant breaths. Simber plunged under the surface of the water and plowed through it. Sky and Alex held their breath and hung on, and soon Florence's thirty-four carpets were above them. Simber glided upward until Alex and Sky felt a bump, and they knew that Florence and her carpets were now resting on Simber's back. The overworked carpets began to pop and disappear in the water as they traveled along.

When Simber slowed, Alex watched through the water as Florence nimbly rose to her haunches, half out of the water, balancing on Simber's back. They sank a bit as the carpets popped and disappeared, but the cheetah flapped his wings and kicked his legs, trying desperately to keep the warrior from sinking them all completely.

A minute later, the water grew brighter and Alex could tell the sun had appeared above them. They'd made it out of the hurricane's circle! And just when Alex's lungs were about to give out, a large shadow came over him. He looked up through the water. *The ship!*

Soon a rope slapped the surface above him, and Alex needed no further urging. He pushed off of Simber's wing and swam to the surface, grabbed on to the rope, and looked around for Sky. She was on the other side of Simber, holding a rope of her own and beginning to scale the side of the ship. Lani and Henry stood at the ship's railing, pulling her up. Alex began climbing as well, with Samheed pulling him from above.

Florence cautiously rose to her feet and grabbed the ship's railing, trying to lighten Simber's load a bit. Once Alex and Sky had made it on board, everyone ran to the opposite side of the deck to help balance the weight and hung on tightly while Florence began an awkward climb, rocking the vessel crazily from side to side, but managing to keep all the passengers on board.

LISA McMANN

The crew cheered when she eased over the edge. Finally Florence centered herself on the deck, and the ship sat steady once more. Almost everyone flopped to the deck, either from being sent off balance or simply because they were exhausted and breathless. A moment later, Simber rose up out of the water and shook himself dry as the Artiméans greeted him with great enthusiasm.

Brushing off the praise, Simber simply nodded his greetings and took his usual place hovering over the back of the ship. Within minutes, everything seemed strangely back to normal again.

Well, almost.

Once Captain Ahab had steered the ship all the way around the hurricane to the other side of the island, and once Spike's faux diamond–studded spike was flashing prettily in the sun nearby, they turned toward home.

Simber, flying off to one side, took a long hard look at the vessel's unusual patch job, and shook his head. He turned toward Alex and the others, who were resting on the deck, soaking up the sun, and asked, "What in the worrrld have you done to Marrrcus's ship?"

Doubts Arise

After stewing half the night over the troubling meeting with General Blair, Aaron spent the morning alone, pressing oil, deep in thought. It was unsettling. Why had the general been so dismissive of Aaron? Was General Blair only using him for the oil? Didn't he see that Aaron was a worthy and smart leader? After all, Aaron had offered him a portion of the mansion once they took over Artimé. Why wouldn't he let Aaron take part in the actual battle?

Granted, he'd mucked up the first one, but he was older and wiser now. He wouldn't make the same mistakes again.

Besides, he was the high priest of Quill. That he had made it to this point must mean something. Yet the general had become extremely standoffish with Aaron now that he'd gotten the oil he needed. And his commanding Aaron to hide in the secured palace until it was all over seemed especially unfair. What was the general planning to do—keep him locked away, and then come and fetch him once the Quillitary had taken ownership of the mansion?

With a jolt of fear, Aaron froze in his work. He looked up, and then all around, a sort of dazed expression on his face. "Wait a second," he muttered. Did the general have a secret sinister plan of his own? What if General Blair moved into the mansion and then decided he didn't want to share it with anybody?

Aaron left the contraption mid-press, stumbled from the room, and ran up the stairs, all the way up to Liam's quarters at the very top of the palace, and pounded on the door.

"Good heavens!" Liam shouted. "What's the matter?" No one had ever come up to his room before, so it was rather startling.

Aaron flung open the door. "General Blair is working

against us, Liam. I've figured it out. He's using me for the oil, and when he attacks, he's going to take over Artimé and keep everything for himself!"

Liam's jaw dropped. "What?"

"He wants the mansion, you fool! Don't you see?"

Liam rose from his desk, where the sack of components rested. "High Priest, I'm afraid I don't see. What in Quill are you talking about?"

Aaron's eyes blazed. "I'm talking about the general's dismissive nature once I gave him the oil. Did you notice it? He wouldn't let me participate in the discussion, and he basically told me I'm to board up the palace and wait inside for him to win the battle. Didn't you hear that? Weren't you there?"

"Of course I was there," Liam said. He was really getting irritated with the way Aaron spoke to him. He bit his tongue, remembering Eva, and said smoothly, "I think that General Blair is just trying to hold up his end of the bargain. You provided him with the oil, and now he will do his part by attacking Artimé and taking it over on behalf of Quill."

Aaron shook his head. "No, Liam. You don't get it. I have made mistakes before, but I'm not going to make another one, and General Blair is a mistake! He's trying to keep me out of the way so he can dethrone Alex and take over Artimé. He's trying to steal what is rightfully mine!"

Liam stared.

Aaron closed his lips. He held Liam's gaze, and then grew pale. "I mean . . ." He faltered.

It was like a waterfall of understanding pouring over Liam. He stood quietly as the pieces fell into place in his mind—things he'd failed to grasp all this time. His eyes darted to the bag of useless components that Meghan had given him to trick Aaron, and then he looked at the high priest once more, seeing him for what he was: a pathetic, regretful young man who couldn't seem to figure out for himself who he was and what he truly wanted.

"Rightfully yours?" Liam asked softly.

"That's not what I meant!" Aaron said.

"Do you wish you were an Unwanted?" Liam asked, just as softly as before.

"No!" cried Aaron. "That's not what I meant at all!"

"Well then, what did you mean?" Liam asked, raising his voice and forgetting himself.

The two stood facing each other in the tiny, stuffy room, Aaron's expression finally betraying years of agony, and Liam's face blanching with the fear of having gone too far. Accusing the high priest of wishing to be an Unwanted was probably the worst of all the infractions in Quill.

After an excruciating moment, Liam spoke to try to save the treacherous walls from crumbling further. "I'm sorry," he whispered. "I believe I misspoke. Did you instead mean that as the high priest of Quill, you are the rightful ruler of the entire island and all of its parts?"

The blood in Aaron's body began to pump once more. A shadow passed over his face, and he dropped his gaze and let out a breath. "Yes, of course," he said, his voice shaking and straining to find its usual patronizing tone. "How dare you assume anything else?"

Liam's chest tightened. "I-I'm so very sorry, High Priest."

Aaron straightened up and stood tall, ignoring his trembling limbs and recovering his high-priestly air. He pointed to the sack of components on Liam's desk. "I'm ready for the components now. I assume I'll find the verbal incantations and all instructions inside?"

"Yes." Liam dropped his gaze to the floor, knowing what had to be coming next. There was no way, with Aaron's temper, that Liam would spend another night in the palace. It was off to the Ancients Sector for him once more. Only this time, he wouldn't live past dawn to tell about it.

"Very well, then." Aaron reached past Liam to pick up the sack.

Liam flinched, waiting for the command.

Aaron retreated to the doorway and then paused, looking back over his shoulder. "I'll let you know if I have any questions about these," he said. He turned away once more and closed the door behind him.

When he heard the click of the door, Liam looked up.

He was still alive. For the moment, at least. And with life, a tiny ray of hope.

A Return to the Office Desk

Downstairs in his office, Aaron dropped the sack of components on the floor, collapsed at his desk, and buried his face in his hands. He felt like his gut was being torn to shreds. He didn't even understand what had just happened. What was so wrong about Aaron wanting to rule over the entire island, including Artimé? And what was so wrong about wanting to do it from the nicest location in the land? Just because the mansion happened to be magical, and just because it happened to be created by Unwanted trash, and just because it was surrounded by wickedly awful creative people, did not make

LISA McMANN

Aaron sympathetic to the Unwanteds, or worse, some sort of jealous admirer.

Artimé *was* rightfully his, but not because Aaron deserved to be Unwanted—no one knew about his infractions but he and his brother, who had taken the blame when they were ten in order to save him. And no one knew what Aaron's life would be like now if he'd taken responsibility for his own creativity. Alex's sacrifice had been a gift that any intelligent person wouldn't think twice about accepting! For that was what Aaron was. Intelligent. Strong. Wanted. Period.

And none of this changed the fact that something sinister was happening with General Blair. Aaron didn't trust him—not now. Not after that meeting.

He lifted his head and stared across the bare, gray room, and his heart sank. He was on his own again. He didn't have the Quillitary after all. He was on his own, and undoubtedly about to fail once more. It was the story of his life.

At least he could let General Blair do the hard work of conquering Artimé. That was an easy enough decision—it was going to happen whether Aaron wanted it to or not. And of course he wanted it to happen. The impossible part would come after that, when Aaron would have to take over the man-sion from General Blair. And if General Blair really was just using Aaron, did that mean that the general was also planning to get rid of him when he was no longer needed?

Aaron groaned into his sleeve. The uncertainty and the anxiety were killing him, he was sure of that.

His mind turned to Secretary. The old woman grew more dear to him the longer she was gone, and he wished her back in this room again. She'd know what to do. But there was no bringing her back from the panther's jaws.

The panther—just one of his many failures. There had been so much promise there. It was such a shame that all the jungle and its creatures were useless to Aaron now. He couldn't trust them to obey him, even though they seemed like they wanted to.

Aaron massaged his temples. Maybe he had moved too fast with the jungle animals. Maybe he hadn't spent enough time teaching the panther what he wanted her to do. Could that have saved Eva? He was always so impatient. And now he would never know.

Three days left until General Blair attacked Artimé, and

LISA McMANN

here Aaron sat, helplessly awaiting the general's takeover, and not really sure he had a place in the angry man's future plans. Perhaps a takeover of the palace was next. Maybe that was why General Blair wanted him to lock himself inside—to make his own capture that much easier.

"I'm such an idiot," Aaron muttered, flopping down on the desk in despair.

"Yes, you really are," came a woman's voice from the hall.

It was the elusive Gondoleery Rattrapp.

Aaron lifted his head and frowned. "What do you want?"

Gondoleery stepped into the room. "I was just nosing about to see how you were coming along in your quest to take over Artimé," she said. "Care to fill your favorite governor in on the plan?"

"Not really."

"What's that you say?"

Aaron shot her a pointed look. "Things are coming along fine," he said. "I'm working with the Quillitary and we're going to attack soon."

"Soon? When?"

"Soon enough," Aaron said. "That's my private information."

Gondoleery laughed. "I'll go ask Blair myself if you like."

Aaron recoiled. "How did you—how do you—?"

"How did I know he was still alive?" Gondoleery purred, obviously delighted to see the surprise on Aaron's face. "Maybe because I've been working with him too."

Aaron stood up, feeling the heat rise to his face. "I knew it! I knew he was—! You traitor!" He whipped around the desk and lunged at Gondoleery.

She pointed at him, and a skewer of ice coupled with an arctic blast shot from her fingers and flew toward Aaron. It struck him, the point burying itself into his arm. He yelped and fell back against the desk. The spear of ice hung from him, and then crumbled and dropped to the floor.

"Next time I won't stop it from going straight through you," Gondoleery said with a sickly sweet smile. "Don't touch me, Aaron Stowe. Don't ever, ever, touch me."

Aaron's mouth hung open. He righted himself and rubbed his arm where the icy spear had jabbed him. Without taking his eyes off her, he slowly walked around to the other side of the desk, putting it between them for his protection. He glanced at the sack of spell components, out of reach on the

LISA McMANN

floor, and useless until he knew the proper things to say with them. He looked down at the drawer that had once contained heart attack spell components, but he'd used them up on the panther.

He was out of luck.

"I'm sure you didn't mean to threaten me," Gondoleery said cheerily. She picked at her teeth with a fingernail. "Did you?"

"No," Aaron said through gritted teeth.

"Good." She stopped picking. "Now when did you say the Quillitary attack will be?"

Aaron worked his jaw. "Three days," he said.

"Very good. I look forward to the festivities and the rewards. I'll tell General Blair you said hello next time I see him." She turned and sauntered to the door. And then she turned back and added, "You know, everyone in the palace can hear everything you say when you and Liam are shouting together up there in that echo chamber."

Aaron's eyes widened. What did she mean?

Gondoleery laughed again as she walked away, talking loudly to herself. "General Blair, still alive. Amazing. What a cunning little mastermind. I didn't expect it of him!"

As Aaron's breath grew hot in his nostrils and he began to seethe, he looked at the puddle on the floor, a small hunk of ice remaining. It reminded him of the day he'd gone to Gunnar Haluki's house and found water dripping from all surfaces, and a single puck of ice on the table—the only other time he'd seen or felt ice in his life.

And that's when Aaron Stowe really got scared.

A Mansion and a Jungle

Aaron had two options if he wanted to protect himself from General Blair, and now from Gondoleery, who had quickly vaulted to being the number one person on his list of people to fear. The first option: the bag of spells. And the second? Another visit to the jungle. It probably wouldn't do any good, but he could try.

Aaron spent the rest of the evening sorting through the spell components and reading the instructions for their use. A small, hard, green component would turn a person into a frog if he yelled "Hey-o froggy face!" while casting. A wispy piece of grass would give the receiver terrible allergies and render them incapacitated if Aaron yelled "Aaah-CHOO!" A squiggly forked stick would poke somebody in both eyes when accompanied by a rousing chant of "Neener neener neener!"

Aaron pored over the incantations earnestly, memorizing them and remembering the components that went along with each. This particular batch seemed ridiculously silly, and he knew he'd be rather embarrassed to yell out some of the strange things, yet he pressed on. He had no choice. It only reinforced in his mind—not that he doubted, of course—that Unwanteds were silly and stupid, and he was most definitely not one of them.

The next morning, Aaron loaded up his pockets, wishing for one of those handy vests that his brother wore to carry all of the components in, and slipped out of the palace. He strode quickly to Haluki's house, made his way inside to the office, and took the tube to the mansion.

Normally he spent only a split second there before hitting all the buttons, which would take him to the jungle. But this time he hesitated. It was quiet in the little kitchenette. He poked his head out of the tube and stole a glance beyond the room to the hallway and into the currently unlit office on the other side.

LISA McMANN

He listened carefully but heard nothing stirring, so he stepped out of the tube and snuck to the door frame. He peered out and to the left, down the intricately beautiful expanse of hallway. It was empty except for a small, ugly statue that looked strangely familiar, but at present Aaron couldn't remember where he'd seen it before. A moment later he was tiptoeing across the hallway and into the office.

He'd been in there before. And like that first time when he'd just discovered his brother was alive, the room made him long for something. The feeling was much stronger now, perhaps because he was getting used to seeing the unusual, colorful world.

On that day, Mr. Today had been sitting at the desk with Alex.

They had been so surprised to see him coming through their strange paper doorway that worked like a real door. They'd been happy to see him. And they'd invited him to stay.

He wondered how things would be different now if he'd said yes. Would Mr. Today still be alive?

Aaron pressed his lips together and dropped his gaze. He didn't like the gnawing feeling that dug into him.

After a minute he slipped back to the kitchenette and into the tube. He pressed all the buttons, and the warm comfort of Artimé was replaced by the cool, minty scent of the jungle. Aaron took it in and looked around.

The rock was there, with the panther curled up in one of its crevasses, sleeping.

Aaron remained still in the tube for a moment, looking out at the softly lit refuge. He'd liked it here before the horrible incident with Eva and the panther. It had an entirely different feel from home and from Artimé. It was the most welcoming place of all, he thought. Populated by misfits and failures of all shapes and sizes. Talk about unwanted.

He cringed. Aaron didn't like to admit to himself just why he felt so comfortable here. But it was pretty obvious. Despite his one success, Aaron was a misfit and a failure too.

He stepped out of the tube, and his soft tread upon the jungle floor sent the panther jumping to her feet. She took one look at Aaron, bounded toward him, and screamed in his face, just like old times. She brushed her body against his legs, nearly throwing him off balance, and nudged his hand with her head, prompting him to pet her.

Aaron's mouth twisted into a half smile and he did what she wanted, checking her all over to make sure she was intact.

"Hey, you, your tail's gone again," he scolded. "What do you do to that poor thing, bounce on it? Bite it off?"

The rock opened his craggy yellow eyes. Its cave mouth spread into a smile. "I was hoping we'd see you soon," the rock growled. "You seem to know just when to come."

Aaron smiled. It was strange how he hadn't thought about the jungle for weeks, and then it just popped into his mind. "It's good to be back," he said, and despite everything that had happened with Secretary, he meant it. He knew the panther hadn't meant to do anything wrong. It was his fault, not hers.

He took a length of vine and fixed her tail, magically melding the pieces together like before, with only a small fraction of the anxiety this time.

The panther screeched in appreciation. Aaron bent down so his face aligned with hers. Her fangs glistened.

"You're so smart," Aaron told the panther. "You know that, right?" He tapped a finger nervously on his knee, debating what to do. Finally, he just decided to explain it, wanting the rock to hear as well.

"I have two tricks I'd like to teach you, Panther," he said. "The first one is called down. When I say 'down,' I want you to sit next to me and not move, no matter what is happening around you."

The panther lunged, licking Aaron with her cold stone tongue and knocking him off his feet.

"Yeah?" Aaron asked, getting up. "Do you understand me? I highly doubt it," he said. "But you will."

The panther panted and screamed.

"She understands. But that doesn't mean she'll do it." The rock moved a few feet closer. "That's the reason she's here, you know. What's the second trick?" he asked.

Aaron looked up. "I'm afraid there's trouble brewing in Artimé, my rocky friend. The second trick I need to teach the panther is called attack."

The rock's eyes drew closer together in concern. "Are you sure that's a good idea?" it growled.

"No, I'm not," Aaron said, surprising himself with how forthcoming he was being today. "But to be honest, it's the only hope I have."

Calm Seas

The patchwork ship soon left the Island of Shipwrecks and the giant hurricane far behind. The Artiméans were so glad to be dry again, and Alex was even gladder to have Simber back with them once more. A quick consultation with the cat convinced Alex that Artimé was not in imminent danger. Simber reassured Alex that everything was under control and running smoothly, and that he would give him more details of future concerns once they had the ship in order.

And the ship was going to be a great task. It had lost most of its original rigging and tools, and because of the hurricane the

LISA McMANN

Artiméans had to stow all of the salvaged replacement items, food, and rainwater belowdecks to keep them from blowing away. By the end of the day they had repositioned everything in its proper place, and the non-statues quite fairly collapsed in exhaustion at the first hint of darkness after their harrowing day.

By morning, once all the shipboard duties had been portioned out and things were running efficiently on the calm waters, Alex and the others finally had time to tell Simber all that had happened while he was gone.

Simber took specific interest in the shipwreck that contained the military vehicles.

Alex explained, "Ishibashi—he's the guy you scared half to death—said that nobody was on board when the ship wrecked. Isn't that weird?"

Simber frowned. "Yes, it's a little strrrange, unless they abandoned ship when they firrrst enterrred the storrrm. Even strrrangerrr, I rrrecall Marrrcus saying something yearrrs ago about a ship just like it that had come limping to Quill back when he and Justine initially inhabited the island, beforrre the wall went up. The ship had been thrrrough some wrrretched storrrm, I guess. Perrrhaps it was the same hurrricane you've been living through."

"Maybe . . . but if they escaped it and made it to Quill, how did they end up right back in the hurricane again? You'd think they'd know enough to steer clear."

"You'd think. But they did drrrop some of theirrr vehicles on Quill to lighten theirrr load. That's how Justine got them. Perrrhaps therrre werrre two ships, and only one was able to make it to Quill." He fell quiet for a moment, thinking. "If I rrrecall, Marrrcus said something about a warrr." The cat shook his head. "I don't rrremember. I wasn't that interrrested in the storrry back then, so I doubt I asked many questions." He puzzled some more as he flew.

Alex puzzled along with him on the deck below. "I suppose there's a book about it somewhere," he said, rolling his eyes. "There always is."

Simber chuckled. "I suppose. Marrrcus did a lot of wrrriting."

"It'll be nice to be home," Alex said after a time.

Henry joined them and entertained Simber for hours with stories of Ishibashi and the greenhouse, though he stayed true to Ishibashi's instructions and didn't mention the glowing seaweed.

Every now and then Henry checked his vest's interior pocket to make sure the container was still there, and it always was. When he had exhausted all his stories, he went in search of a bit of wire. Once he found something that would suffice, he fashioned a magical fastener for the container's pocket that would only open on his command. He felt proud that Ishibashi trusted him to make wise decisions, and he took Ishibashi very seriously when he said the seaweed should never fall into the wrong hands. Henry imagined someone horrible like Aaron Stowe getting ahold of it, and imagined what would happen if a tyrant like that had the ability to live forever. It would be absolutely terrible for everyone else, he knew that much. It could cause the downfall of the whole world!

By midafternoon, Captain Ahab, who was functioning more like a normal, non-insane statue ever since Ms. Octavia cleaned out the inside of his head, shouted out for all to hear: "Land ahead!"

Simber confirmed the sighting, though no one else could make it out. That prompted Alex to ask Simber for his story.

"Now it's your turn. Tell us everything," Alex said, "from the time you left with Sean and Carina until you scared the stink out of Ishibashi. And what took you so long coming back?"

"Afterrr yourrr adventurrrous storrries," Simber said, "I'm afrrraid mine will borrre you." He flapped his wings a few times. "But I'll give you the highlights."

Others gathered to listen.

"Ourrr jourrrney home was a difficult one," he began. "It took much longerrr than I expected because of Sean's leg. If I flew too fast, the wind buffeted him arrround in his hammock. So we took it verrry slow. He's doing much betterrr now."

"Thank goodness. And what about Artimé?" Alex asked. "Is everything all right? I've been anxious to know what prompted Ms. Morning's seek spell."

"Ah, yes," Simber said solemnly, and he recounted the story of Eva Fathom's tragic death, and the confusion about whose side she was really on. Simber saved some of the more sensitive information about Sean and his secretive work with Eva for a time when he and Alex could talk privately.

"Well if that was all that went wrong," Samheed asked

LISA McMANN

after a while, "what took you so long to come back?"

Simber took a moment to sample the air and check to make sure Spike was nearby, and then he began anew. "You might not believe this," Simber said with a rare, wry grin, "but shorrrtly afterrr we got to Arrrtimé, and just as I was about to rrreturrrn to you, a most extrrraorrrdinarrry thing happened."

"What?" Alex asked.

"The Quillitarrry and the Necessarrries began tearrring down the wall that surrrounds Quill."

"That's crazy!" Lani said.

Ms. Octavia just shook her alligator head in disbelief.

"It's trrrue," Simber said. "They werrre going at it with some vigorrr when I left."

"And is Aaron still high priest?" Alex tried to picture Aaron making that decision, knowing what he knew of his brother. He added sarcastically, "How much time did they spend tearing it down before *someone* changed his mind and demanded it to be rebuilt again?"

Samheed snickered.

"That's what I was wonderrring," Simber said, "and of courrrse we werrre all concerrrned about the motives behind

LISA McMANN

that action. So I decided it was best that I stay forrr a while, at least, to see if we could deterrrmine what was coming next. Of courrrse we anticipate an attack eventually."

"But you changed your mind and decided to find us anyway?" Sky asked.

"When you didn't rrreturrrn, I began to worrry," Simber admitted. "The Quillitarrry continued theirrr demolition, planning to topple the entirrre wall, level the rrrubble, and chop up the barrrbed-wirrre ceiling. It seemed rrreasonable to me that they wouldn't do anything to us until theirrr task was completed.

"In the meantime, Clairrre and Meghan have rrreinstated Magical Warrriorrr Trrraining for everrryone, including teaching defensive spells to the Warrrblerrr childrrren. Carrrina is worrrking harrrd on incrrreasing the medicine supply. Sean and Sigfrrried Appleblossom and some of the youngerrr Unwanteds arrre building up ourrr stock of spell components. And of courrrse the girrrinos arrre keeping a close watch on the borrrderrr between Quill and Arrrtimé. They've rrrecrrruited help from Jim, the winged torrrtoise, and the ostrrrich statue, and a varrriety of otherrr statues to stand guarrrd along the borrrderrr, since we no longerrr have a wall at all."

"That must look so strange," Sky said.

Lani nodded. "I can't even imagine it."

Alex was flabbergasted. He couldn't picture a scenario where his brother would do such a rash thing, so opposite of what Justine stood for. "This is very strange," he muttered. "I don't think Aaron is working alone. This is not something he would ever do—I just can't see it."

"You know him better than anyone," Ms. Octavia said. "It's one of the reasons Marcus chose you to be the next mage. Let us know if you think of anything that would help us defend Artimé, for I fear that's what he's after. Why else would he expose Quill by taking down the wall, if it's not to have better access to attack us?"

Alex absently rubbed the patches of fuzz on his chin. "Yeah, of course," he said, lost in thought. "I'm not sure what to think, quite honestly."

Samheed nodded. "We've got time to figure it out. I hope." He looked out over the water toward home.

Alex knit his brows, unaware of the others watching him curiously. "He would have been one of us, you know. He had a chance to join us early on, before that first battle. I remember . . ." He trailed off.

Sky glanced at Crow. This was news to them. She looked up at Simber, who stared ahead in stony silence.

"I remember he almost did it," Alex said, finishing his thought. "He was tempted." He shook his head and sighed. "Things would be a lot different for us if he had."

Samheed snorted. "Yeah. A lot worse."

Lani nudged him with her elbow. "Take it easy," she said, nodding her head in Alex's direction. "He's having a moment."

Samheed raised an eyebrow and glanced at Alex, and then he shrugged and turned back to the water. After a minute, he craned his neck and stood on his tiptoes, straining his eyes. "I see it," he said, pointing. "Just there. The mysterious island number six."

A Strange Message

Everyone but Alex crowded at the starboard railing, anxious to catch a glimpse of the next island. As with most of the islands in the chain, they knew nothing at all about this one as they approached for the first time, and the conversation turned animated.

"I wonder what grave danger awaits us there," Lani said in her storytelling voice. "Strange thorn-necked undergrounders?"

Sky and Copper grinned.

"A reverse aquarium, perhaps?" Lani went on. "Or a tall, bronze, handsome stranger?" Lani swung her head dramatically and made googly eyes at Florence, who groaned and put her hands over her face to hide her embarrassment.

"Or," Lani continued with a bit of sarcasm, "everyone's personal favorite, a never-ending-hurricane island?"

"Hey," Henry objected. "I liked that one. I had a special bonding time."

Fox and Kitten made faces at each other. They both hated the hurricane island and were anxious to get home to the lounge band once more.

"What do you think this island has in store for us?" Lani asked Alex, nudging him from his reverie with her foot. "Come on—come look."

Alex let Lani pull him to his feet and he joined the others. "I think we're due for a fun island, aren't we?"

"Yes," Lani said. "I know—a carnival island."

"What's a carnival?" asked Henry.

"It's a place with fun rides and cotton candy," Lani said wisely, for she'd read it in a book.

"Candy made of *cotton*? That's like eating your shirt. Disgusting!" said Crow, and the others agreed.

"Yeah," Lani admitted. "I didn't get what was so great about that either. Apparently cotton tastes sweet, though."

"Huh," Samheed said. He slipped his arm over Lani's shoulders and pecked her on the cheek. "Just like you."

"Gross," muttered Henry.

Fox nibbled at the tail of Henry's shirt and made a face. "Maybe it's an island covered with rabbits," he suggested, and he wanted it so much that he almost believed it could be true.

"Mewmewmew," Kitten said.

"No, not mice," Fox replied. "That one on the hurricane island was enough."

Simber sighed and shook his head.

Fox looked up with caution and smiled meekly at the giant cat. Simber glared back at him. Fox tiptoed to the other side of the ship, with Kitten scampering behind.

"I would wish it to be an island of art supplies," Ms. Octavia said. "I miss my classroom. Especially my paints. I haven't done a painting in so long, I've nearly forgotten how."

"You'll never forget," Florence said. "But it'll be good for all of us to get back to normal." Several of the others nodded.

"I miss painting too," Alex chimed in. He was feeling melancholy from the news about Quill's wall coming down, and he was feeling weird about Aaron. The talk of Ms. Octavia's

LISA McMANN

classroom made him long for home. He stood off to one side of the group, leaned forward to rest his elbows on the railing, and stared out over the water.

"It's probably boring and deserted," Samheed said.

"I kind of wish for that," Alex admitted. He stood up straight and took a deep breath, trying to chase away his glum mood. "And besides, it doesn't matter. We're not stopping there."

The announcement was met with a few halfhearted expressions of disappointment.

"We need to get home as quickly as possible," Alex said, deciding it right then and there. "Artimé needs us. I don't know what Aaron's up to, but if the Quillitary is helping tear down the wall, it sounds like he's got them on his side, which seems suspicious to me. He's never had their support—in fact, they're probably the ones who threw him out of university because he messed up their plans."

"With a little help from me," Samheed added.

"Yes, you made it happen back then, didn't you?" Alex said with a grin.

Samheed shrugged, but he couldn't brush off the smile. After being so closely associated with the evil Will Blair, he'd

LISA McMANN

had to prove his innocence, and he'd certainly done it.

"Anyway," Alex said, glancing at the sixth island, which grew larger as the conversation continued, "our island hopping needs to end for now. We're heading home at top speed, and we're not stopping for anything."

Later, as the low-hanging sun turned orange off the bow and everyone had scattered, Sky joined Alex at the railing.

"It's smart to go home," Sky said. "We all need it, and Artimé needs us."

Alex nodded.

The sixth island loomed as large as life now. It was one of the bigger islands in the chain, from what Alex could see, and it was very green and lush. He leaned over the railing and pointed to the mountainous end of it, which was quite a bit higher than the other side. A huge waterfall gushed from the top of it and slipped down the side, disappearing behind the trees.

"Look how beautiful it is," Alex murmured. He glanced at Sky, whose face lit up at the discovery.

"Stunning," she agreed. "Maybe we can visit another time?"

"Yeah." Despite the island's beauty, Alex couldn't tear his eyes away from Sky. Her face was so expressive, and he loved how she delighted in simple, beautiful things. She had such a wonderful appreciation for them, just like the Unwanteds did after having lived in the colorless world of Quill.

He blurted out, "Do you think your experiences in Warbler turned you into this amazing human being, or were you just born this way?"

Sky's lips parted in surprise. She caught his gaze and held it and didn't answer his question. Instead she sighed and smiled. "At last."

Alex tilted his head. "At last what?"

"At last, the real Alex has returned," she said. She tapped a finger to her lips and grinned, adding, "You know, you can be very attractive when you let yourself be vulnerable."

Alex had trouble comprehending her words. He could only stare at her finger on her lips, and wish his lips were there in its place. "The real Alex?" he managed to say.

Sky nodded. She dropped her arm to the railing, letting it rest millimeters from his, but held his gaze. "The guy from the roof," she said.

Alex lowered his eyes. "Oh, him. That Alex was a mess," he said. He wasn't proud of that Alex. That Alex had so many shortcomings, so many breakdowns.

"That Alex was the one I—" She stopped.

Alex's stomach lurched. He lifted his gaze. "You what?" he whispered. He drew an inch closer to her, and she to him. Was she really about to say what he thought she was going to say? It made his heart tremble.

"The one I . . . ," she said again, and swallowed hard.

Just then a shout rang out.

Alex and Sky bolted apart.

"What?" screeched Alex. "What's wrong?"

Samheed and Lani came thundering across the deck, leaping over Florence's leg, and pointing to the island. "Look!" Samheed shouted. "Look at the shore!"

Alex and Sky spun around and searched the area where Samheed was pointing.

"I don't see . . . ," Alex began, and then he sucked in a breath.

Spelled out in white bones on the brown sandy shore of the island was a single, enormous word. "HELP!"

LISA McMANN

Ominous Island Six

Bones!" gasped Sky. "That's crazy!"

"Do you see anyone on the shore?" Lani asked. She, Samheed, Alex, and Sky craned their necks toward the sixth island, searching all around the word "HELP" for signs of life. Nothing moved.

"I don't," Alex said. "Simber, do you?"

"No, not frrrom herrre."

Alex tapped the railing nervously as he considered his options. "We can't stop here. We can't," he said, as if he were trying to convince himself. "We have to put our own people first."

"Of course we do," Lani said, "but what if someone's in trouble?"

"What if our own people are in trouble?" Alex said, frowning.

Lani shot him a look.

Alex sighed. "Right. Okay, Sim, let's take a quick ride over the island. See if you can detect any life. I mean, that help sign could be years old. The person who wrote it could be dead by now. Or rescued," he added.

Simber dipped a wing. Alex climbed on and slid to Simber's back, and they were off.

"It'll be dark soon," Alex said, glancing at the half circle of orange that remained in the western sky. "I won't be able to see for much longer."

"Don't worry, I can see," Simber said. They flew over the waves and above the shore, Simber weaving across the area nearest the bone message. The island below was thick with trees and bushes. Sections were covered with beautiful flowers. A river flowed from the waterfall on the mountainous side, leading into the thick center of the island.

Alex peered around Simber's wing, but in the waning light,

LISA McMANN

he could only see occasional movement of leafy branches, probably from the wind.

Simber crinkled his nose. "I don't see anyone, but therrre's definitely life down therrre. Severrral species, I think. It's harrrd to tell. But therrre's not a strrrong human scent." Simber glanced back at Alex. "Do you want me to coverrr the otherrr half of the island too?"

Alex glanced back at the ship, which now glowed warmly, lit by magical torches that someone had fashioned. "Nah," he said. "If someone made the help sign, you'd think they'd stay near it. If you don't see anyone, let's head back."

Simber soared over the sign once more. As they began turning back toward the ship, they heard an earsplitting roar. Out of the corner of his eye, Alex saw something move near the waterfall. He turned to see a huge, silver creature leap from a ledge on the mountainside and disappear into the overgrowth.

"What was that?" Simber growled. Whatever it was, it moved swiftly across the ground, leaving a battered trail of broken foliage in its wake.

Alex leaned forward to watch it as Simber circled back and followed the action from a safe height. A moment later a wild

LISA McMANN

pig shot out from the bushes onto the beach, running at top speed. The silver creature exploded from the brush, chasing after it. It lunged for the pig and tackled it, and with a roar and a squeal, the two went rolling across the sand.

"Holy gorillas!" Alex's heartbeat thrummed in his eardrums. He gripped Simber tightly around the neck and pressed his cheek against the cool stone. "I think that's what that thing is called, anyway," he said quietly. "But it's eight feet tall at least. And check out those teeth." Two saber-shaped fangs no less than six inches long curved downward from the gorilla's mouth.

The gorilla grabbed the squealing pig and got to his feet. The pig looked tiny in his hands. The beast roared again, gleaming fangs dripping with saliva, and brought the squealing pig toward its mouth.

Alex cringed and looked away just in time. The pig went silent.

When Alex dared look again, the gorilla was loping back through the overgrowth toward the mountain.

"Wow," Alex breathed. "That was intense."

Simber nodded. "Quite. I have a feeling that whoeverrr made that help sign—"

LISA McMANN

"Has long ago been eaten," Alex said. There was no doubt. No one could survive with a beast like that around.

Simber turned toward the water. "Maybe this is one island we can safely avoid in the futurrre."

"Definitely," Alex said.

As darkness fell, they flew back to the ship.

When they arrived, the Artiméans had gathered and were waiting for details.

"We heard a roar," Samheed said. "What happened? What did you see?"

Alex slid off Simber's wing and landed on the deck. "Oh, just a lush forest, sparkling waterfall, rugged mountain . . . and an eight-foot-tall saber-toothed mountain gorilla that hunted down a pig and killed it in about four seconds," he reported.

Lani grabbed his arm. "Are you serious?"

"Yep."

"Eight feet tall? No way. You can't be serious."

"It was huge, Lani."

"Saber-toothed?"

"Six-inch spears jutting down out of its face. Not kidding."

"Wow," Lani said, imagining it. "But it didn't *eat* the pig . . . did it?" Lani's face was aghast. "Gorillas aren't carnivorous."

"I admit I didn't watch that part," Alex said.

"It ate the pig," Simber confirmed. "Two bites."

As the captain continued guiding the ship toward home, Lani fielded questions from Fox and Kitten about what gorillas were supposed to look like. And Alex used some burned bits from one of the lamps to do a charcoal sketch on the deck of the monster he'd seen, fangs and all.

Later, as Samheed, Lani, Sky, and Alex lounged under the stars before falling asleep, Sky said, "It was such a beautiful island. I'm sad we can't ever visit there."

"Yeah," Alex said. "That waterfall looked refreshing."

They lay in silence for a while.

"I wonder if any of our spells would be strong enough to freeze the gorilla," Lani mused.

Alex and Samheed simultaneously shot her warning looks.

"No," Alex said.

"Not a chance," Samheed said. "Don't get any ideas."

Sky looked on, amused.

Lani smiled innocently at the stars. "It was just a thought.

Sheesh," she said. But it got her mind whirring. Perhaps she could come up with a special spell. . . .

One by one, their eyes fluttered closed and they drifted off to sleep.

By morning the sixth island was just a spot on the horizon behind them, and a new, tall rise of land greeted them from in front of the ship, still some distance away.

"Wow, it's island seven!" Crow said when he woke and saw it. "I can't believe we've seen all seven of them."

"It's pretty cool," Henry said. After breakfast and chores, they hung over the railing as they sailed by, not as close as they'd been to the sixth island. The others gathered to look at it too.

The seventh island, which was the one just east of Quill, jutted up from the water like a canister wearing a giant spiky crown. Lush growth sprouted from the top, with vines hanging between the spikes a short length down the side of the smooth vertical wall.

"I wonder how you get up there," Alex mused. "It looks impossible to climb."

"Look, there are birds circling above it," Ms. Octavia said. "And diving down to the water."

They could hear the cries of the sea birds, and watched as one particularly large-beaked bird flew just above the surface of the water and scooped up a fish without stopping, gulping it down its floppy gullet. They didn't seem alarmed to see Simber or the ship. They just went about their birdly business.

There seemed to be no way to access the island, and nothing was happening on it that they could see, so the Artiméans moved on without discussion.

By midafternoon, the seventh island was long gone, and the Artiméans grew anxious for signs of home. They were more than ready. And it was way past time.

A New Discovery

Aaron immersed himself in the jungle, spending the rest of the day training the panther to stay when he commanded her to. Whenever the panther obeyed, Aaron would pet her, and whenever she did not obey, Aaron ignored her and played with the little sharp-toothed dog that often spent time in the clearing near the tube.

Every now and then, when the panther would slink away or run off, and the dog and rock would nap, Aaron whiled away the time by fashioning things out of all the vines around him. He twisted long pieces together without any particular purpose in mind at first, but then noticed the connected vines resembled a large, long-legged spider.

Inspired, Aaron went in search of something that would make a good head for the spider. Eventually he settled on a ball of mud from the riverbank and a handful of acorns for the eyes. He used extra mud to hold everything together.

The rock watched with interest. And the panther seemed very curious as well. She didn't like it when Aaron spent time paying attention to other things, even when it was because she disappeared. And whenever the panther came bounding back to demand Aaron's attention, Aaron would work with her a bit more on the "down" command, until she did it ten times in a row, perfectly.

"That's excellent," Aaron praised, giving the panther an awkward hug. "You did it!"

The panther screamed in his face, pleased with herself as well.

Since things were progressing so well, and Aaron's forced seclusion in the secured palace was now only two days away, he decided to spend the night in the jungle—after all, he didn't have much time.

The next day, he worked on the "attack" command with the panther. This one was easier, since the panther seemed to prefer attacking things to sitting down. Aaron fashioned all sorts of fake enemies out of sticks, vines, and branches for the panther to go after, including an army of spider figures.

Quite often during the attack training, Aaron called out "Down!" to make sure the panther didn't forget that trick—the most important one. And the panther obeyed almost every time. It was the "almost" part that caused Aaron to panic. He wasn't sure why he was panicking, since he of course hated all Unwanteds and thought they probably deserved their fate. But the girl with the orange eyes that he'd seen in his brother's mansion right before the neighboring island attacked—she wasn't an Unwanted. He was sure of that. He'd have remembered her. So maybe she didn't deserve to die.

As much as he tried, he couldn't seem to feel good about the panther running around and randomly attacking people. He didn't want to witness that—it was too horrifying. He only wanted the panther to attack General Blair, and only if the general double-crossed Aaron and took over Artimé's mansion.

"I know what I need to do," he said to himself during a

break. The little dog came over and climbed in his lap and began nibbling on his fingers with his razor teeth. Aaron shook his hand free and stood up. "I need to make a General Blair decoy." And so he fashioned one from jungle materials and began calling it General Blair. He taught the panther the decoy's name, and lined the General Blair decoy up alongside the spiders and several other decoys Aaron had made.

"Panther," Aaron said to the panther, as he'd begun to call the creature, "attack General Blair!"

The panther bounded over to the lineup, hesitated, and grabbed the nearest spider, shaking its viny body in her teeth.

Aaron tried again, and again the panther attacked the decoy closest to her. Over and over, the panther started out with good intentions, or so Aaron surmised, but the temptation to attack the nearest object won out every time. When Aaron moved the General Blair decoy to the front of the pack, Panther attacked him soundly. But when Aaron moved him behind, the panther just couldn't ignore the easiest catch.

The rock watched with fascination. This was no doubt the most entertainment he'd seen since Marcus Today had extracted the giant hunk of ebony from his mouth.

"I have an idea," the rock interjected when Aaron collapsed to the ground after hours of failure. "Perhaps you should only use the command when the enemy you wish the panther to attack is nearest you."

Aaron sighed deeply, staring up at the canopy of leaves that held up the sky above him. Light was fading once more. Dirty, exhausted, and dejected, Aaron lay there for several minutes before admitting, "You're probably right."

The rock thought for a moment but decided to say no more. It moved away, down a path, leaving Aaron alone.

Aaron struggled to his feet and looked at the decoys, many of them mangled beyond recognition. Aaron picked up his original spider and petted the vines as if the creature were alive. He marveled over his ability to put these things together like this. He'd never done anything like it before—not in front of anybody, anyway. He'd never been caught as a child pretending the mop was a fluffy dog, or the worn old broom a hedgehog. Not even Alex knew about that.

He drew a hand over the spider's mudball head and vine body, thinking about what it would be like to have an animal companion. Certainly it would be better than any human friend.

The only thing human friends were good for was advancing one's self above them and fearing their revenge later. But an animal was no competition. *I wonder what it would be like if this spider came alive*, he thought. Could he make it happen? He knew he could fix the panther's tail by attaching a vine and concentrating on it becoming a part of the living creature . . . but what about starting with something that was completely not alive? It had to be impossible. Still, Aaron closed his eyes. *Come alive*, he thought, and pictured the spider moving about. *Come alive.*

The vines grew fuzzy under his fingers. Aaron opened his eyes and let out a horrified shout as the spider began moving in his hands. He threw it to the jungle floor and moved backward to get away from it. The spider found its legs and ran frightened down the path that led deep into the jungle. Soon it had disappeared.

"What the—good grief!" he cried. He wiped his hands on his pants, trying to get the creepy crawling sensation off them, and then stood there alone for a long moment, contemplating what had just happened. And wondering anew just what exactly he was capable of.

LISA McMANN

In the Middle of the Night

I t was dark in the jungle when Aaron decided it was time to go. He hadn't quite accomplished what he'd wanted to, teaching the panther to stay down and attack on command, but in a way, he discovered much more about himself than he'd ever imagined. Still reeling from bringing the spider to life, he stumbled back to the tube and pressed the button. From the mansion, he quickly continued on to Haluki's closet, then made his way through the dark house and outside, into the pressing heat. There was very little breeze tonight, and Aaron was surprised by how much he missed the cooler air they'd had since the wall came down.

He walked up the road to the palace and slipped through the portcullis and past the sleeping guards, reminding himself to send them to the Ancients Sector in the morning for not doing their jobs. As he approached the palace, he looked up. The windows in the tower were dark—Liam must be asleep. Inside the entryway, all was dark and quiet. Even the interior guards were away from their posts. Aaron could hear them rummaging around in the kitchen for food. At least they were awake, but they shouldn't all leave their posts at once. Aaron frowned. If he sent them to the Ancients Sector too, he'd run out of guards.

No matter, Aaron thought, and shrugged. By morning the place would be teeming with Quillitary soldiers, shuttering Aaron inside "for protection," or so General Blair said, as the rest of the Quillitary attacked Artimé. But Aaron knew differently. He was being imprisoned. Kept out of the way until Blair was safely in charge of everything.

Aaron thought briefly about disappearing back into the jungle, but he feared his absence in the morning would tip off General Blair that something wasn't right. And Aaron needed General Blair to attack and take over Artimé—Aaron couldn't do that alone. So all he could do was sit tight and wait it out, and then, when he was free to move about Quill once more, he would go back to the jungle, round up Panther, and make his move.

But first he desperately needed sleep.

On the way to his sleeping quarters, he stopped in his office and saw a roughly scribbled note from Liam, who was still quite new at writing. *Didn't see you today. Hope all is okay for big day tomorrow.*

Aaron crumpled up the paper and tossed it on the floor. Liam was a bit of a moron, which was good, because it probably meant that he'd forgotten the uncomfortable conversation they'd had the other day, the memory of which made Aaron's stomach churn. But Liam was loyal. That was more than Aaron could say for Secretary, he supposed. He had never known exactly where she stood, even to the end. What had she been doing in Artimé, anyway? He still had no idea.

Aaron sat down and began emptying his pockets of spells into his desk drawer, then thought the better of it and reloaded them in case things got ugly with the Quillitary in the morning. He closed the drawer and straightened his desk, his thoughts once more turning to the spider in the jungle. Had he really made it come alive? Every time he returned from the jungle, he doubted what had really gone on there. It never seemed real when he was surrounded by the lifeless gray walls of the palace. It was almost as if Quill had been dulled purposely to dampen everyone's imagination and will. In Quill, nothing really seemed possible. In the jungle, everything did.

Aaron pinched his eyes shut, knowing he was exhausted and not thinking clearly. But he couldn't leave his thoughts of the spider behind. When an idea occurred to him, he looked around the sparse room. He got up from his chair and walked to the closet, opening it wide and looking at the box of junk he'd stashed there when he took over the palace—Haluki's junk, which he'd never gotten around to throwing away. He pulled the heavy box out of the closet and carried it to his desk, setting it down hard.

He looked inside, wondering if he'd find anything he could shape or mold into a creature. "I wonder," he muttered. "Can I make a living creature here in Quill? Or is there something about the jungle that gave me the powers?"

He picked up an ugly gargoyle statue with a silly pink ribbon tied to one horn and set her down on the desk, then rummaged

357 « Island of Shipwrecks

LISA McMANN

through the rest of the stuff, finding only a few books and writing utensils. Nothing pliable. Nothing with which to make an animal. "Drat."

He tossed the box on the floor and looked again at the statue, narrowing his eyes. "You look fairly harmless," he said, "though extremely ugly." She wouldn't be his own creation, but he could at least see if his powers to make her come alive worked here in Quill.

The statue returned his stare with a blank one of her own.

Aaron picked her up and turned her around, inspecting her all over. He shrugged and closed his eyes, placing his hand on her back, and concentrated on her. "Come alive," he said, picturing her walking across his desk. "Live."

The statue didn't move. Aaron opened his eyes, and found her staring at him just as before, frozen and dead.

His heart sank. Maybe he wasn't as powerful as he'd thought. There must have been something magical in the jungle that had given him the ability. He frowned and made a face at the gargoyle.

Just then, his office door burst open. Before he could turn his head to see what was happening, the lights went out and

LISA McMANN

footsteps thundered all around him. He heard the zing of swords being pulled from their sheaths, and the clash of them striking walls and the desk. Aaron froze, letting the statue slip from his fingers. She clattered to the desk. A cold piece of metal slid across Aaron's throat and a muscled arm pulled him backward against an enormous man's chest. In the moment he was so shocked he didn't utter a sound, and so afraid of the steel at his neck that he dared not make a noise once he felt capable again. His chest heaved uncontrollably.

Someone barked an order, and in seconds Aaron was blinded by a bright light pointed directly at his eyes. Beyond the light, he could see shadows of a number of men. Instinctively he reached for the spells in his pockets, but the man holding him grabbed his arms and wrested them behind his back.

Aaron's shoulder popped and he squealed in pain.

The man turned his sword on Aaron's neck, introducing a sharp point, and pressed it hard into Aaron's skin. "Shut up," the man growled. "Don't move."

Aaron froze.

"Well?" said the captor in a gruff voice to his companions. "Is it him, or isn't it?"

Aaron heard the rustle of a paper as someone held it up next to his face in the light. He gulped and stared into the light, his Adam's apple rolling along the sharp point at his neck.

"Aye, it's him all right, Captain."

The captain chuckled evilly. "Let's be gone, then."

They shoved Aaron to the floor and gagged him, and four of them each took a limb and hung him between them, facedown. Aaron's injured shoulder burned like fire, and he felt like his arms and legs were going to pull right out of their sockets. He fought to keep from crying out, muffled though his shouts would be, fearing retaliation.

They carried him out of the office and down the stairs, past the empty entryway and the room where they'd locked up the guards when they'd first snuck in hours before, and out the door into the night. They crossed over the driveway and skidded down the rocky bank to the water. And then, on three, they threw Aaron face-first into a small boat. There wasn't time for Aaron to swing his arms around to brace his fall. His head hit the wooden seat, and his body crumpled to the damp floor. Everything went black and quiet.

» » « «

Inside Aaron's office, Matilda picked herself up, climbed down the desk, ran to the wall, and jumped as high as she could, straining to reach the window ledge. When she finally managed to get a fingerhold on the sill, she pulled herself up and scrambled to her feet, watching as a group of small boats pushed off the shore toward a large pirate ship that sat in the calm water.

She stayed there, keeping watch, as the large ship pulled up all but one of the smaller boats and set sail, heading east.

A quarter of the way around the south side of the island, another gargoyle stood on a window ledge watching, waiting for the ship to pass.

Preparing for a Civil War

A t dawn Meghan, Carina, Ms. Morning, Gunnar Haluki, and Mr. Appleblossom gathered their troops and sent them to their stations to wait for the surprise attack that wasn't really a surprise. This was thanks to Liam, who had paid another visit to Meghan three days prior, letting her know that the Quillitary was coming. It was quite a bit sooner than anyone in Artimé had expected, considering that the wall had not come down all the way.

Meghan wondered if Aaron had gotten word that Artimé was suspicious, and had decided to leave the wall destruction to the Necessaries and put the Quillitary on order to attack. Liam hedged a bit, saying he thought it was more likely the Quillitary who was making decisions, but he didn't know much.

"Are you saying the Quillitary is running this attack, not Aaron?" Meghan had asked him.

"Truly, I don't know," he said. He looked more uncomfortable than ever.

That left Meghan puzzled, but it was all she could get out of him before he'd hurried away. Still, she was grateful for the information.

Now, as the leaders stood in the mansion to confer before joining their teams, Charlie the gargoyle tugged at Ms. Morning's component vest.

"Not right now, Charlie," Ms. Morning said, distracted. "Unless you've caught sight of Alex and Simber and the ship—have you?"

Charlie shook his head.

"Too bad. We could use them. Any other emergencies or imminent danger?"

Charlie thought for a moment, and then shrugged and shook his head again.

LISA McMANN

"We'll talk after this confrontation is over, then, all right? Head upstairs and stay safe."

Charlie nodded and climbed back up the steps to Alex's office, where he spent so much of his time.

"Everybody ready?" Meghan asked. She'd stepped into her new leadership role as a Magical Warrior trainer in Florence's absence, and she was very good at her job. Now she stood alongside Ms. Morning, the commander in chief, as an equal. She was armed, dangerous, totally committed, and prepared to fight to the death for Artimé. This young woman who stood by the front door of the mansion today was a far cry from the scared little red-haired girl who had arrived on the property at age thirteen. Meghan Ranger was muscular and cunning. She knew it, and she was proud of it. She only hoped she was cunning enough to keep Artimé's losses to a minimum and lead her people to victory.

Claire looked around at the other leaders and nodded solemnly. "Yes, we're ready. Let's go." They followed Meghan out of the mansion.

Several teams sat upon the lawn, looking quite like they were having a normal day enjoying the weather and each other's company. They were seated this way to give the Quillitary a sense that Artimé was not expecting an attack. But each group was set up behind a magical glass wall, which created clear barriers that were undetectable from a distance. These groups were on high alert, ready to fight at a second's notice.

Other teams lined the border, stationed high up in the trees that had once helped to camouflage the ugly gray wall. Squirrelicorns circled now and then as they often did, this time prepared to report to their groups in the trees any change in the status in Quill.

Still other fighters remained on alert inside the mansion, prepared to attack if the enemy got in, ready to defend their home at all costs.

The absence of Simber left everyone just a little bit unsettled. Surely the Quillitary would notice he wasn't there, and no doubt they would take advantage of it. There was a chance they wouldn't notice the absence of other key fighters, including Alex, at least not right away. Meghan could only hope that Artimé's weaknesses were not exposed too soon. She'd done everything in her power to design this defense, and lives depended on it working right.

Claire and Mr. Appleblossom climbed into neighboring trees near the traditional entrance to Artimé, where the gate had once been. There was no sign of the Quillitary from there.

"I certainly hope we weren't given false information," Claire said.

Mr. Appleblossom smiled at his longtime friend. "In ages past we'd climb these trees for fun. What matter is it, if it's all for none?"

Claire couldn't help but grin. "You're right of course, Siggy. There's nothing to lose by making this a practice run."

The warriors of Artimé bided their time through the slow morning hours, watching, waiting, and listening for the squeals and chugs of the Quillitary vehicles. And just when they thought Liam's warning was fake, a squirrelicorn darted to Meghan's side. Meghan signaled to Claire, Claire whispered to a party stationed on the ground, and someone from that party whispered to someone in the next party, and so on and so forth all across the lawn, until someone slipped inside the mansion to alert those inside.

"They're coming."

Gondoleery Makes
a Move

When Gondoleery finally got around to being curious about the planned attack on Artimé, she left her house and made her way to the palace to see how Aaron was handling things. She heard a loud boom as she walked. The ground shook below her feet. "Stupid wall," she muttered.

Quillitary vehicles whizzed past her at speeds she'd never seen before. Some headed to the palace, others toward Artimé. Gondoleery sighed. They just didn't learn. Artimé wasn't a land of stupid people, and it was a big mistake to treat them as such. They'd be ready for the Quillitary, no doubt.

LISA McMANN

"Now," she muttered, "if only I could get everyone in the same place."

She shoved past the groggy-looking guards at the portcullis and raised a newly redrawn eyebrow at the throng of soldiers who stood alert, guarding the palace.

"What's happening?" Gondoleery asked, walking up to them.

"We're safeguarding the palace, Governor. Protecting the high priest from potential attacks."

Gondoleery snorted. "Well, that's a relief." She approached the door. "Let me in," she said to the soldier standing there.

He hesitated, looked to his superior, who snarled at him, and stepped aside to let her in.

Gondoleery entered and looked around. The entry area was empty. Shrugging, she clumped up the stairs and went down the hall to Aaron's office. Empty as well. Papers were scattered on the floor. Gondoleery frowned and went in. She scrutinized the papers to see if there was any useful information, and then walked to the window where a statue stood, and peered out. There were soldiers surrounding the palace as far as she could see.

After a minute, Gondoleery left the office and listened at the rickety stairway that led up to Liam's room, but she could only hear a light snoring sound echoing from the tower. She turned around and went to the conference room, finding the oil press standing alone on the table. Aaron wasn't there, either. She slunk down the hall to Aaron's sleeping quarters. The door stood open, and the room was dark.

"Aaron?" Gondoleery called. There was no answer. Where was he?

Gondoleery scratched her head and began to chuckle, just as Liam descended the stairs from his room, yawning.

"Good morning, Gondoleery," Liam said. "It appears I've slept late this morning. Is, ah, is anything new going on in Quill? Or anywhere else?" He'd tossed and turned until very late, finally falling into a hard sleep. Now he fought to hide his anxiety as well as his knowledge of the attack on Artimé, for he didn't know how much Gondoleery knew about it.

"Oh, there's something new all right," Gondoleery said with a laugh. "General Blair has apparently taken great pains to protect the high priest, as you'll see by the scores of soldiers surrounding the palace. But no one actually bothered to make

LISA McMANN

sure the high priest was inside it before they locked it down."

Liam frowned. "What? You mean Aaron's not here?"

"I certainly can't find him. Have a look for yourself. He's given them the slip! I didn't think he had it in him. People are surprising me left and right these days." She shook her head and laughed again. "Shall we break the news to them, or just let them discover it on their own?"

Liam paled. This wasn't part of the plan. Where had Aaron gone? The only place he could think of was Artimé, to fight. He was surprised Aaron hadn't confided this plan to him, and he wondered now if Aaron really did trust him as much as he seemed to. "Are—are you sure?"

Gondoleery shrugged and filed a fingernail on her teeth. "I said have a look yourself—wait, what's that?" She tilted her head toward the stairwell that led down to the entryway. "Do you hear something?"

There was a faint pounding coming from behind the closed door to the servants' kitchen. Liam looked at Gondoleery, then ran down the stairs and to the door. He tried opening it, but it was stuck. He slammed up against it, but it wouldn't budge.

"Who's in there?" he shouted.

The reply was a muffled series of shouts and groans. Liam ran to get something with which to leverage the door, and tried wedging it into the casement. The rotting wood split and the broken door fell open.

Before him, six guards lay gagged and tied.

"Gondoleery!" Liam called. "Come quickly!"

He began working to unfasten the knotted rope around the first guard's wrists and ankles. The rope was stiff, like new—unlike any rope Quill had seen in decades, he was sure.

Gondoleery appeared in the doorway, but she didn't deign to help. Instead she peppered the guards with questions once a few of them were able to remove their gags.

"Who did this? When did it happen? Where's Aaron?"

The head guard coughed, trying to speak. Liam rushed to get him a cup of water from the bucket while Gondoleery continued with more questions. "Did the Quillitary do this? Or did Aaron? What is going on here?"

Finally, the guard could speak. "Neither. We were ambushed last evening. Twenty or more strangers broke in and overtook us. They shoved us in here and tied us up. A few hours later we heard another scuffle, then nothing more

LISA McMANN

until you found us." He coughed. "We don't know who they were, but it wasn't the Quillitary. And I don't know where the high priest is, or if he was involved. I heard a muffled shout that sounded like him last evening, and then silence. I can only guess he was captured and taken away."

Liam and Gondoleery exchanged looks.

"Captured?" Gondoleery asked slowly. "Taken away?"

The words sank in. With a strange look on her face, Gondoleery turned and walked out of the room. At the door leading outside she paused, her singed fingertips on the handle. And then a wicked smile spread across her face. She opened the door, looked over her shoulder at Liam.

"Governor," she said, "you are relieved of your duties. I'm taking over as high priest, and I declare that your time in Quill is done. Please make your way to the Ancients Sector."

Liam's mouth fell open. His stomach knotted with fear. He gripped the banister as sweat broke out on his forehead, and the knot in his stomach twisted and churned. "What?" he whispered.

Gondoleery cackled. "You heard me." She turned to go once more, when a flurry of activity stopped her in the open doorway. A small group of bedraggled Necessaries was running up the driveway, covered in rock-wall dust, fresh wounds bleeding through torn bits of clothing. Some carried children.

Gondoleery sneered. "What do you want?" she asked the first one to reach her.

"There was an accident, Governor! The last section of the wall collapsed. It fell inward, on top of the workers, and it crushed several houses."

Gondoleery sighed. "What a shame."

"Rows twenty-five through twenty-seven in the Necessaries Sector are completely demolished!"

"What do you want me to do about it?" Gondoleery tilted her head as if she hadn't a clue.

"Tell the high priest, for one!" cried the Necessary. He looked around desperately at the stragglers behind him.

A man approached, carrying two crying toddlers. "These children are orphans—their parents died in the collapse."

Gondoleery looked at the children like they were diseased animals. "Well, I surely don't want them," she said.

The man sighed, exasperated. "They aren't for you, they're for the high priest—"

"That's what we're trying to tell you," interrupted the first. "The high priest's father was working on the wall when it collapsed. And it crushed their house, where his wife was with the children. The Stowes—they're both dead, you see. We pulled the babies from the rubble. They're the high priest's sisters."

"I'm sure he would want to look after them," said another Necessary.

Gondoleery stared at them.

Liam stared at Gondoleery, still in shock from what happened earlier, and now this. . . .

Gondoleery looked from one bloody, bruised face to the next. "Aaron's sisters, you say?" she asked slowly.

"Yes," said the first Necessary. He took one of the girls and held her out to Gondoleery.

She narrowed her eyes, but took the child gingerly in her arms, and then reached out for the other, a look of disgust apparent on her face. "I'll see to it that Aaron gets them," she said. "Soldiers," she said to the Quillitary members stationed by the door, "please escort the Necessaries outside the palace gates where they belong."

She didn't wait for the Necessaries or the soldiers to

respond. Instead she stepped back into the palace and closed the door with her foot. Then she shoved the twins into Liam's arms. "Here."

Startled, he took them. "What am I supposed to do with babies?"

"You'll take them with you to the Ancients Sector," Gondoleery said. She wiped her hands on her blouse, then opened the door to make sure the Necessaries were gone and stepped out once more. "Let the proprietor know I want all three of you put to sleep by morning."

Liam gaped. Gondoleery slammed the palace door, shoved past the Quillitary guards, and got into an awaiting vehicle. Through the window he could see her barking orders, and soon the jalopy roared off. He looked at the girls. One of them tugged at his ear, and the other began to fuss. "Mama," she whimpered.

"What in Quill?" Liam whispered, and a fearful breath escaped him. *Babies? To the Ancients Sector?* No one had ever heard such a heartless command, not even in Quill. Liam's eyes darted around the palace, from the empty staircase to the servants' kitchen where half a dozen guards had heard every command given by the new self-declared high priest. They would see to it that her wishes were carried out—that was the way of Quill. His chest tightened, and he could taste something sour burning his throat. Gondoleery was a monster. A monster who was now in control of Quill. And Liam and these babies would be dead by morning.

He had no choice in Quill but to obey. He tightened his grip on the twins as first one then the other began to cry. "Shh," Liam said. He glanced up the steps.

Seeing Liam's hesitation, the lead guard cleared his throat and approached, followed by two more. "We'll arrange your ride," the lead guard said, his voice cold as ice.

Liam whipped his head around at the sound, his eyes wild and panicked.

When the guard opened the door to call for a driver, Liam darted out, twins in tow. He broke through the confused line of Quillitary soldiers and ran across the driveway, half sliding, half hopping down the bank toward the sea, knowing that his wasn't the only life that depended on his stamina and speed. And hoping against hope that the thundering of footsteps behind him that grew louder by the second would stop . . . or he was never going to make it.

Home at Long Last

They'd spotted Quill at dawn looming large on the horizon, and now it was only a matter of time before Alex and the team would be home. Alex stood with his friends at the bow, the sun warming their backs, their faces to the breeze, thinking about their soft beds and all the wonderful food in the kitchen awaiting them.

"I'm going to collapse in my room and order up everything on the menu," Samheed said. "I'm glad Ishibashi-san gave us all these fruits and vegetables, but I'm hungry for some real food."

"Me too," Lani said. "And ready for home cooking."

Alex's stomach growled thinking about it. He could just barely see the top of the mansion reflecting the morning light. But he was anxious, too. "I hope everything's okay." He glanced at Simber overhead.

"It seems quiet," Simber said. "People arrre sitting on the lawn. Earrrlierrr I saw a cloud of dust rrrise up frrrom the farrr side of the island. I'll bet that was anotherrr chunk of the wall coming down."

Alex shook his head, trying to imagine Quill without its wall. "What else can you see?"

Simber flapped his wings. "I'm not surrre what to think of this, but at dawn I could see the outline of a pirrrate ship behind us, heading east. We must have passed it durrring the night."

"Strange," murmured Alex. "Or maybe not. I've never seen another one, but that doesn't mean they aren't out here sometimes."

Simber was quiet for a moment, and then he said, "Look towarrrd Arrrtimé. Tell me if you see something."

Alex and the others did so.

"There's a tiny sparkle," Henry said.

LISA McMANN

"A bunch of them," Sky said. "They're all over the lawn."

Alex nodded. "I see them too." He looked up. "What do you think it is, Simber? Can you tell?"

"I've been seeing the little glints of light forrr some time, and I think I've just figurrred out what they arrre."

Alex held his hand up to his eyes to protect them from the glare on the water, straining to see Artimé. "What are they?"

"They'rrre glass shields," Simber said. "The people on the lawn arrre all sitting behind them. We'rrre seeing the sunlight rrreflected off them as we move along."

Alex leaned forward. "Why would they all be sitting behind—" He stopped short, and then, along with Samheed and Lani, said, "Ohhh." The three friends looked at each other as the realization came over them.

Samheed looked up at Simber. "What's going on?"

"I think they arrre expecting company. And not just us."

Alex's heart raced. "Do you think Quill is going to attack? Like, now?"

Simber focused intently on the things no one else could see. After a minute, his eyes widened.

"What is it?" Alex asked.

LISA McMANN

"Therrre's a steady strrream of dust rrrising frrrom left to rrright on the nearrr side of the island," Simber said slowly. "The kind of dust a line of vehicles would make if they werrre headed frrrom the Quillitarrry yarrrd towarrrd Arrrtimé." He looked down at Alex. "I think they'rrre on theirrr way."

"Alex," Samheed said. "We have to do something."

Alex nodded. "I know. I'm thinking." He looked all around the ship, seeing Florence leaning forward and listening. He ran to her side. "They're going to need our help. The ship is at full speed—I think I should go ahead with Simber. What do you think?"

"Absolutely," Florence said. "Take a few others with you— as many as Simber can hold."

Alex nodded. "Okay. That feels right." He turned back to the group at the bow and considered his options.

"Samheed, Lani, and Henry, I want you guys to come with me."

They nodded.

"Everybody else," Alex said, "hand over whatever spell components you have left. Once you reach the lagoon, Florence will assess the situation and give you instructions, and, Ms. Octavia?

I need you to stay on board and guard the ship."

"Of course," the octogator said.

The components were gathered into a miserable little heap on the deck. Lani sorted them and handed them out, leaving a few for Ms. Octavia in case the Quillitary decided to attack the ship. Alex arranged his components in his pockets the way he liked them, wishing for ten times the number, then signaled to Simber that he was ready.

Simber dipped a wing. Alex grabbed hold of it and vaulted onto Simber's back. He scooted forward so Lani, Samheed, and Henry could hop on behind him.

As soon as Henry was settled, Simber called out, "Hold on tightly!" And they were off, soaring at Simber's top speed. He updated them as they flew with whatever details he could make out. The closer they drew to Artimé, the more alarmed Simber's voice became, for he could see clearly now that Artimé was indeed under a severe attack.

"The Quillitarrry is sprrread acrrross the entirrre southerrrn shorrre of the island," Simber said. "They'rrre attacking frrrom vehicles and on foot!"

Alex could hardly see—the wind was making his eyes water

LISA McMANN

furiously. He wiped them and tried again. They were closing in now, and Alex could make out the figures on the lawn, fighting from behind their glass shields. Quillitary soldiers waving their rusty metal weapons were everywhere, running and plowing into glass shields with their vehicles, causing all sorts of problems, but Alex could tell Artimé was holding its own by the number of frozen Quillitary soldiers on the grounds. Every now and then he saw a body flying backward and sticking to a tree or the side of a vehicle with scatterclips.

Alex turned to address Samheed, Lani, and Henry. "Let's make our first pass from the air. Get ready to pepper them with whatever spells we have, and keep your aim measured and tight—we don't want to waste anything. Sound good so far?"

The three agreed that it did.

"Great. Who has a large stash of components in their room and can get access to them fast?"

"I do," Samheed said.

"Okay, perfect. So we'll make that first pass, then when we get near the mansion, we'll drop Sam off and keep fighting with our remaining spells until Sam comes back with components. Clear?"

"Clear," the three called out.

"Simber?" Alex prompted.

"Got it," said the cat.

The next minutes dragged by, Alex clutching Simber's neck and leaning forward, as if that would propel them even faster. He hated the Quillitary's presence on his land. It made him furious to see his people having to risk their lives without him right by their sides. "Hurry up, Sim," he muttered, not intending for Simber to hear him, but realizing too late that of course he did—he always did.

Instead of getting angry, Simber risked a glance at the mage and nodded. "It feels terrribly helpless, doesn't it?"

Alex let out a deep sigh. "Yeah," he said. He patted Simber's neck.

"We'rrre moments away." He began his descent and circled, then called out, "Coming in frrrom east to west. Lining them up forrr you—no extrrra charrrge."

Alex heard nervous laughs behind him. You could count on Simber to lighten the mood during the intense times. It made Alex feel more relaxed. Mentally he planned out his spell lineup and grabbed the first two components.

LISA McMANN

Simber swooped in, almost unnoticed by anyone on the ground because they were all concentrated on their battles, and one by one, the four excellent spell casters on Simber's back released their components and rendered four soldiers useless. A second later, four more went down.

When the Artiméans on the lawn realized what was happening, a cheer rose up. Their mage had returned.

Alex, Lani, Samheed, and Henry didn't stop. They shot off another round, and another, all the way along the southern shore into Quill, until they were almost out of components.

"Back to the mansion," Alex called out. "Samheed, be ready to run!"

"Got it!" Samheed slid to the end of Simber's wing as the statue swooped down, and he jumped off, hitting the ground running.

Simber lifted off again, and the three remaining on his back continued firing components until they ran out. Once Alex's supply was depleted, he was able to sit back and look out over the island, trying to spot areas of trouble. He spied Meghan near the mansion, but she was too busy fighting to notice them.

After a minute, Samheed burst out of the mansion, his pockets bulging and a burlap sack in one hand. He fought off the Quillitary with spell after spell from his free hand, waiting for Simber to find an open spot to swoop in. Unable to get through the crowd to hop onto Simber's back, Samheed finally gave up.

"Here!" he shouted, and tossed the sack of components to Lani so they could continue fighting from the air. "Go on without me—I'll stay down here!"

Lani caught the sack, and Simber flew up and away to take on soldiers farther inland.

Samheed reloaded and glanced around, trying to figure out where his allies were. He spotted Meghan and shouted to her.

She looked up, surprised and pleased, though there wasn't time for niceties at the moment, seeing as she was nearly surrounded and a trickle of blood was blocking her vision in one eye. She took out the nearest soldiers and glanced back at Samheed, who was moving toward her.

"Are you okay?" Samheed asked, seeing the blood. He took out two more soldiers and muscled through the throng of fighters, narrowly avoiding a crack to the head with a

LISA McMANN

rusty iron rod. Once through, he raced to her side.

"I'm fine. Feel like giving me a hand?" She shot him a wry grin. It was good to see her friend after so long.

"I suppose," Samheed said. He reached out to give her shoulder a squeeze and gave her a kiss on the cheek while simultaneously tossing a pin cushion spell at a soldier nearby. The soldier convulsed in pain from hundreds of pinpricks. "You didn't have to go through all this trouble just to welcome us home, you know."

"We do things right here in Artimé," she replied. "It's incredibly good to see you."

"You too. Is Sean all right?" Samheed whirled around to toss scatterclips at a soldier running toward him, sending the chap flying backward toward Quill. He faced Meghan now, and hastily froze two young Quillitary soldiers heading toward Mr. Appleblossom, who left his tree and was fighting on the grounds nearby.

"He's better than when he got here," Meghan said over the din of clashing metal. "Still in the hospital wing."

An attacker sliced into Meghan's arm, which made her furious. She sent her to the ground with a dagger spell to make her regret it. When Meghan turned back toward Samheed to express her disgust, she gasped. Looking over Samheed's shoulder, she saw a stealthy figure coming up in the distance behind him. And when she caught sight of the man's face, she grabbed Samheed by the shirt. "Samheed!" she screamed. "Look out!"

The General's Vendetta

Samheed whirled around, components drawn and ready to cast, and then he gasped too. Not twenty feet away was a small group of soldiers advancing on him and Meghan, weapons poised. And behind them stood a man, a head taller than the rest. The man's eyes bulged and his nostrils flared.

"General Blair," Samheed whispered.

Meghan gulped and whispered back. "I see him. I thought he was dead." She came to her senses and pulled some components from her pocket. "I'll take the left guards, you take the right, and I'll leave you the honors of handling the general."

"I appreciate that," Samheed said. He looked at the components in his hands and then shoved them into his pocket, opting for a different arsenal. He chose the components he wanted. "Ready?" he said under his breath. "Go."

One after another, he and Meghan sent four guards flying backward, pinning them to the nearest trees, and four guards running screaming into the sea. And all the while, General Blair, a wild look in his eye, advanced as if nothing were happening to his group of protectors. Finally Samheed reloaded and pulled his arm back to take out the general, but the general was quicker. He held a circular piece of jagged metal in one hand and a pistol in the other.

"Don't move or you're dead," the general said, his voice thundering loud enough for people all around them to hear. The angry scar on his neck pulsed with each word.

Samheed froze.

"You see this weapon here? It has your initials on it, Burkesh. I found it imbedded deep inside my neck."

The general held Samheed's throwing star.

"I've come to return it. Now put your weapons down and take what you deserve!"

LISA McMANN

"He's gone mad," Samheed muttered.

"Stay still," Meghan whispered. "Can you put up a glass shield without moving?"

"Good idea." Samheed concentrated and whispered, "Glass." A shield appeared in front of him. Immediately Meghan moved to the edge of it and without hesitating, fired off a heart attack spell.

A nearby soldier jumped in its path, took the hit, and fell to the ground. She shuddered and was silent.

"Don't make me angry!" the general roared. And before anyone could figure out what was happening, there was an ear-splitting blast. The glass exploded and shattered at Samheed's feet.

Meghan screamed and moved to Samheed's side, fumbling with her pockets.

General Blair fired the gun again, but there was only a click.

Samheed saw his chance and searched his pockets for the spell he needed to finish the general off. But he'd shoved components in his pockets so quickly and without any planning that he couldn't find what he needed. At last his fingers landed on the familiar heart shapes. He snatched them up.

Fuming, General Blair tossed the pistol aside. He switched the throwing star to his right hand, reared back, and let it fly. At the same time, Samheed wound up and sent two heart attack spells soaring.

Meghan looked up just in time. "No!" she yelled. She leaped into the air, shoving Samheed aside as his heart attack spells hit the general square in the chest.

The man's eyes widened, and his shaking hands gripped his shirt. At the very same moment, the throwing star found its mark, sticking fast into Meghan's chest. Without a sound, she tumbled to the ground in a heap.

The shuddering General Blair dropped to his knees, gasping for breath, and fell forward, his face in the lawn. The onlookers from both sides began shouting. They burst into an intense battle, fighting for their lives and their honor.

"Meg!" Samheed cried. He staggered to his feet, fell, and crawled toward her, but the enemy was quickly closing in around him and he couldn't reach her. He lunged for more components, sending a round of heart attack spells at every soldier in range, and planted two more in the general's back to make sure the job was done.

LISA McMANN

A cry went up from a Quillitary soldier. "They've killed the general! Fight to the finish!"

"Simber!" screamed Samheed in a horrible voice no one had ever heard before. Finally he was able to stand. A new wave of soldiers approached, slashing the air, trying to get a piece of him. He ducked and darted away from their lashings, and began shooting off lethal versions of scatterclips. "Die a thousand deaths!" he cried with every throw, and one by one each scatterclip caused the fall of another Quillitary soldier. Yet behind each fallen soldier was another to take his place.

From the roof of the mansion, Carina heard Samheed's cry for help. She shouted for Simber and began pelting the soldiers from her spot up high. Heart attack spell after heart attack spell went soaring, and lethal scatterclips went flying as fast as Carina and Samheed could send them.

"Somebody please get Meghan out of here!" Samheed begged, his voice hoarse, but the battle was so fierce that no one could pause for a moment to help any of the wounded. He was sure she'd been trampled, and there was nothing he could do but fight to stay alive.

Finally Simber swooped in, and Alex, Lani, and Henry all

jumped to the ground and began casting lethal spells alongside a bruised, broken, and bloody Samheed. The fight continued to rage with wave after wave of soldiers running to attack the person who had killed their general, until there were only a handful of Quillitary soldiers left alive.

As their components dwindled along with the enemy's numbers, Ms. Morning and Mr. Appleblossom finished off the remaining Quillitary near the former gate area and ran toward Samheed and the others to assist. There they helped finish the battle. The last soldier went down with a deathly poem from Mr. Appleblossom.

And then the world was silent.

Heaving and gasping for breath that wouldn't come, Samheed sought out Lani, and then his eyes rolled back into his head and he crumpled to the ground next to Meghan. Neither of them moved.

And then, in the very moment that all the friends rushed in to help Meghan and Samheed, the land beneath their feet turned slick. Not with the blood of their enemies or friends, but with a thick layer of blinding white ice—ice from the veins of the most evil one of all. Gondoleery Rattrapp.

393 « Island of Shipwrecks

Artiméans everywhere slipped off their feet and went sprawling, landing hard. Quillens, too, apart from the fighting, were frozen inside their homes or fell while doing their jobs. The few Quillitary soldiers who had survived the battle now watched in horror as their vehicles slid off the road and skidded down the embankments to the frozen shoreline. And the pirate ship nearing the lagoon in Artimé stopped short, its hull encased in a sea of ice.

Aaron in Trouble

It was midday before Aaron gained consciousness. When he could pry his swollen eyelids open, he found himself flung out across a bench in a little fishing boat, alone, bouncing and churning and lurching against the waves. His stomach lurched too, but there was nothing more than bile inside it to expel.

His face throbbed. Gingerly he reached up to touch it. His skin was on fire. It was more pain than he'd ever known. Every rise and fall of the boat caused his sight to waver and his nose to feel like it was going to explode. He pushed himself up and peered fearfully over the lip of the vessel's side, and then he sat up and gripped the bench. The sea swam before his eyes, and briny water sloshed about at his feet. The only solid thing in sight was the pirate ship, to which his little fishing boat was attached by a heavy gold chain.

He could hear voices coming from above him, on board the ship, but he couldn't make out any words. "Hey," Aaron said, but little sound came from his parched throat. His bottom lip was split, he could feel it. "I'm the . . . I'm the high priest. . . ."

Every effort to remain conscious took more out of him, and eventually Aaron gave up. He sank back to the floor of the boat and closed his eyes.

The Queen of Ice

Almost no one on the island of Quill had ever seen ice before. It felt cold before it stung, and with little warning it became awful to touch. Alex, who went down hard on his back, caught his breath and scrambled to his feet, and promptly slipped and fell again. "What's going on?" he whispered to Simber, who was splayed out, legs in all directions.

"I don't know," Simber said under his breath. He flapped his wings to help him get to his feet.

From somewhere in Quill, a dark, magical, thunderous

LISA McMANN

voice rang out above all other sound on the island, and spread beyond to the icy circle of the sea around it.

"Greetings, my people," boomed the voice.

Claire Morning froze. "Who *is* that?"

Mr. Appleblossom shook his head.

"I am your new high priest," the voice said. "I want to take a moment to thank Artimé for destroying the Quillitary. I didn't care which side won, I just wanted one of you out of the way. So it's Artimé I welcome back into the fold—you are a part of Quill once more. We are a complete nation again."

She paused. No one moved.

"Enjoy the ice," she said. "It's my little way to keep you all *safe* until I get my kingdom sorted out. It's only temporary. Probably. Or maybe not."

Alex and Sky exchanged horrified glances.

"I'll keep you informed. Try not to freeze to death in your little ice desert." With that, the booming voice faded away.

Those near Alex turned their frightened eyes to him. He stared back, rapidly trying to figure out what was happening.

"Okay," he said. "I don't know who that was. We'll figure it out. But first we need to take care of our injured. I need a

LISA McMANN

team to somehow get to the mansion door and wait for Simber and the squirrelicorns to airlift our wounded and deliver them to you."

A few able volunteers raised their hands and began sliding on hands and knees toward the mansion.

Alex looked around at all the injured, his heart filling with dread. Artimé was a disaster. Swiftly he sought out the friends he knew he could count on. "Henry, Carina, pick an additional team to take inside so they can help treat the incoming patients."

"Got it," Henry said. He and Carina began recruiting help from uninjured people all across the lawn.

And then Alex's eyes landed on Meghan and Samheed. Sam's face was hidden, but Meghan's was ghastly white. The ice was red beneath them. "Oh no," he breathed. He stepped gingerly toward them on the ice, trying not to slip. Each step was agonizingly slow. "Everyone, get moving!" he shouted. "Crawl if you have to! Let's get the injured inside now!"

Simber chose to fly. Immediately he scooped up an unresponsive Meghan into his mouth and carefully dug his claws into Samheed's component vest, lifting them both. They

LISA McMANN

hung limp from Simber's grasp. Alex took his own advice and dropped to the ground, sliding himself along the side of the mansion to the door to help Simber.

A moment later squirrelicorns filled the air, picking up injured Artiméans far and wide and delivering them to the mansion.

Alex's hands burned against the ice. He crawled up to the threshold of the mansion, past the Artiméans stationed there to help transition the injured inside. He rose to his knees and grasped the handle to open the door, praying that the ice was external only.

It was.

"Phew," he said, pulling himself into the mansion and getting to his feet just as Simber lowered Alex's two friends to within reach.

Alex stretched out his hands and pulled Meghan gently from Simber's jaws. His face paled when he held her.

"She's cold," Simber said.

Alex's heart fell. "From the ice, you mean?" he said, faltering.

Simber was silent. He dropped his eyes.

Alex's eyes burned. "From the ice? Simber?"

"Just get herrr into the hospital warrrd!"

Wild with fear, Alex started off. "You guys grab Samheed so Simber can rescue more injured," Alex croaked over his shoulder to the Artiméans at the door. "And tell Carina and Henry to hurry! Meghan's . . . she's bad off." He ran with his best friend in his arms into the hospital wing, and laid Meghan gently on the nearest bed. Her freckled face was gray.

He couldn't breathe. He put a shaking hand to his mouth.

From across the ward, Sean sat up, his leg in a cast and held up in the air in a sling. "Oh, thank goodness you're all right, Al. Is everybody okay? That voice—did you hear it? That was Gondoleery Rattrapp! Eva told me about her, she's—why, wait . . ." He sat up farther and peered at the figure in the bed. "Is that—is that Meg?"

Alex could barely hold it together as Henry and Carina burst into the mansion and came running toward him, and others rushed into the room carrying Samheed. He shot Sean a fearful look. "Yes," he said in a voice that sounded far away. "It's Meghan." Numb, he backed off from the bed to let the healers get close, and then tripped over a side table as Sean,

LISA McMANN

helpless in his bed, strained to see what was happening.

Carina began barking out orders to the nurses, and the more intense her voice became, the more Alex felt his world crashing in on him. He stumbled to the hospital ward entrance, useless, yet knowing there were many other wounded, and he had to help them.

Blindly he returned to the front door and picked up the next body that had been left there. He ran with it to hospital ward and deposited it on a bed, and then doggedly went back. Body after body he transported from inside the front door to the hospital wing until his limbs and lungs burned.

At first he tried to block the screams and shouts that were coming from Sean, and from around Meghan's bed, but the cries were endless. Mentally he begged for a spell that would cause his hearing to fail while he did the job he had to do, but there was none. He couldn't unhear the horrible truth. His dear friend Meghan, his freckled classmate and fellow Unwanted, was dead.

When Sean cried out Alex's name and grabbed his shirt as he passed by with yet another body, Alex looked at the horror in his friend's eyes and croaked, "I'm sorry! I'm sorry, okay?

There was nothing we could do to save her!" He ripped his shirt from Sean's grasp and stumbled out of the hospital ward, hot tears singeing his eyes and throat as he went back for the next injured person. And all the while a sort of fatalistic mantra began forcing its way into his head, whether he wanted it there or not. It was the only thing that kept him going.

We can only save the ones we can save.

By the time Florence and the rest of the ship's crew had scuttled the distance across the frozen lagoon and reached the shore, Alex had almost singlehandedly delivered the last of the injured Artiméans to the hospital ward.

Hours later, as darkness settled over the island, only Henry remained beside Meghan's now empty bed. He was crying inconsolably, his hands shaking as they clutched an unopened tin of fluorescent blue seaweed.

LISA McMANN

Another Shipwreck

With no water or food and in blinding pain, Aaron slid in and out of consciousness. As the pirate ship pulled his little fishing boat along, he didn't notice the cylindrical island with the rocky crown on top as they passed by, and he didn't notice the lush, larger island with the jutting mountain and waterfall on one side and the word "HELP!" spelled out on the beach with bones. Every time his eyes opened, all he could see was water. Where were they taking him?

Now and then the pirates above peered over the railing at him. Sometimes they jeered. Whenever Aaron cried out for water, some of them would spit at him and laugh. Aaron knew this was the end of him. His tongue swelled with thirst until he reached over the side of the boat and sipped a handful of sea water, but that only made him more thirsty.

His stomach twisted in pain, his shoulder felt like fire grew inside it, and his face swelled and throbbed. The sun beat down on him during the day, burning his skin, and when it went down at night, he shivered until he thought his teeth would fall out.

He drank more sea water and became delirious, shouting, "I am the high priest of Quill. Let me go!" And when the pirates laughed, he growled, "Take yourselves to the Ancients Sector!"

Other times he shook and sobbed, though he was so dehydrated that he couldn't produce tears even if he wanted to. "I don't know what you want with me!" he cried, his voice growing so hoarse that the pirates couldn't hear him anymore.

Finally he slid to the bottom of the boat, into the sludge, and passed out. And in his unconscious state, he dreamed of his brother, and of a better life.

» » « «

It was dark and choppy when the pirates unhooked the chain. The wind slapped waves against the sides of the little fishing boat, and the current, though not strong enough at this distance to pull the pirate ship into its grasp, was more than mighty enough to control the small vessel. The boat succumbed to the outer reaches of the hurricane, and went sailing into it without a struggle as the pirate ship pulled away and grew smaller. Soon the pirates' laughter was drowned out by the whistling wind.

But Aaron heard none of it. He flopped about, shivering on the floor as the tips of waves licked the lip of the boat, and he rolled from side to side as the sea swelled. It was only when the rain came in sheets that Aaron roused. Perhaps it was instinct as the pure liquid touched his lips. Fresh water. He forced himself to lift his head, barely raising an eyelid, and opened his mouth wide to let the cool, driving liquid hit his tongue and the back of his throat. Sweet relief.

As the rain quenched his thirst, the ride grew rougher and more waves splashed in. Aaron grabbed on to the side of the boat and hoisted his battered body to a sitting position against the bench. He stayed hunched over so the driving rain didn't sting his broken face. The strengthening wind whipped his loosening clothing and made his cheeks shudder, and once his mind returned to him, he grew scared.

"Help!" he rasped as a pitchfork of lightning crackled in the sky. "Please help! What's happening?" The boat began to move faster through the water.

The waves grew and thunder crashed. The wind whipped the rain until the drops flew horizontally. They felt like hard pellets hitting Aaron's face, nailing his eyes and nostrils and eardrums, no matter how he tried to shield them. He grew dizzy with the speed of the watercraft and all the rocking and rolling. Soon, it was all he could do in his weak state to hang on. And before his muddled head could think, the fishing boat was darting past slices of rock jutting out of the water.

As lightning became more frequent, Aaron could see the path forward. Dangerous obstacles peppered the shoreline of a desolate island. Waves swelled and rolled, dragging the little boat with them. Aaron's screams were barely audible above the roar of the sea, and the wind sucked the breath from him.

Aaron clung for dear life to the side of the boat as it careened crazily toward the maze of boulders and wrecks, narrowly missing one after another, and causing Aaron's heart to leap. The boat went faster and faster, and began to bump against rocks, throwing Aaron from one side to the other.

When the next series of lightning made the sky glow, Aaron's gasp stuck in his throat. He barely had time to close his eyes before the boat's front end flew up and went airborne over a rock, flinging Aaron to the floor, and then it crashed on another, splintering the little boat into a thousand pieces and sending Aaron flying into the sky. When he came back down, he landed hard on a rock with a stomach-churning thud, and was still.

The next giant wave rolled in and poured over top of him. When it receded, the high priest of Quill was gone.

In an Icy Land

Meghan Ranger wasn't the only one who had given her life for Artimé. And she wasn't the only one to die saving another person. Artimé was filled with heroes.

While Alex and Lani worked diligently around the clock to assist the living in whatever way they could, Meghan never left their minds. The days that followed the battle blurred into one long, horrible nightmare for all of them—Alex and Lani, Sean, of course, and Samheed, once he recovered enough to hear the horrible news.

Everybody mourned in his own way—they'd seen evidence

LISA McMANN

of that when Mr. Today died, and were reminded of it now as Unwanteds poured every ounce of strength and grief into breaking through the layer of ice that covered the land so that they could dig graves for the fallen. The final toll was eleven, with more than thirty injured severely enough to remain in the hospital ward. The Quillitary death count was much higher, yet no one came to claim the bodies, so the Artiméans buried them, too.

Sean's manner of grieving for his sister was loud and quick. He was completely inconsolable for a day. Not even Carina, who had pushed aside the fight they'd had, could comfort him. But after that, he pulled his sadness inward. He was alive, and he had work to do. Alex needed him. And he knew the most about what was happening in Quill.

Well, almost. Charlie actually knew the most, and he did his best to share the information he had, but no one had a moment to listen.

When finally Alex could take a break from the endless task of caring for his people, he and Lani sought out Sean and helped him walk into Ms. Octavia's empty classroom where they could talk in private. Simber, Florence, Claire, and Haluki joined them, while the rest of Artimé had dinner in the dining room. It was a somber meeting.

"I'm certain that voice was Gondoleery Rattrapp's," Sean said. The circles were deep and dark under his eyes, and his tone was reserved. "She's one of the new governors, and I fought against her—she's one of Aaron's Restorers. Or at least she was, until she did this." He pointed out the window at the ice-covered world.

"So she took over power from Aaron?" Alex asked. He had to admit this was the most burning question on his mind. What had happened to his brother? His stomach had been knotted and unsettled for days—he could only guess the worst.

"Sounds like it," Sean said. "Eva told me Gondoleery was up to something. She's been doing some sort of elemental magic, I guess. Ice, fire, stuff like that. Eva said they used to make rain with Marcus and Justine back when they were children on Warbler. And that once Marcus gave them their memories back, Gondoleery started working on her magic again."

"I didn't know they had that kind of magical ability," Lani said. "But I guess Mr. Today brought a rainy day to Artimé now and then just to change things up, didn't he?"

"He did," Claire said. "I'm sure I don't know the spell for it, though."

"Maybe there's a book with a counterspell to the ice," Alex muttered. "Somewhere in that mess of a library in the Museum of Large. I'll see if I can find something on the topic of elemental spells." He pinched the bridge of his nose to ward off the headache that threatened at the thought of digging through all of Mr. Today's books.

Lani looked out the window longingly. "I'd just love to get in there and fix it up."

"Maybe if you were just a little bit better at magic, you could see the secret hallway," Alex said. He meant to tease her, but the dull way the words came out made it sound like an insult.

Simber cleared his throat. "Why don't you paint a 3-D doorrrway to the Museum of Larrrge? That way you could let whomeverrr you want up therrre."

Everybody turned to look at Simber. The suggestion raced through their brains as they tried to find a flaw in the plan.

"It's just a suggestion," the cheetah added.

It seemed like a valid one, and Alex was chagrinned that he hadn't thought of it before. "That's really good thinking, Sim.

LISA McMANN

We'll have to keep it quiet, though," Alex said. "I don't want just anybody getting up there."

There was a shuffling of feet behind Alex, and he turned to see Charlie peering at the group.

"Charlie!" both Claire and Alex exclaimed at once.

Claire put her hand to her forehead. "I'd nearly forgotten all about you."

"Me too—I'm sorry," Alex said. And then it occurred to him that Charlie might have very important news. "What can you tell us?"

Charlie began signing rapidly. Lani narrowed her eyes, trying to decipher the language, but she gave up and looked to her father.

Gunnar Haluki gave Charlie his full attention, while everyone else watched the expressions on his face change. When Charlie stopped, Haluki let out a breath and shook his head.

"What is it?" Alex asked.

Haluki pursed his lips. "It sounds like it's going to be a long story," he said. He glanced carefully at Alex. "Charlie says Aaron was kidnapped."

LISA McMANN

Tough Answers

K idnapped?" exclaimed Alex.

Haluki nodded. He watched Charlie intently as the gargoyle explained further, and then Haluki interpreted once more. "Matilda saw the whole thing. A group of ten pirates burst into Aaron's office while Aaron was trying to make her come alive magically." Haluki paused. "She adds that she faked being a frozen statue the whole time, of course."

"What?" Alex said.

Gunnar shrugged. He watched Charlie and continued. "The pirates had shiny weapons. Swords, cutlasses, that sort of thing. They grabbed Aaron and held a paper to his face, and agreed he was the one they were after. They picked him up and he tried to reach some magical components that Liam had given him—"

"Wait. What?" Claire asked, her face furious.

Haluki shrugged again, but Sean spoke up. "It was Meg," he said, his voice hollow. "She created a sack of fake components to trick Aaron."

Alex was confused by a number of things, but he couldn't worry about them now. "What happened to Aaron?" he demanded.

Simber lifted his head and regarded Alex, but Alex was focused intently on Haluki.

"They carried him out of the palace and down to the sea. They threw him face-first into a small boat and rowed out to the pirate ship. And then they chained his boat to the ship, left him there, and climbed aboard. And then they sailed away, pulling him behind them."

"Back to their island? What would they want with him?" Alex was stumped. "He'd be absolutely useless as a slave."

Haluki and Charlie conversed for a moment.

LISA McMANN

"They went the other way," Haluki said, his voice puzzled.

"You mean east?" Lani asked, exchanging a look with Alex. "Why?"

Haluki shook his head. "Matilda doesn't know. Charlie saw them, too, from the mansion window. They passed by during the night, definitely heading east."

The group was quiet for a moment, contemplating the news.

Charlie signed some more, and Haluki translated. "Then, in the morning, Gondoleery arrived at the palace and there was a bit of a ruckus. Matilda could hear some of the exchange from her post by the window in Aaron's office. When Gondoleery found out that Aaron was gone, she declared herself high priest and sent Liam and some others—she's not sure who—to the Ancients Sector."

Ms. Morning leaned forward, eyes narrowed. "Oh," she said. She massaged her temples and was silent, while Sean just closed his eyes and let his head fall back against the back of his chair, defeated.

Alex's mind whirled with information, but he knew he had to get down to the bottom of Gondoleery's intentions. "Let me get this straight," he said. "Gondoleery Rattrapp took over

Quill. Okay, I get that. And I get that she cast this ice spell and it affected Artimé and even a bit of the sea all the way around the island. But other than this severe inconvenience, does Artimé have something to worry about here? Seems to me she's got her hands full trying to get Quill figured out, and we're just victims of the spell because we happen to share the island. Is that the correct assessment?"

Haluki began to sign the questions to Charlie to make sure the gargoyle understood the complexity of what Alex was asking, but before he could finish, Sean spoke up. "No, Alex," he said. He paused and looked wearily around the circle. "She wants the mansion. She is the one person in Quill who has the magical ability to keep Artimé alive if you die. And believe me—she wants all of us dead."

They sat in silence. And once they'd each thought about it, no one was particularly surprised. Hadn't the people of Quill always wanted the people of Artimé dead? It was a common theme.

"Well, that's just great," Florence said. "Can I please just go pay a visit to the palace and have a little *meeting* with her?"

Alex might have laughed if the day weren't so bleak. "Sure. And then two days later the next person will take over and decide Artimé should be destroyed. And the next, and the next." He sat up. "You know, I'm starting to have an identity crisis. Why does everybody hate us so much?"

Even Sean managed a small smile. "We're the most despised people in the whole world," he said. "Just because we like to create things. No, not just create things, because everyone creates things. The problem is that we create things that they don't think are the *right* things. And that's what makes us so despised."

"Which makes it even more strange that the pirates captured Aaron, of all people. You'd think if they despised us and were out for revenge, they'd have come here." Alex tapped his finger to his lips, and then he said, "Charlie, can you ask Matilda what was on the paper that the pirates held up?"

Charlie nodded and a moment later he signed something to Haluki.

Haluki knit his brows, and then he looked at Alex. When he spoke, his voice was guarded. "She says it was a drawing of Aaron's face."

One by one, the advisors looked up, and then at Alex. And as the truth dawned on him, Alex's face grew pale.

"Oh," he said softly. "They thought Aaron was me."

LISA McMANN

A Confession

After the meeting, Alex pinned a large canvas to the wall next to the Museum of Large. He lit the hallway brightly so he could see all the nuances of the door, and he began to paint. It had been such a long time since he'd had a chance to paint anything at all, and even though he was exhausted and his heart ached for Meghan, he found comfort in working on his art again. And it was important for him to get the 3-D door finished quickly to allow Lani access to Mr. Today's personal library so she could help him look for a book about elemental spells. Thankfully it was a simple door, so it wouldn't take much time to replicate.

LISA McMANN

While he worked, he thought about the whirlwind that had consumed every moment since he'd arrived back in Artimé. His community had never seen this much grief—they'd never lost so many people before. His best friend was gone, just like that. He still couldn't process it. It was so strange . . . so horrible. He hadn't even had a chance to say hello, much less good-bye. And poor Sean! He loved his sister so much. They had a very special sibling relationship. It was something Alex envied. But he didn't envy Sean now.

Alex thought about his relationship with Aaron, and he knew he couldn't relate to what Sean was feeling, even though it seemed possible that Aaron could be dead now. As much as Alex had wanted a relationship with his brother like the one Meghan had with Sean, it wasn't meant to be.

After a while, Alex heard a sound at the mouth of the hallway and looked up. It was Samheed, hanging on to the wall and hobbling toward him.

"Thought I'd find you here," Samheed said, breathing hard.

"They let you out of the hospital ward?" Alex asked, hurrying into his living quarters to grab a chair for his friend.

"Nah, I snuck out. Figured I could hide up here. I just needed to get out of there."

Alex nodded and picked up his paintbrush. "Are you feeling better?"

"I guess." Samheed's face clouded over.

Alex glanced at him. "What's wrong? You thinking about Meg?"

"Yeah. I'm so stinking mad at her, I can't see straight."

Alex paused his brush stroke, and then continued painting, saying nothing.

"She jumped in front of me," Samheed went on. "She pushed me out of the way. You know?"

"Yeah."

"Why'd she have to do that?" Samheed's voice was filled with pain.

"You'd have done the same for her."

Samheed was quiet for a moment. "Yeah. But still . . ."

"I know." Alex put his brush down. "All I can think to say is that she'd do it again if she had the choice. All of us would. You, Lani, me—none of us would think twice about pushing

LISA McMANN

each other out of the way." He sighed and started painting again. "That's what made us such a good team, I guess." His vision misted over, forcing him to paint blind for a time, but he couldn't stop or he knew he'd break down.

Samheed closed his eyes and rested his head against the back of the chair. He sat there in silence until a tear trickled out, and another. He wiped them away and took in a deep breath, letting it out slowly. "I hate this," he said.

Alex looked over his shoulder at his friend. "Me too."

They stayed together in the hallway for a long time, Alex painting and thinking, Samheed watching and trying not to lose it, until finally Samheed said, "I heard about Aaron."

Alex's hand wavered, and he cursed under his breath, trying to fix the errant line he'd made. He drew his thumb along it, dabbing the excess paint onto his pants. When he'd fixed his mistake, he replied, "They were coming for me, you know."

"Makes sense."

"I'm sure Aaron has no idea what's happening. Or why he was captured."

"If he's even alive," Samheed said.

Alex frowned at his work. "Why would they kidnap him

if they were just going to kill him? Why not just kill him?"

"I don't know."

Alex painted a while longer. "I think he's alive."

"Yeah?"

"Yes. I don't know why. I just—I just think I'd, you know, *feel* something if he died. I'd be able to tell." He let out a small laugh. "Sounds weird, I know."

Samheed shifted in his chair. "You always were a little weird when it came to Aaron."

"I suppose. I mean, we were very close. Or . . . or I thought we were."

Samheed gave an exasperated sigh. "Look, I know he's your twin, but he's a bad person. And you're not. And I think . . . if it's possible . . . you should just forget about it. About him. Because I, for one, am kind of glad he's gone."

Alex cringed and stepped back to look at his work. "I suppose you're happier with Gondoleery in charge," he said, sarcasm creeping into his voice.

Samheed was quiet.

Alex snuck a glance at him. He could see that Samheed was trying to hold his tongue, which wasn't easy for him.

LISA McMANN

"No, you're right," Samheed said eventually. "We're worse off until we figure out how to stop her kind of magic. That's true."

Samheed's admission surprised Alex, but he took it without question. They fell silent again.

Slowly, as Alex finished sections of the 3-D door, the corners and edges pushed out from the wall. Soon the drawing was finished. Alex took a tiny rubber component and cast it at the drawing, muttering "Preserve." The component hit the canvas in the center, spread out, and rippled to the edges so it would never tear. He released the drawing from the wall and began rolling it so he could deliver it to Lani.

"You ready, bruiser?" asked Alex. "Let me help you back down to the hospital ward."

Samheed frowned. "Can't you just bring me to my room?"

"No way. The nurses will kill me."

"Fine. Let's go."

Alex tucked the 3-D door under one arm and helped Sam out of the chair. They walked slowly toward the balcony, where Artiméans bustled about, going in and out of their respective hallways.

As Alex helped Samheed descend the steps, he caught a

glance from Simber, who stood in his familiar spot at the front door. By the time they reached the bottom, Simber's attention was elsewhere, his ears flicking this way and that, and his head tilted to one side. He leaped off his pedestal and stood at attention by the door.

Alex's heart fell. "What is it, Sim?" he asked in a low voice. They weren't ready for another attack. Samheed's hands went automatically to where his vest pockets would be if he were wearing it, but he was unarmed. Alex grabbed components from his robe and shoved them at Samheed before taking some in his own hands.

Simber narrowed his eyes. "Somebody's coming. But I don't . . . I can't tell if . . ."

"Claire? Ms. Octavia?" Alex called out. "Are you around? We have visitors."

Ms. Octavia and Claire Morning came out of their classrooms and joined the head mage, preparing to attack as well.

There was a soft bumping at the door, more like something falling against it than a knock.

Alex looked at Simber in alarm. "Shall I open it?" he whispered.

LISA McMANN

Simber hesitated, and tried peering out the window. Seeing nothing from the strange angle, he nodded.

"Stay here," Alex muttered, and left Samheed standing alone near the banister. He went to the door, turned the handle, and opened it.

There, slumped against the door frame, was a disheveled, shivering man with two identical packages in his arms.

Both packages were crying inconsolably.

Sisters

A lex and the others stared.

Simber growled. "Carrreful," he said. "Could be a trrrick."

Ms. Morning peered at the figure through narrowed eyes. She took a few steps toward him to get a better look. "Liam?" she asked, incredulous. "You're alive? What are you doing with those children?" She glanced at Alex. "Don't let your guard down. I'm with Simber. This could be a trap."

Alex, Samheed, and Ms. Octavia remained steady and watchful as Ms. Morning looked out the door, this way and that. When she was satisfied that there was no one else

LISA McMANN

nearby, she reached out to the partially frozen Liam and took the babies, who were wrapped inside ragged pieces of cloth. Liam's arms dropped and his head fell against the door frame. His eyes were closed.

Alex rushed to Liam's side, slipped the man's arm over his shoulders, and hoisted him to his feet. Ms. Morning quickly stepped inside with the crying girls and rushed them into the hospital ward to have them checked out.

Alex followed her, dragging Liam along, but before he could reach the hospital ward, Liam snapped his head up and struggled to stand on his own. "I'm fine," he said, his voice hoarse. "Just make sure the babies are all right. I didn't know where else to go."

Ms. Morning handed the children over to the nurses and came back to the entryway, where Alex helped Liam take a seat on the steps near Samheed. Ms. Octavia brought him a blanket. His unshaven face was proof enough that he'd been living precariously for at least a few days.

"We heard you'd been sent to the Ancients Sector," Ms. Morning said. "It's a shock to see you alive, much less carrying children."

Liam didn't dare look at her. He pulled the blanket around

his shoulders, still visibly shivering. "It's true. Gondoleery sent me to the Ancients Sector, and she commanded me to bring the babies there with me, but I didn't. I couldn't. They did nothing wrong. So I've been on the run." He looked wearily at Alex. "You know about Aaron?"

Alex nodded.

A nurse who'd seen Liam come in returned with a steaming mug of warm liquid. Liam took it, grateful to warm his hands, and sipped from it. After a moment, he went on. "I took to the shoreline. After everything turned to ice, it took me all this time to get here, sliding along a little at a time so I didn't fall with the children." He glanced anxiously into the hospital ward. "They're starving. I'm so sorry. I only had a little bread in my pocket, and I had to melt ice to give them water."

Samheed looked over the banister at Liam. "Gondoleery sent little children to the Ancients Sector? Since when did Quill start doing *that*?"

"Since Gondoleery took over. But I have to tell you that I don't think she has a plan much beyond freezing everybody in place. I think she saw the opportunity when Aaron was captured and she took it."

LISA McMANN

Simber spoke. "So you don't think she's planning to attack us furrrtherrr at this time?"

Liam, who wasn't comfortable at all around the large stone beast, shifted away from him. "I-I can't say for sure, but I feel quite certain she froze the island because she needed to figure things out. She doesn't have any allies as far as I know. Well, maybe Governor Strang, but I doubt it. The two are total opposites."

"That's good to hear," Alex said, beginning to pace. "It buys us some time to figure out how to counteract the spell. In fact, that reminds me. I need to get Lani into the library. . . ." He stood still as his thoughts turned back to the task at hand, then he picked up the 3-D door and handed it to Samheed. "Get this to Lani, will you? You'll see her before I do, I'm sure. I'm going to start searching. Tell her I'll meet her up there."

Samheed nodded and took it.

Alex looked at Claire. "Is this whole thing," he asked, waving his hand toward Liam, "under control?"

"We'll take it from here," Ms. Octavia said. "Go save our island."

Alex bid his thanks and his good-byes and turned to Liam. "Thank you," he said before starting up the steps.

LISA McMANN

"Yes, of course." Liam stood. He dropped his eyes. "I'll be going, then. Thank you for the, ah, the drink."

"What?" Alex asked. "Where will you go?"

"T-to the Ancients Sector," Liam said. "That's where I've been sent."

Alex narrowed his eyes. He'd forgotten the strange ways people thought in Quill. "No, Liam. Don't be ridiculous. You will not go back there. We'll—we'll find you a place. Some-where. Here or in Quill." He looked at Ms. Morning, letting her make the call.

Ms. Morning sighed. "Fine. You can stay here, of course. Then you'll be closer to your children."

Liam looked at her in alarm. "My—my children? The girls aren't mine! They're Alex's. I thought . . . I thought you all knew that."

Alex's eyes nearly bugged out of his head. "What are you talking about?" he asked.

Samheed raised an eyebrow.

"Oh. Oh dear." Liam grew pale. "Y-you didn't hear this part? About the wall—and your parents? Oh my, I'm afraid I've quite bungled this. . . ."

LISA McMANN

"My parents?" Alex stared at Liam. Then he slowly turned to peer into the hospital ward where the children were being cared for, and slowly turned to look at Liam once more. "Explain, please," he said in a terse voice.

Liam wavered. "Oh dear. Alex," he said, "I'm so very sorry. I have some, ah, some horrifying news." His mouth went dry, but he pressed on. "When the last of the wall collapsed, it fell inward on the workers, and it crushed three rows of Necessary houses. Your parents were both . . . killed."

Alex continued to stare.

Liam swallowed hard. "Oh dear, you don't know a thing, do you. I'd thought—I'd thought you'd have had contact with them by now." His eyes darted around, making sure no one was about to attack him, and chastised himself under his breath. "You see, Alex, the children are your sisters. Twins, just like you and—" He stopped.

Shock registered on the faces all around.

"And, well, since Aaron is . . . ah . . . ," he added weakly, and then finally he gave up trying to be sensitive and blurted out, "You're their only kin. You see?"

In the long moment that followed, Alex appeared to have

turned into a stunned statue. No one else moved either.

"You're saying my parents are dead," Alex said finally, "and I've inherited these screaming babies." It wasn't a question. He shook his head slowly in disbelief. First Meghan, then Aaron, then this craziness . . . it was all too much. What was Alex supposed to do with two helpless babies on top of everything else he had to do?

"Yes," Liam whispered.

"No," said Alex. "I do not accept this. Not any of it." And then, without another word, he turned and walked up the stairs.

Simber started toward the stairs to follow him, pain and worry etched on his stony face, but Ms. Morning touched his shoulder. "Let him go."

The cat frowned. Every instinct he had urged him to go after the mage. But sometimes Claire understood human things better than he did. He stood at the base of the staircase for a long moment, and then he bowed his head and returned to his spot by the door.

Heartbreak and Loss

Alex stared unseeing at the library shelves in the Museum of Large, trying to process everything he'd been through in the past few days. He still couldn't believe Meghan was gone forever, along with ten other Artiméans. Then his brother was kidnapped, and Alex had no idea where he could be. Then Liam told him his parents were dead, and he had somehow inherited two crying babies that he'd never laid eyes on before.

He closed his eyes and gripped the shelves, wanting to pound his head against the wood, but ultimately deciding to rest his forehead against it instead. Meghan had been the closest thing to family Alex had known for years. Ever since Alex's parents had told him that he was Unwanted at age ten, they'd distanced themselves from him. He'd always pretended it didn't hurt, because that's what a good Quillen would do.

And now Meghan was gone, his parents were dead, and Aaron . . . Alex squeezed his eyes tighter, trying to tamp down the pain and tears, but his breathing grew heavy and wretched, and before he could pull himself from the grip of reality, he found he was hurtling toward it. He cried out in anguish—a deep, ugly groan that began at the depths of his gut and burst from his throat, and then he dropped to the floor and pounded it, sobbing incoherently about the unfairness of life and his awful childhood.

Growing up in Quill, being taught not to feel—those lessons would never quite leave him completely, no matter how hard he tried to forget them. He hated Justine for it, and Aaron, and all of Quill for inserting their fears and rituals into his mind. He hated his parents for it. Even in their death, he hated them.

As he sobbed, feeling terribly sorry for himself, it began to occur to him that maybe the only reason he was so troubled by

LISA McMANN

the injustice of growing up in Quill was because he had experienced life differently since then. He'd experienced something that his parents and Aaron had never known. And that maybe, if he hadn't been Unwanted, he'd have been just like them.

"I wouldn't!" he said, but immediately he doubted himself. And then he began to regret that he'd never reached out to his parents from Artimé once he'd had the chance. He'd always thought of it as their job to come to him if they wanted to see him, and they'd chosen not to do it. They'd chosen to let him be sent to his death, and they'd chosen to stay in Quill once Artimé was exposed. That was their decision! Even when Alex saw his father near Mr. Today's grave, Mr. Stowe had hurried away from him, as if Alex were somehow dangerous. What was Alex supposed to do? Beg? After what they'd done to him? But he'd never asked. And maybe they assumed Alex would hate them. They'd have been right.

Maybe if he had invited them to Artimé, they would have come. But he hadn't, and now they were dead.

His heart tore anew when he thought about Aaron. Aaron had been close, once. Close to joining Alex in Artimé. He'd been tempted—Alex had seen it in his eyes. But when he'd reached out, Aaron ran the other way. It was too late for him.

Alex sometimes wondered what would have happened if he'd let Aaron get the infraction. Would Aaron have turned out differently if they'd both been Unwanted from the start? Would they be friends now? He'd never know.

"You're so stupid!" he cried into the floorboards, and then he pounded them once more as another wave of anger and remorse flowed over him. "Aaron," he pleaded now, "you had so many chances. So many." He grew quiet as the waves of emotion softened. "And I never let go of you. How could I?" He lay there for a moment, as pain began to swell inside him, this time sharp and physical, like half his soul was breaking away, being torn from his body and hovering just out of reach. Alex gasped in agony and surprise and pushed himself to his knees, holding his side where the pain ripped through him. A revelation came over him as he knelt there, alone in the stacks, clear and vivid as any dream, and as certain as the pain that split his soul.

"He's dying," he whispered. "Right now, this minute, he's dying. Oh, help me. Someone . . . anyone . . ."

Element-ary

Alex pushed through the pain and tried to take hold of the truth—his brother was dying, and he was never coming back to Quill. But the pain in his side remained sharp and steady, no matter what Alex tried to do. He stared at the library shelves and tried to focus, but he wasn't making much progress.

Soon, after pasting the 3-D door in her bedroom, Lani showed up, and together they sorted through piles of books, making hardly a dent. It was easier with Lani there. And it was nice to spend the time in silence, or chatting now and then about things other than death and dying.

Finding no luck after a day or two, Alex asked others to join them in the search. Samheed and Carina helped Sean up the stairs and through the traditional way, and Sky came with Lani through the 3-D door.

Alex was glad to have Lani take charge of the organizing. He remained quiet, mostly, preoccupied with the pain that never left his side.

In the evening, after the others left, Sky stayed with Alex. The two sat shoulder to shoulder together on the museum floor, in silence for a while, until Alex couldn't hold his thoughts anymore. They came pouring out.

Sky listened. And listened. And listened. All night long, until years' worth of Alex's private thoughts and feelings and actions were strewn out across the endless floor like the scattered piles of books. Stories about his parents. Stories about Meghan and her bravery. And stories about Aaron and what life was like for them in their little dusty room in Quill that was now demolished, buried under tons of rubble.

They talked, and dozed, and sorted, and talked, and dozed some more, until Lani returned to start a new day of work and shooed them out to get something to eat.

And while Alex and Sky wolfed down a most delicious breakfast at the kitchen bar, Florence wandered in, saying over her shoulder, "Come on little ones. Let's get a snack."

Behind her, the twins toddled, laughing and trying to keep up with Florence's long strides. One wore purple, the other red. When Florence noticed Alex and Sky, she grinned and picked up the girls, which made them laugh harder, and set them on the countertop near where Alex and Sky were sitting.

Alex, nervous, sat back in his chair. "Uh, hi there."

Florence pushed the girls toward Alex and guarded the edge to make sure they wouldn't tumble off. "These are your sisters. As you can see, and as I'm *sure* you were wondering, they are doing quite well now after a few days of spoiling by the nurses."

Alex managed a weak grin. "They look . . . fine," he said. "Nice. I mean, I don't really know anything about babies."

"Carina and the nurses think they're probably a little less than a year old."

"Oh," Alex said. "That's . . . a good age." He didn't really know what to say.

One of the twins leaned forward and stretched out her

hand, trying to reach Alex's face. He backed up, and she took interest in his plate of food instead. She grabbed a crust of toast and shoved it in her mouth.

Sky laughed, but Alex looked at Florence in alarm. "Is she—is that—?"

"She's fine. She just wants to share your snack."

"Okaaay." Alex frowned.

Sky tore off a crust of bread from her plate and offered it to the other twin. "What are their names?"

Alex looked up, curious. "Yeah," he said. "What are they called?"

Florence shrugged. "No one knows, and we don't want to stir up any suspicion in Quill by asking around, since we don't want Gondoleery to know they're here and alive. I think you ought to give them a fresh start, Alex."

"Me?" Alex sputtered. "I don't know anything about that. You guys just go ahead and do it."

"Alex," Sky said, disgusted, "don't be ridiculous. They're your sisters. And," she added more gently, "it's pretty likely the longer Aaron is gone that you're all the family they have left."

LISA McMANN

Alex cringed as the pain in his side throbbed. He knew deep inside him that something terrible was happening with Aaron, but what? If he was dead, would this pain last forever?

Florence leaned in. "Even if Aaron returns, you have a chance to give them the childhood you never had. Aren't you excited about that?"

Alex flinched. "That's a fine point, Florence, and you know I want that, of course."

Sky squeezed his knee under the counter. After their long talk last night, she knew as well, now.

Florence tipped her head, waiting. "Well, then. You should name them."

"All right," he sighed. "Let me think about it, though." He peered at the girls as if seeing them for the first time, trying to figure them out. "It might take me a few days to come up with some options."

"A few more days won't hurt," Florence said. "I'll take them back to the hospital ward for now so you can get back to your search. They've set up a nursery in the corner for them, though they like to escape and visit Simber and me." She grinned. "But you can stop by and visit them now and then, you know?"

LISA McMANN

"Yeah, I guess." It would take some getting used to. But they seemed like nice enough children when they weren't crying. And they *were* his sisters. "I'll come by," he promised. When Florence swept them up, they waved over her shoulders, and Alex found himself waving back.

Sky and Alex finished their breakfasts, feeling ready to hit the library again. But just as they were leaving the kitchen, Lani came pounding down the stairs and flying around the banister carrying a small book high over her head.

"I found it!" she cried, leaping into the air. *"Element-ary: A Guide to Elemental Magic!"*

On the Island of Shipwrecks

When Ishibashi exited his shelter during the hour of calm, he carried a few of his newly recovered tools to the precious ship that Alex-san had so thoughtfully transported to the island. Now the three scientists could explore it once again after so many years.

Having such access to the ship fulfilled the scientists' greatest wish, and as far as Ishibashi knew, he'd never expressed that wish to Alex—the young leader had figured it out on his own, which made the gesture even more thoughtful.

And likely, with the long future that seemed to be ahead of

LISA McMANN

the three scientists, it would give them something to fill in the endless hours. Now more than ever Ishibashi wished for a few more hours of calm each day, since the machinery on board the ship was too heavy for the three old men to dismantle and move into the shelter. They had precious little time each day to explore and marvel over the equipment they had thought they'd never see again.

On this day, Ishibashi did as he always did. He shuffled to the ship as quickly as possible, with Sato and Ito right behind, and he climbed the iron ladder up the side. Because the ship's bottom wasn't flat, everything tilted to one side, but Ishibashi didn't mind. He was old, but he was nimble, and after the first couple of days, he found footholds and handholds all around to allow him to look at everything.

As Ishibashi disappeared inside the hold, Sato and Ito climbed the ladder. Sato was the slowest and weakest, so he stopped at the top and looked around the island while catching his breath.

On the barren beach, a new shipwreck caught his eye. It appeared to be part of a fishing boat, but the storm had ripped it to shreds. Sato put a hand above his eyes to shield the weak sunlight that managed to come through the clouds. His eyesight wasn't very good anymore. He saw what looked like a sack of goods farther down the shoreline. They would have to pick it up before the storm took it again—perhaps there was something exciting in it from the other world. Sato didn't see any people, but he didn't expect to. Most shipwrecks lost their passengers well before they reached the shore.

Carefully he climbed into the ship, and for the next while the old men examined the contents and tinkered with the machines, trying to dry out their waterlogged guts to see if they would work again. If only they had more time! If only the storm wouldn't drench everything again, day after day!

Instinctively, when the sky darkened and the wind picked up, the three reluctantly climbed back out of the ship and made their way carefully down the ladder to the ground. Sato told the others about the new shipwreck, and all three went to look it over before going back to the shelter.

"Another fishing boat," Ishibashi said to the others in their language. He picked up a jagged plank and tossed it aside, then pushed on the chunk of the hull that sat on the rocky ground to see how heavy it was—it might make a good container for plants. But it was too bulky to carry with so little time left today. If the storm didn't devour it, he would go back for it tomorrow.

Sato walked farther down the shoreline to the sack of goods. But when he reached it, he gave a shout. He knelt next to it and turned it over as the other two scientists hurried toward him. It was a young man, all curled up, covered in a paste of wet sand. The waves licked at him.

When the others reached him, Sato looked up, his expression deeply troubled. He spoke rapidly to the others.

Ishibashi reached down to feel the boy's pulse. He shook his head. The young man was cold and unresponsive. He was most certainly dead.

Sato spoke more firmly, and began dragging the boy toward the shelter. Ito and Ishibashi helped, moving as fast as their old legs could go, with Ishibashi and Sato arguing the whole way. Ishibashi did not want to take the body of this dead stranger into their living quarters. But Sato won out.

As thunder rumbled and a sudden blanket of rain poured down on them, the scientists maneuvered themselves into the shelter and pulled the body inside the main room. Sato took

LISA McMANN

one look at the victim and gasped. The rain had washed the caked sand from the young man's face. And while bruises were evident, the young man was clearly recognizable.

"Alex-san!" Ishibashi cried. "No!" Wildly Ishibashi, Sato, and Ito scrambled to resuscitate their dear friend who had been so kind to them. How did he end up here? Had the enormous flying cheetah dropped him on the rocks to die?

Sato and Ito pounded on the young man's chest, and as Ishibashi watched in horror, he grew more desperate the longer their friend did not respond. He gripped his hat and wrenched his clothes and begged for life to return to the leader of Artimé, but nothing was working.

Finally Sato shouted to Ishibashi in a voice that sounded like a command. Ishibashi cringed. He nodded, and with a heart full of anguish, he ran to the greenhouse, ripped open the container of glowing blue seaweed, and took the tiniest pinch. He raced back to the others and knelt down.

Ishibashi looked at the glowing seaweed between his finger and thumb. He closed his eyes, his heart ripping apart. What he was about to do went against everything he believed. Everything. Yet . . .

"Please forgive me, Alex-san," Ishibashi whispered. With that, he plunged the seaweed into Aaron's mouth, massaging it between his cheek and gums for several seconds. When there was nothing left to do, he slowly backed away. Sato and Ito stopped their reviving techniques and sat back too, their worried eyes darting from the young man's face to his chest, searching for any sign of life.

Broken Souls

Three islands away, Alex joined Lani on the ice-covered lawn. And as she chanted the words from a thin spell book that would remove Gondoleery's grip on the island, the sharp pain in Alex's side snapped and disappeared, and the broken half of Alex's soul that had hovered outside him for days took flight. Alex clapped a hand to his ribs and gasped. In an instant, as the rest of the islanders watched a different show orchestrated by Lani, Alex could only see the one that was happening inside himself.

"He's alive," he whispered, clutching his side while the world changed beneath his feet.

The ice disappeared, and the grass and flowers sprouted up once more. The pirate ship and Claire's speedboat were set free from the frozen stretch of sea, and in the distance, Alex could see the flash of a faux diamond–studded spike slicing the air, followed by Spike Furious herself, jumping and splashing in shallow water again.

"Yes!" Lani cried, turning to him. "We did it, Al!" She hugged Alex as the people of Artimé cheered and ran to the lawn to celebrate. "Artimé is alive again!"

But Alex hardly noticed what was going on around him. Strange thoughts appeared in his head and churned through his mind. *He's alive.* He stumbled away from Lani's grasp, a dazed look on his face. Lani watched him quizzically as he stripped off his robe and thrust it at her.

"Here," he said in an odd voice. "I . . . I need you to take care of things. My sisters, and Artimé, and everything. Just for a while. Something's happened, you see, and I . . ." He searched the crowd, looking for someone, and finally he found her. "I've got to . . ."

Lani grabbed his shirt, forcing his attention back to her. "Alex, what in the world are you doing?"

LISA McMANN

Finally he looked into Lani's eyes. "I've got to go," he said simply.

And before his stunned friend could reply, Alex ran to Sky's side, took her hand, and spoke earnestly into her ear. Her eyes grew wide. And then she nodded. Alex kissed her cheek and darted off alone, almost completely unnoticed by the rejoicing Artiméans. He veered off the lawn to the shore, and continued toward the lagoon. And once he arrived at the spot where platyprots often perched, he splashed through the water, dove, then surfaced and climbed into the gleaming white boat named *Claire*.

He stood at the controls, and at his command, the magical boat roared to life. Alex swung it around, pointed it to the east, and without a single look back at the land and people he loved, he set out, full speed ahead, in search of the broken half of his soul.

Acknowledgments

Many thanks to all of you Unwanteds out there who are reading this series and telling your friends about it. I'm so grateful!

Thanks as always to my family: my husband Matt, who puts up with my moments of panic so others don't have to; my son, Kilian, who makes me look cool at schools because his character drawings are such a hit with students; and my daughter, Kennedy, who keeps me organized because of her great help behind the scenes. Thanks to my extended family as well for your constant support—parents, brothers, sisters, nieces, and nephews.

You all rock!

This book would not be possible without the hard work of the entire Aladdin team. Saying thank you hardly scratches the surface of my gratitude. Special thanks to my amazing editor, Liesa Abrams, whose passion for kids' books is limitless; to publisher Mara Anastas, whose energy knows no bounds; and to Karin Paprocki and Owen Richardson, whose stunning artwork and designs never cease to delight all who lay eyes upon them.

This is my fourteenth published book, and every time I pen the acknowledgments I find myself profusely thanking my agent, Michael Bourret. I am running out of ways to express myself, therefore I will simply say that I am so very grateful for you and for the person you are, and my adoration only grows.

I hope you enjoy this fifth installment in the Unwanteds series!